DIRE STEPS

Also by Henry V. O'Neil

The Sim War series
Glory Main
Orphan Brigade

DIRE STEPS

The Sim War: Book Three

HENRY V. O'NEIL

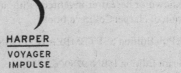

HARPER
VOYAGER
IMPULSE

An Imprint of HarperCollinsPublishers

EPub Edition SEPTEMBER 2015 ISBN: 9780062359230

Print Edition ISBN: 9780062359254

10 9 8 7 6 5 4 3 2 1

This book is dedicated to the members of the
West Point Class of 1985
For Excellence We Strive

Discover the force of the heavens, O Men;
once recognized, it can be put to use.

—Johannes Kepler

CHAPTER ONE

The man sat at a metal table in a small room with pale walls. Lights directly overhead beat down on blond hair cut military-close and the travel uniform of a captain in the Human Defense Force. The man's hands were folded in front of him, and he was concentrating on keeping them still.

The room's one door opened with a ripping noise that the captain recognized as soundproofing. A uniformed guard held the door's handle, allowing a tall man to enter before pulling the hatch shut again. The captain raised his eyes to study the figure before him, noting a frame that was lean and strong despite the signs that he was no longer young. The captain recognized his visitor's gray uniform, but tried to hide his fear as the newcomer sat across from him.

"What's your name?" the tall man asked.

The captain frowned, but quickly smoothed his features. "I would hope you'd already know that, given that you're detaining me against my will."

"You're an officer in the Human Defense Force during time of war. Legally, you have no will. What is your name?"

"Antonine Nabulit. I'm assigned to the staff of the Twelfth Corps, on leave from the war zone, and if you will just allow me to contact—"

"Your boss? The commanding general of the Twelfth Corps? We already communicated with him, and he was unable to explain your absence from his command."

Nabulit's face lost some of its color.

"Do you know who *I* am?" The tall man placed his fingertips on the table. His hands were large, and the overhead lights made the scar tissue shine.

"No."

"But you do recognize my uniform."

"Yes. You're with the security detachment for the Chairman of the Emergency Senate."

"Close. I'm not *with* Chairman Mortas's security. I'm in charge of it."

"You're Hugh Leeger."

"Very good. This will go much more smoothly if you don't pretend you're anything but the chief interrogator for Twelfth Corps."

"Listen, I know what this is about now, and I was only doing my job. I was ordered—"

"To interrogate Chairman Mortas's son when he was injured and starving? To threaten to kill him if he didn't answer your questions, and say you'd never tell his father that Lieutenant Mortas had been found alive?"

"Yes. Exactly that. I was ordered to do all that. And you would have understood, if you'd been there. The transport carrying the Chairman's son went missing, the whole corps was looking for him, and he turned up at Glory Main—excuse me, the top secret corps headquarters—with a Force psychoanalyst who turned out to be an alien impersonating a human. We needed answers, and we needed them right away."

"I see. But the abuse didn't stop once you got those answers, did it? Jander told you everything he could, and you took him along when you abandoned Glory Main, but he remained a prisoner."

"Again, I was acting under orders. This is my job, my training." The captain appeared to warm to the subject. Straightening in his chair, he waved a hand at the cramped space. "You keep the subject guessing about everything, especially his whereabouts, which is exactly what you're doing to me. The last thing I remember, I was being sealed in my Transit Tube, and when I woke up from the voyage I was in a detention cell. I have no idea where I am right now."

"You're in Unity Plaza."

Nabulit swallowed. The Unity Plaza complex was the personal headquarters of Olech Mortas. His eyes roved over the walls, as if trying to imagine the towering buildings all around him. Or above him.

"I'm not your enemy, and certainly not the Chairman's. My interrogation actually helped Lieutenant

Mortas. I proved that he didn't realize he was bringing an enemy alien to a corps headquarters. And how could he? It was almost impossible to guess that thing wasn't human, until we got them both into the scanning tubes."

"The tubes you said were for decontamination."

"We had no idea who—or what—they were. They showed up at Glory Main in a commandeered enemy ship, no advance warning, so we reacted accordingly. And the scanners proved we were right to do that. Once the alarms went off, the alien burst into a million flying particles, and we burned it up while it was still confined in that tube. It was the right thing to do."

"Oh, but you are actually wrong."

"How can I be wrong? Were you there? Lieutenant Mortas was returned to duty, and because we detected and destroyed that *thing* he brought with him, we were able to alert the rest of the Force that a shape-shifting entity had entered the war. There's been no reported sighting of anything like that creature since the first one, so how could that be wrong?"

"I wasn't talking about the alien, or your mistreatment of the young man whom I practically raised." Leeger's eyes slipped toward a blackened observation window on the side wall, and then back. "I meant you were wrong when you said you know why you're here."

"Why am I here, then? What's the point of this?"

"You should be able to figure that out on your own. You can start by dropping that lie about being on leave. Your boss certainly has."

"I have travel orders stating I'm in a leave status.

I'm a returned war veteran, and you're preventing me from traveling to my home planet."

"I wouldn't call an interrogator from the worst corps in the war zone a veteran of anything, but that's beside the point. You see, Nabulit, once we learned of the alien's existence, we put all of our networks on lookout for any indication of our new opponent. Most of what we've found was just a rehashing of our own disinformation campaign, but every now and then there's a tidbit that catches my attention. And when that morsel contains details about the alien that only a few people should know, you can bet I look into it closely.

"You visited a number of alliance planets before we scooped you up. You've been briefing some very important officials about that creature, and you've also made some side trips to meet with people we haven't identified yet. That's why your general has disowned you. We told him about the nice commissions you've made by selling what you know to people who weren't on his list.

"You've violated a whole host of wartime security regulations, any one of which carries the death penalty." Leeger stood. "I'm going to give you a little time to think about that."

The tall man slapped the door twice with the palm of his hand. It opened immediately, but he didn't leave. "And Nabulit? Don't think this is one of those silly head games they taught you in Interrogator 101. No one is going to come in here and offer you a deal. You're going to give us the names of everyone you've met, and everything you told them. Then we're going to decide if you get shipped off to a war-zone penal unit—or if we kill you right here."

"**H**e'll talk. He knows that his protector's abandoned him."

Leeger spoke in a darkened room next to the interrogation cell. Three large wall screens provided a dull illumination, one showing Captain Nabulit nervously seated at the table while the other two held blurred images of video footage paused in midplay. Leeger's boss, whose son had been tormented by their prisoner only months before, stood facing the screens. As tall as his security chief and only two years his senior in age, Olech Mortas nodded judiciously.

"Look at this here."

Mortas activated one of the tapes, revealing a setting that both he and Leeger had seen before. The recording showed a sterile white room at Glory Main, containing two transparent cylinders that ran from floor to ceiling. A figure in an armored fighting suit entered the space, followed by Jander and the alien that had been impersonating a Force psychoanalyst named Captain Amelia Trent. They were the only survivors of a group of four who'd been marooned on a hostile planet, and their tattered uniforms were covered in dirt and blood. Jander was the taller of the two, but they shared similar features in that their hair was dark, both of them were in their twenties, and they looked like they could use a meal. They were directed to remove all their clothing before entering the cylinders, which were referred to as decontamination tubes.

Trent was visibly shaken by the command, and fixed frightened eyes on the tubes while slowly peeling off her ragged flight suit. Seeing her discomfort, Jander reached out and touched the bare flesh of her left side. "Hey. Thanks for not dying on me."

Olech paused the tape. "That mark on her ribs was where the alien was impaled by flying debris when they were stealing the shuttle. The thing had healed itself, but Jan didn't know that."

The tape started again. Naked and filthy, Jander and Trent began walking toward the now-open cylinders. In a childlike gesture, they took each other's hand. Looking at Trent with concern, Jander spoke again. "It's all right. They're just gonna wash us off, and then we'll get nice clean clothes and some hot food, and then they'll have the docs check us out."

Apparently those soothing words were not enough, as Olech's son continued to speak. "Listen. You just look at me while this is going on. All right? Look right in my eyes, until they hit us with the suds of course, but you just look right at me and everything will be fine. Heck, we got this far, what's a little shower?"

Trent responded with a weak smile. "Thank you, Jan. Get me through this, okay?"

Olech stopped the footage, turning toward Leeger in the gloom.

"They never showed us that part." Leeger murmured. They'd both seen footage of what had followed, the flashing lights and mechanical alarms, and the creature transforming into a swirling cloud of mothlike specks before fire had blown through the tube and incinerated it.

"Exactly. Doesn't seem too important, until you hear this."

Olech activated the third screen, where a graph jumped into life with the oscillations of audiotape. Jander's voice, shouting in anger and fear, a scene with which Olech and Leeger were familiar. When Jander's hijacked Sim shuttle had approached the barren space rock that held Glory Main, the headquarters defense systems had seized control of the vessel and set it on a collision course with the surface. Yelling over the radio, Jander had revealed that he was the son of the feared Chairman of the Emergency Senate.

"Answer me, damn you! Whoever you are, you will *not* survive the *shitstorm* when my father finds out what happened to me! *And he will!*"

The words were accompanied by the whine of the shuttle's straining engines, but then Trent's voice was heard. Soft. Resigned. Calm.

"Jander." A brief pause. "Thanks for getting me here, Jan."

Olech stopped the playback, already knowing that the invocation of his name had saved his son and his duplicitous companion.

"Something else they held back on us. Never heard her say that on the other tape," Leeger mused, trying to imagine why the senior officers at Glory Main had edited the recordings they had forwarded with the original report.

"But they included them in the package our friend"—Olech waved a hand at the screen showing their prisoner—"was showing around. Which means they considered them significant."

"Think they figured out something more happened in the tubes?" Despite weeks of interrogation, Jander had managed to keep his captors from learning that the alien had communicated with him telepathically while they were both trapped in the cylinders. When Jander had been released, he'd told his father how the shape-shifting creature had explained the entire ordeal in a sort of deathbed confession. That Jander and the others had been taken prisoner while being transported unconscious in the faster-than-light travel known as the Step. That the alien had already taken the place of the murdered Captain Trent by then, and how the quartet's marooning on the planet now known as Roanum had been a setup right from the start.

"I doubt it. If that were the case, Command could have scooped Jan up for further questioning at any time after he returned to the war zone."

"Maybe they're just trying to learn everything they can about the thing. For their own ends." Despite its shocking capabilities and near success at infiltrating a major headquarters, the alien's advent had not been repeated. The entire Force in the distant war zone had gone on high alert, but nothing like the creature had been seen in the seven months since the incident.

"That's quite possible. The thing has an astounding potential. Did you detect anything in the scuttlebutt suggesting the alien could act as a translator between us and the Sims? So far Ayliss has been the only one to think of that." The war had been in progress for forty years, and the possibility of finally being able to communicate with their humanoid enemy was something Olech found enticing.

"No, nothing we intercepted has suggested the thing could act as a go-between. Perhaps our alliance partners are curious because they don't believe the alien picked your son at random. Reena thinks they are." Leeger spoke of Olech's lover.

"After all this time, and all the goodies I've handed them, you'd think they would have learned to at least trust my judgment. Even if they don't trust me personally."

"Your little land grab didn't increase their confidence." Six months before, having learned that alliance members were staking claims to captured planets in the war zone, Olech had turned the tables on them by claiming the prizes for the Veterans Auxiliary. A popular agency, the Auxiliary had been tasked with setting up colonies for discharged soldiers on the captured planets.

"Those bandits want the natural resources, not the planets themselves. I made it abundantly clear that they'd all continue to share in the exploitation of those worlds. Their operations haven't skipped a beat, so there's no reason for them to resent my decision."

"But they do. And you should remember what

happened to the man who held the job you hold now, when he got that gang angry."

"Hard to forget, really. Considering I was there." Olech's somber face turned from the glow of the screens, wearing a wraithlike smile. "I just realized something. The man who used to have the job *you* hold got killed that same day in that same room, shielding me from the bullets."

Leeger returned the grin. "Why do you think I'm so concerned?"

Olech's hand came out of the shadows to rest on Leeger's shoulder. He turned back to the screens, staring at the prisoner. "All right, then. We need to find out exactly who our friend has been talking to, and what they were planning to do with this information—if he knows that part."

"And then?"

"Have him executed. It'll be a good message for our overly curious partners."

"No."

"No what?"

"I won't have him executed." Leeger started for the door. "I'll do it myself."

Heavy clouds blotted the sun when Olech emerged from the building where the prisoner was being held. Unity Plaza was almost the size of a small city and still growing, but its central tower wasn't far away, so he decided to walk. All around him, stone buildings rose out of manicured lawns, structures that housed the workings of humanity's highest level of government. In spite of that lofty status, Olech had insisted on large expanses of green grass with walkways as the complex grew. Thousands of people lived and worked at Unity, and the Chairman of the Emergency Senate was now surrounded by men and women hustling from one place to another.

Tensions among the alliance planets had reached even this place, and Olech knew that several of the faces in the crowd were Leeger's security people working incognito. Olech had flatly rejected the assignment of a bodyguard detail while inside Unity, but Leeger had insisted on the hidden escorts. Drone messengers flitted across the gray sky, and the Chairman knew that some of them were surveillance robots assigned to protect him.

Despite the threatening clouds, Olech wore a sunny smile as he walked. He was greeted by many of the different staffers as they passed, and returned most of the salutations by name. Mixed with the oppressive sense of a distant, lurking danger was a different sensation, one of expectancy and even relief that manifested itself in the humanity flowing around him. Olech Mortas had always considered himself a man of the people, and he still prided himself on his ability to take the pulse of a crowd.

He suspected that this particular crowd was feeling relieved because his daughter Ayliss was due to depart the next day, after a six-month residence. As an officer of the Veterans Auxiliary, Ayliss was being placed in charge of one of the newly-formed veteran colonies in the war zone. She'd spent the previous weeks being trained in her new duties by Olech and Reena, which some had viewed as an unwelcome rapprochement between the absentee father and the resentful daughter. For years, a rumor had circulated that Chairman Mortas hired attractive young men and women in a subconscious effort to replace the two motherless children who had grown up disliking him. The presence of his daughter at Unity had damaged the psychological ecosystem for many of its personnel, and they were glad to see her go.

The sun broke through the clouds for half an inhalation, momentarily casting the smiling faces in a bleached-out light. For that instant, in Olech's mind, they took on the pale, empty visages of dead men and women. Olech recognized some of the blank masks as people he'd sent to the war, all of them young, all of them killed. It was not the first time he'd hallucinated in this fashion, though the experience was relatively new.

Olech maintained his pleasant façade when he reached the security wall around the enormous stone tower that was his home. Moving through the scanners on a side gate, he wondered just how the carefree staffers would feel if they could see what he sometimes saw in them. Or if they knew that Ayliss was not the only Mortas who was about to leave them.

Nabulit looked up when Leeger reentered the interrogation room. He didn't speak, so Leeger placed an object on the table within his reach. It was a small dagger with a black handle inside a worn scabbard, and it made Nabulit look away.

"We found this hidden in your effects, along with the recordings of the Chairman's son. Jander told me about the man who owned this dagger. Cranther, the Sparta-can Scout who died saving his life on Roanum. Jan was carrying this knife, and a longer one, when he got to Glory Main. Decided to help yourself to a souvenir?"

Nabulit looked down at the weapon, but made no move to touch it.

Leeger took the dagger, and drew it from its sheath. The black blade showed some wear when he placed it directly in front of the other man. "Go on. Pick it up. I'll fight you barehanded, and you can use the knife. You win, we'll let you go."

"That's a lie."

"It's a chance. Troops just like Jan and Cranther are taking chances all over the war zone even as we speak. Pick it up."

"No."

Leeger walked to the observation window. He laced his fingers behind his back, and began examining the dark, non-reflective pane. His heart rate slowly increased as he waited for the sound of the chair, but after a few long seconds he knew nothing would happen. He returned to the table.

"This is what I hate the most about guys like you." Leeger retrieved the weapon and seated it in its carrier. "You didn't even *try*."

The double slap on the hatch caused it to open, and the dagger went outside. Leeger sat down.

"Now you're going to tell me everything I want to know."

Olech stood in another darkened room, meeting with another man who specialized in personal protection. They were far beneath Unity's central tower, looking through a sheet of bulletproof glass at a broad indoor firing range. The vista resembled a wooded country-side, a mock-up with rolling terrain, trees, bushes, and failing light. A lone figure with blond hair and black fatigues lay prone just in front of them between two fake hillocks, sighting down the barrel of a long Scorpion rifle.

"Watch this." Olech's companion was large, and his head was shaved almost bald. He extended a paw-like hand to press a button on a control console just below the window.

Far downrange, where the trees and bushes blocked the view, the silhouette of a human figure hopped up and began running toward them in a crouching zigzag. In the semidarkness, it was little more than a shadow. Before the moving shape had gone three steps, another one popped up from behind a mound many yards to the left and rushed forward. The first runner dived headfirst behind a low rise in the ground, and a third figure materialized off to the right, charging ahead.

The prone shooter might as well have been a statue.

The moving men repeated their brief moments of exposure in a seemingly random fashion, never more than two of them up at the same time, each exposed for only a few seconds. Olech studied the runners' movements, how they tried to reach the cover of low ground but sometimes opted for the concealment of the fake shrubbery. He noted with a combat veteran's eye that they never popped up in exactly the same spot where they'd gone to ground, and that they alternated the direction in which they crawled or rolled before rising again.

A speaker in the room broke the silence with a sharp crack, and the prone shooter seemed to flinch just a bit. The runner on the left, two strides into his rush, flipped over backward when the slug hit him. A second shot followed almost immediately, knocking down the middle runner just as he was rising from cover.

The shooter shifted minutely, swinging the long rifle to the right before firing three rapid shots. Tall fronds of faux grass jerked and twitched with the passage of the rounds, then the last runner was up too, having been flushed out by the near misses. The shooter fired twice more, drilling the projectiles into the fleeing figure's back and toppling it to the ground.

"Well done." The voice of the bald man boomed out over the firing range, but the shooter made no effort to acknowledge the compliment. The light in the room brightened just enough to show the three robot targets, human in every regard, coming to their feet where they had been gunned down. Glowing circles showed where the rounds had struck them, and they stood there in mute machine accusation.

"Resetting. This iteration the opponents will utilize smoke obscurants." The light went down again, and the robots hustled off.

"You've done a fine job with her, Dom." Olech gave a brief nod to the security man, Dominic Blocker. Deep lines crossed Blocker's forehead, but he radiated physical vitality.

"If I couldn't teach her how to shoot in six months, I ought to hang it up. She's a natural, by the way."

"Takes after her old man. I was the best shot in my platoon in Basic."

"That's funny. The official history says there wasn't time for Basic before you and the other kids shipped out." Blocker's voice was deep, the words unkind. Olech Mortas had joined the war against the Sims in its third year, when the conflict had been going so badly that a special waiver had dropped the volunteer age to twelve. Fifteen years old, he'd been thrown into battle with an army made up mostly of children. Badly wounded on a planet in a distant solar system, Olech had returned to Earth as one of the few survivors among the waivered recruits, a revered group still known collectively as the Unwavering.

"Sometimes the official story is different from the truth."

"Is that what Ayliss and I are going to find out on Quad Seven?" The colony Ayliss was slated to administer was on a planet code-named FC–7777, the two-letter prefix standing for Force Colonized. "That what you told her here is different from what she'll find there?"

"Reena and I told her the truth, while failing to convince her to take a different colony. It's going to be rough out there."

"You've got that right. A recently conquered planet, already being mined by Zone Quest, colonized by some worn-out combat vets who think they're going to inherit the place. Deep in the war zone, in a part of space routinely worked by Sim raiders and human pirates. And your daughter is the Veterans Auxiliary minister who's supposed to organize that circus."

"Don't sell those troops short. You're a combat vet, older than most of the ones you'll meet out there, and you're not worn out."

Blocker ignored the compliment. "It's a guaranteed losing situation no matter how you cut it. The Zone Quest managers are going to ignore her, and when the vets see that happen, they're going to reject her."

"Zone Quest will play ball with her just fine. They know they're only operating on that planet because I'm letting them."

"That won't hold up. The troops believe you gave the planet to the Auxiliary, and when they see that Ayliss is all chummy with the outfit that's mining the place without their permission, they'll turn against her."

"Listen to that pessimism. Not the Dom Blocker I remember."

"The Dom Blocker you remember was seventeen

years younger. He couldn't make you listen to him then, and apparently he can't do it now."

"I didn't listen to you because you didn't want me to do the one thing that was going to keep Ayliss and Jan alive."

"Your kids would have been just as safe if you'd let Faldonado and me track down Lydia's murderers. They poisoned your wife, robbed your kids of their mother, and what did you do? Pretended you didn't care, about your wife or your own children."

"You keep forgetting it worked."

"And you think that was a good thing? I don't know who else bought your charade, but Jan doesn't trust you at all, and Ayliss is worse. The woman I've been working with for the last six months is nothing like the little girl I left with you. She's fueled by blind rage, and that's your fault. You're just lucky that she found somebody else to hate."

The prone figure glanced back at them, and an impatient voice came over the intercom. "You going to give me something new to shoot, Dom?"

Blocker activated the intercom. "What did I teach you? You shoot, you move."

"But I got them all."

"You never get them all. Move."

They watched as Ayliss slowly wormed backward, away from the notch that had been her firing position. Slipping into a minor depression, she cradled the rifle in her elbows and began crawling toward another spot.

"Did you hear that? The eagerness? In all of the

ranges I've been on in my life, no matter what the target looked like, I never once fantasized I was shooting a living being." Blocker pointed. "I believe your little girl imagines she's shooting someone every time she squeezes the trigger."

"Me, you mean? I doubt that. We've been spending a lot of time together these past few months."

"No, I don't think she's shooting you, or even that bastard Python. She got one hell of a rush when she pushed him over that railing. I think that's why she took this job, why she picked Quad Seven, and why she's set aside her anger at you."

Olech's voice was low. "You mean she's kill-crazy?"

"Worse. In the fifteen years I spent in the war zone, I only saw a few guys who'd gone batshit over the blood. They were easy to spot; got all goofy whenever there was a chance of a fight. No, Ayliss is different. She knows she had to kill Python, but I think she was very surprised by how much she enjoyed it. She wants that feeling again, and she knows you can get away with a lot out in the zone."

The crawling figure in fatigues had found a new firing point at the base of a fake tree. Slowly extending the Scorpion, Ayliss looked down the barrel to familiarize herself with the new view.

"Look at the concentration. She's actually having fun out there. Reminds me of her mother."

Olech snorted. "That's the first time I ever heard that one. Everybody says Ayliss is just like me, and that Jan is just like Lydia."

"People don't see beyond the obvious. Ayliss resembles you, so of course she's just like you. Same for Jan and Lydia. Add in the way she died, and all the time that's gone by, and basically everybody forgot what she was like."

"I remember."

"Not sure you do. Or that you remember what *you* used to be like. You had the right medals, but she had the brains. She wasn't murdered to bring you to heel; it was to stop her from feeding you ideas that some people didn't like."

"Whoever they were, they've learned differently, haven't they? I *am* the Chairman of the Emergency Senate, you know."

"You wield a lot of power, but you spend a lot of time trying to keep everybody happy."

"Keeping everybody happy?"

"You look the other way on all sorts of things, in the name of keeping the alliance going. Like the slavery on Celestia. It's barbaric."

"Funny choice of words, there. Did you know that Horace and the rest of the Celestian leadership refer to the war zone as Barbaricum? Old Roman term for basically anything outside the Empire."

"They use a lot of funny words on Celestia. It's important to call a slave something else if you want to sleep through the night."

"Not sure how we ended up talking about Celestia."

"Yes you are. I'm an old personal-security man, and I can tell when something big is in the works. You're taking a trip off-world. You're going to use Ayliss's departure to cover your own, and something tells me you'll be stopping to see Horace Corlipso."

"I'm managing a war that stretches across entire star systems, Dom. And the Step lets me go anywhere. So if I did decide to go somewhere, what makes you think it would be Celestia?"

"Because Reena's going too. The only reason you'd take the chance of both of you disappearing is because you need her along when you see her brother."

"You make visiting the man who runs Celestia sound like a bad idea."

"It could be. I was long in the war zone when President Larkin got nailed, but once the Purge was done, a lot of new faces started showing up as recruits. Familiar faces. People who used to work security for some of the senators who died with Larkin."

"Yes?"

"They told me that Horace's bodyguards came to work that day loaded for bear—and that they killed Larkin, as well as several senators Horace didn't like. Not by accident."

"I've heard that rumor before. What are you saying?"

"Horace assassinated half the human government and made it look like an accident. I'm saying a guy like that could easily poison the troublesome wife of a promising politician."

Olech finally reached the last shadowy room of the day. This one wasn't far from the shooting range below Unity's main tower, and it was almost as big. It contained one of mankind's most important secrets, and so it was even more secure than Olech's personal quarters.

The woman who shared those quarters stood very close to one of the room's looming walls, the fingers of one hand resting on a glass frame just below eye level. The entire wall, and two of the others, was covered in panels just like the one she was touching. The lights in the room were low, giving a golden hue to the parchment-like material inside each of the frames. Her own face, framed by dark red hair and tinged with concern, looked back in a ghostly reflection.

At one time, Reena Corlipso had spent endless hours in that room, studying the almost-hieroglyphic messages. The meaning of the pictographs had been deciphered long ago, shortly after the panels had been found inside a deep-space probe that had mysteriously reappeared near Earth. The ease of decryption was not surprising, as the pictures were meant to be understood. They described the miraculous technology that had carried the probe back to Earth. The Step.

The faster-than-light method of travel had allowed humanity to reach out across the solar systems, colonizing habitable planets until the dark day when they encountered the Sims. Although the Step's origin was an old secret shrouded in rumor and outright lies, the people who knew the truth sometimes wondered if the gift had been a cruel trick by a malicious and still-unidentified entity.

The room's small door opened, and Reena knew

without looking that her lover had arrived. She turned toward the tall figure and watched it resolve into the man she knew so well. Olech wore a dark suit cut in a military style with a high collar, and the blood-red ribbon that marked him as one of the Unwavering stood out on his chest. Strong hands slid around her waist, exploring the swell of her hips and the fabric of her dress. Cut low to show off her considerable bosom, it was informal attire that she usually reserved for the bedroom.

They kissed, acknowledging the approach of a series of voyages that might separate them forever. They embraced in silence while Reena noted the unusual way that Olech's weight bore down on her. She slid her palms onto his cheeks and raised his face from her shoulder.

"You know, two people who are finally going to get married really should look a lot happier than we do."

"Honestly, if I haven't learned it by now I'm just going to have to figure it out once I'm there." Ayliss Mortas had joined her father and Reena in the subterranean room. Her blond hair, which she'd kept long her whole life, was now cut off just below her ears. She wore well-used walking boots, into which a coarse set of olive drab trousers were tucked. A long tan shirt hung down over her hips, and a leather belt crossed her waist. Conditions on FC–7777 were austere, and she'd been wearing that rig or military fatigues for most of the prior six months to get ready.

"Just a few final reminders, that's all." Despite the many hours Olech had spent tutoring his daughter in the past weeks, he appeared slightly nervous. "Whatever you do, don't favor one side too much. The veterans will try to manipulate you as a representative of the Auxiliary, and Zone Quest will try to paint you as being on their side because I let them continue operating there."

Ayliss gave him a smirk. "You know, this all sounds vaguely familiar. As if I heard it over and over these last several months."

"How is Lee doing out there?" Reena asked. The trio stood in the center of the room, near the ancient space probe that had carried the diagrams that adorned the walls. There were many places in Unity where they could speak without fear of surveillance, but few of them were as secure as this room.

"Making lots of new friends. If I don't get out there soon, they'll probably make him an honorary vet—or enlist him." Lee Selkirk had been the chief of Ayliss's security detail until their relationship had been revealed by their nearly disastrous brush with the duplicitous Python. Fired from that role, he'd traveled to FC–7777 two weeks earlier. "You were right about sending him in without a cover story. The veterans had already identified a few moles among them, people they believed were Zone Quest spies, and they weren't gentle when they ejected them."

"Does he think they're willing to listen to you?"

"Hard to tell at this point. There's this one senior

NCO who's in charge, and so far the vets are still following military hierarchy. That solidarity has been reinforced by the friction with ZQ."

"You can get a lot of mileage out of that." Reena spoke softly, having coached Ayliss on the subject of politics and winning her grudging acceptance. "If you work out some compromises on these areas of friction, it will put you above the fray, where you want to be perceived."

"I might have heard that one before, too." Ayliss gave her a brief smile. "Sooner or later, I'm going to end up on one side. And after that, it becomes a fight."

"Precisely why you don't want to end up on any side at all."

Ayliss opened her mouth to speak, but her father beat her to it.

"I know your shuttle's taking off soon, but I wanted to tell you this myself." Olech glanced at Reena, then continued. "When you leave here, Reena and I are leaving as well. We're traveling to Celestia, to get married."

Ayliss regarded Olech with a blank look for several seconds, then an expression of minor revelation appeared. Her eyes moved over the panel-covered walls, and she nodded without speaking.

Olech exhaled audibly before draping an arm around Reena. "We didn't want you to get the news in the war zone. Obviously, we're keeping this very quiet."

"Leeger can't be happy you're going off-world."

"Leeger doesn't like it when I go outside. And he thinks bad things happen in the Step."

"They do." Ayliss's words were a whisper. "Sometimes, entire ships disappear."

"That's true. But thousands of men and women get killed, wounded, and lost every month this war continues. I can't ask them to go in harm's way if I'm afraid to travel between two solar systems nowhere near the war zone."

"That's not all you're doing."

"No it's not." Olech's eyes were somber. "You know I have to try."

Ayliss extended both hands, placing one on each of them but speaking to Reena. "When you get back here, remind your new husband that having both his children in the war zone is enough danger for one family."

CHAPTER TWO

On a planet many star systems away from Earth, Lieutenant Jander Mortas was experiencing something akin to blindness. The darkness surrounding him wasn't total, and every now and then, a break in the tall trees allowed some starlight to penetrate the night woods. Even so, those spots of increased illumination were spread far apart and only turned the gloom into a murky gray.

The terrain was quite varied, and he had to move with caution. More than once he'd fallen into unexpected dips in the ground or tripped over small boulders. That wasn't the worst part, unfortunately, as the various creatures that lived in the forest were making his painstaking journey even more unpleasant. Roughly an hour into his trek he'd stopped suddenly at the edge of a dangerous drop-off, and his abrupt halt had created an unexpected silence. Not far behind him, something had taken a single loud step before stopping as well.

The ground under his boots was covered with many seasons of dead leaves and fallen branches, and so most of Mortas's movement had been noisy. Having been made aware of the creature that was tracking him, he'd delicately negotiated the minor cliff to his front and then checked his course with a small compass. A Force shuttle had passed overhead just then, its running lights offering a merciful view of the obstacles to his front, and Mortas had stepped out quickly. Bulling forward, he'd intentionally come to a dead stop for no reason.

The dark silence was interrupted by a single sound, the crunch of the detritus on the forest floor under a hoof or a paw. Nothing followed it. The night was warm, and he was sweating freely into his fatigues, but a chill crawled up the back of his neck as if something was watching him. Clearly he was being stalked, and he'd tried to remember the species of the planet's indigenous wildlife. Standing there in the shadows, Mortas had realized that he knew nothing about the creatures that called the woods home even though he'd been living and training on this planet for the previous seven months.

MC–1932, seized from the Sims decades earlier and controlled by the Human Defense Force (hence the MC designation, for Military-Controlled) was a major base in that part of the war zone. Numerous units called it home, among them the Orphan Brigade in which Mortas was a platoon leader. Almost destroyed in combat six months before on a planet called Fractus, the brigade was slowly coming up to full strength, and so training was practically nonstop. The jaunt through the forest that had transformed him into possible prey was part of that training, an all-night individual movement without the aid of the multipurpose infantry goggles on which Mortas had come to depend.

The goggles could do wondrous things, and at that moment he was missing the way they let him see in the dark. His well-worn electronic eyes were back in the office he shared with Sergeant Dak, his platoon sergeant and the author of that night's training event. Dubbing the sightless movement through the woods "Goggle Appreciation Night," Dak had sent the entire platoon off individually, spread out across many acres of deep woods. Their start point was only a few miles from the Orphan Brigade's barracks, and the finish line for the walk was just short of their battalion area.

He'd stood stock-still for several minutes, and so had the creature somewhere off in the shadows. Or so he'd hoped. Unable to penetrate the gloom, Mortas had been forced to fight his own imagination and the images of some horrible, fang-toothed beast with razor-sharp claws that might be able to see in the dark and move without making a sound.

The creature finally proved the last part wrong, crunching off into the distance on what had to be at least four paws. Breathing out a noiseless exhalation of relief through his open mouth, Mortas had waited several minutes more before resuming his walk.

The dirt under his boots grew firm and began to rise, pressing thin branches against his helmet, torso armor, and sleeves. The cloying tendrils of a spiderweb passed across his mouth, and the touch of the gossamer webbing sent him into a frenzy. Swinging his arms madly, his palms encountering more and more of the spider's work, he began to twist his entire body while swiping at the exposed back of his neck, certain that the arachnid was dropping down inside his fatigue shirt.

One of his elbows barked against the trunk of a very solid tree, and the jolting pain launched a tidal wave of muttered curses. Trying to put some distance between himself and the web, his hands spasmodically wiping off the sticky material, Mortas caught the toe of one boot on a jagged piece of deadfall. Unable to see it, he felt himself falling just as the broken end of one branch began running up his leg toward his groin. With no other choice, he lifted that leg in the air and made a clumsy hop.

The awkward move freed him from the threat to his privates, but the blackness betrayed him and he landed on the rest of the fallen branch with all his weight on one boot. His ankle turned sideways, and he went crashing to the dirt in a cacophony of snapping wood and full-throated swearwords.

"You all right there, buddy?" a bored voice asked, and a dull light flicked on a few feet away. Sergeant Dak had forbidden the platoon members to carry any kind of illuminants, and as platoon leader, Mortas had considered it his responsibility to follow the rules set by his right-hand man. Looking up at the dim glow, he recognized the voice.

"Ringer, is that you?"

"Oh. Hey, El-Tee Mortas. Lemme help you up." Instead of grasping Mortas's outstretched hand, Ringer's long fingers slipped under his torso armor near his clavicle. The big man levered him into a standing position with little effort. "There we go."

The light clicked off, and Mortas took a moment to rearrange his uniform. Ringer was an old hand with the Orphans, but he'd missed Fractus because he'd been in the hospital.

"How's the hearing tonight, Ringer?" That wasn't actually the man's name. Like so many of the combat veterans of the decades-long war with the Sims, Ringer had sustained a lasting injury that modern medicine could not resolve. The drumming in his ears sometimes made it difficult for Ringer to detect low sounds even up close, and the platoon took pains to pair him off with soldiers with better hearing.

"Kind of a dull buzz, sir. I thought it was insects for a while, but I haven't been bitten by anything, so I guess it's me."

"Well, one of us has wandered out of his lane."

"Oh, that would probably be me. I've done Sergeant Dak's midnight stroll a few times, and finally found this downhill patch that runs all the way back to the barracks. I sorta zigzag around out here, but as long as I don't go uphill anywhere, I always come out in the right spot."

"That's amazing."

"Not really. I never got any good with a compass, so if you take my goggles away, I'm pretty much lost."

"I suppose we could walk together, unless you want to keep wandering." Mortas checked his azimuth, pondering Ringer's statement about the overall downslope.

"That'd be fine, sir. We're almost there anyway."

"Really? I thought I was still a good couple of miles out."

"How long you been in the infantry, sir?" The words were spoken in such an indifferent fashion that it was impossible to take offense. "Anything under ten miles counts as almost there."

When they arrived at the edge of the tree line facing the battalion area, Mortas and Ringer were greeted by most of the platoon and Sergeant Dak. The entire brigade had been ordered to form up on a parade field a half mile distant, and First Platoon had to hustle to get there.

The three infantry battalions of the First Brigade (Independent) of the Human Defense Force each consisted of three companies made up of three platoons, which were in turn made up of three squads. Although the unit was not yet completely up to strength, it still made for a huge number of uniformed men standing in rectangular formations facing a large wooden stage. The assembly order had interrupted early-morning activities all over the brigade, and so different blocks of men were adorned in the T-shirts and shorts of physical training while others sported camouflaged fatigues mottled with green, black, and brown.

Mortas's platoon, standing at attention as part of First Battalion's B Company, was the only unit wearing helmets and body armor. Dirty faces and mud-specked fatigues showed they'd been training hard and, regardless of their personal opinions of Goggle Appreciation Night, the First Platoon troops bore the marks of exertion with pride.

Standing in front of the three squads, Mortas could only see B Company's commander and the commanding officer of First Battalion. Both of those officers, veteran Orphans, had replaced men lost on Fractus. First Battalion was now led by Major Hatton, a bear-sized individual popular with the troops, who had been standing next to the battalion's previous commander when he'd been killed. The battalion staff, including an intelligence captain named Pappas who'd been poached from a much-higher echelon, stood in a row behind Hatton.

B Company was commanded by a young captain named Emile Dassa. Though only twenty, Dassa had been serving in the war for five years and in the Orphans for almost two. Lean and dark-haired, Dassa had given Mortas crucial tactical advice before the brigade's perilous defense of an important ridgeline. They were now fast friends, which Mortas still considered slightly odd because they had fought in prep school five years before, a fight that had sent Dassa to the war zone.

Movement on the reviewing stand caught his eye, and Mortas observed several figures in camouflage fatigues mounting the rostrum. He immediately recognized Colonel Watt, the Orphan Brigade's beloved commander, and then noted the heavyset figure of General Merkit, the officer in charge of personnel assignments across the Force. The brigade's expected dissolution after Fractus had been halted when Merkit unexpectedly arrived on MC–1932, and he'd been instrumental in the unit's rebuilding over the last six months.

Officers and senior NCOs from the brigade headquarters filed into place behind Watt and Merkit, giving some of Mortas's troops an opportunity to mutter choice comments.

"Look at ol' Merkit. Hardly recognize him. All skin and bones."

"Remember what he looked like when he got here? I bet he's dropped fifty pounds."

"That's what you get for hanging around with the walking infantry."

"He sure didn't want to hang out with us at first. They say Colonel Watt had to practically drag him to PT."

Mortas tried hard not to smirk, standing rigidly at attention. The comments continued.

"That was part of the plan. Force the fat bastard to spend time with us."

"It worked, didn't it? Colonel Watt killed him with kindness, and he rebuilt the brigade."

The discussions ended when a shouted command told the Orphans to stand at ease. Spreading his muddy boots to shoulder width and placing his hands against the small of his back, Mortas watched Colonel Watt approach a microphone at the front of the platform.

"And good morning, Orphans."

"Good morning, sir!" Hundreds of voices shouted in return.

"This is a big day for the brigade. Although we're not quite up to one hundred percent, you've all performed so well in our recent live-fire evaluations that we've been put back on the list of active units."

The voices rose again, a chorus of loud shouts and low grunts that quickly subsided.

"I thought you'd like that. Here's something else I think you'll like. We have just received our first mission, and this one goes to B Company of First Battalion. Captain Dassa!"

Dassa popped to attention, and called out, "Here, sir!"

"When we got alerted for Fractus, your company was en route to Verdur to clean up some Sim holdouts. As B Company never got to do that job, I wanted to offer the assignment to you. Same mission: chase down the Sim remnants who've been giving the stations on Verdur so much trouble—and kill them."

Behind him, Mortas heard Ringer's drawl. "Ya think Sergeant Dak will give us our goggles back now?"

At the rear of the platoon formation, the platoon sergeant growled, "Cut the chatter."

On the platform, Colonel Watt looked directly at B Company. "What do you say, Captain Dassa?"

"B Company accepts the mission on behalf of the entire brigade, sir!"

"That's what I expected to hear. It's only fitting, considering how many times on Fractus I had to explain why B Company was wearing jungle fatigues on a planet with no jungle."

The laughter was subdued, as was all joking when it came to the subject of Fractus. Although the brigade had held its ground and destroyed an enormous number of Sims, the cost had simply been too high.

Colonel Watt continued. "On this special occasion, I want to personally thank General Merkit for the invaluable help he's given to our brigade in its rebuilding. Sadly, General Merkit is leaving us later today. I can honestly say that he has become a true friend to the Orphans and that he will be missed."

Watt turned to the florid-faced man standing next to him, and shook his hand. They spoke briefly, words that no one could hear, and then Merkit appeared to be declining Watt's offer to address the troops. The brigade commander would not relent, however, and Merkit finally took the microphone.

When he spoke, his voice shook. "I cannot express my humble gratitude to all of you. When I came out here, it was with the intention of leaving as soon as I could."

Merkit stared at the platform's decking for an instant, and the watching soldiers saw Watt's lips moving. Merkit's somber face brightened just a bit.

"Your colonel just told me that most Orphans feel the same way when they get here."

A low ripple of laughter rose from the formation.

"On my first day, I was being driven to your brigade headquarters when I saw a soldier limping down the road. His fists were balled up, he was sweating all over, and he didn't seem to be getting anywhere. I offered him a ride, and you know what he said? He told me he was rehabbing a leg wound on his own because he was afraid that if he went to a therapy center, he might be reassigned to a unit other than the Orphans. I will confess to you that I have never been more ashamed in my life than I was right then.

"I was out of shape and out of touch, and that soldier's example told me I should learn how to be less like me and more like him. If anyone thinks I came out here and rebuilt this unit, they're wrong. This unit, and the men in it, rebuilt me.

"I watched that limping soldier march in here today, and I couldn't have been more impressed. I found something invaluable here, a genuine inspiration, from selfless people with indomitable hearts and unbreakable spirits. No matter where I go, and no matter where the Orphans go, I will always be ready to join you again.

"Thank you, and good luck to all of you."

A few hurried hours later, Lieutenant Mortas entered the offices of the battalion's intelligence section. He was now dressed in jungle fatigues, dark green with horizontal black stripes and brown smudges, so he stood out from the soldiers in woodland camouflage.

The intelligence section was compiling final estimates of the enemy B Company would encounter on Verdur, and Mortas had been dispatched to find out when the report would be ready.

He passed between desks where different screens showed wire diagrams of Sim unit organizations and satellite footage of the heavily vegetated planet. Stepping into the doorway of Captain Pappas's office, he was surprised to see the intelligence officer dressed in jungle fatigues and stuffing personal items into a rucksack.

"You going with us, sir?"

"Of course." The tall man smiled at him while closing the backpack. "I haven't seen Sammy Sim in the flesh for seven months. What kind of an intel guy would I be if I passed up a chance like this?"

Mortas took a step into the office. "Something going on, sir?"

"Look at you. Less than a year in the zone, and already paranoid." Pappas lifted his torso armor onto the desk. Its detachable canvas covering sported jungle camouflage, and he began adjusting different pouches that hung on its front. "Good for you. Yes, there is a reason I'm coming along. Seven months ago, B Company was supposed to perform a standard cleanup mission, chasing down Sim holdouts pestering our stations. When you got diverted to Fractus, a corporate security force was sent in to do the cleanup. That's not surprising; one of the stations belongs to Victory Pro."

Victory Provisions was a powerful corporation operating all over the war zone. Primarily a supplier of military rations, they'd branched out into farming the conquered planets. They were particularly interested in the Sims' preternatural ability to grow food just about anywhere.

"Apparently those security guys weren't crazy about going into the jungle, and stuck close to the sites. When they pulled out, they said everything was calm and suggested there aren't many Sims left. But ground sensors out in the bush suggest there's a sizeable number of Sammies working the area." Pappas stopped fussing with his gear, and looked Mortas in the eye. "Those sensors are notoriously unreliable, but if the estimates are even close, the Sims on Verdur have been reinforced somehow. Maybe another group of holdouts finally linked up with the original bad guys, or maybe Sam found a way to slip some more troops in."

"Wouldn't the surveillance satellites pick up the heat signatures, if the Sims were moving around in big numbers?"

"And now you know the real reason why I'm coming along. A reliable expert of impeccable judgment"— Pappas winked at him—"to say exactly how many Sims are out there and, if the numbers are correct, how they're not getting spotted."

Though heavily sedated in his Transit Tube, Olech Mortas waited for the dreams. His high rank seldom allowed him to risk traveling in the Step, but as a younger politician he'd used it frequently. On every one of those faster-than-light trips, Olech had dreamt he was being visited by important people from his past. In recent months he'd consulted an expert on this phenomenon, and had been surprised when it was pointed out that almost all of his dream visitors were dead.

His mind slowly entered dream consciousness, a swimmer rising from dark water toward a lighted surface, and when he emerged it was in a familiar place. A crescent-shaped room that resembled a lecture hall, with desks and chairs rising away from a raised speaker's platform. The flags of the different alliance planets hung from the high ceiling over the dais, and a silver-haired man was addressing the assembly.

It was the final session of the old Interplanetary Senate, of which Olech had been a member, and the speaker was Interplanetary President Larkin. Senators from Celestia, Broda, Tratia, Dalat, and all the other settled worlds were standing around Olech, shouting, shaking their fists, outraged by President Larkin's revelation that he'd launched a hundred space probes in an attempt to contact the still-unidentified entity that had given mankind the Step. Larkin stepped away from the podium, unsurprised by the reaction, holding his palms up to quiet them.

Olech's sleeping body twitched in anticipation of the remembered violence, but there was something very different in the dream. The chamber was silent. Clearly the men and women surrounding him were yelling, and yet there was no sound. His eyes began searching the room, flying over the contorted faces and outraged gestures as if he expected someone to approach and speak to him.

He was bumped by someone, then someone else, and then he was being carried forward as the assemblage surged down toward Larkin. Olech joined the shouting then, trying to get the President's attention, hollering for him to get out, just as he'd done on that fateful day, but even his own voice was silenced in the dream. The doors on all sides began to fly open, and instead of the relief he'd felt at the time upon seeing the different bodyguard teams entering the room, Olech felt the surging fear, the dread of what followed. Many of the armed men had merely been trying to reach their charges, and he'd recognized the looming figure of Faldonado, chief of his own security team, forcing his way toward him.

Olech continued downward, magically passing through the desks and the chairs, getting far closer to the doomed Larkin than he had in real life. Flashes interrupted his vision, the first shots, and then he was engulfed in what had felt like a tornado. Buffeted from all sides by bodies, some fleeing, others diving for cover, and many of them falling as the slugs ripped into them. Still no sound, almost reaching Larkin, the walls behind the President chipping and bursting, the blood starting to appear all over the man's suit. Finally tripping, pressed to the carpeted floor, unable to breathe, and then seeing the arms covering his head and feeling the warm wetness on his back. Faldonado protecting his body with his own, his chest armor too light to stop the slugs, dying right there along with more than half of the Senate.

And finally Larkin's face, resting on the carpet right next to his, dark red on pale skin, and the words that were the only sounds in the dream tumult.

"Finish what I started, Olech. They're waiting."

Unable to move, unable to breathe, panic setting in even as the light went out of Larkin's eyes. Wriggling, rocking, anything to gain a centimeter's distance between his chest and the unyielding floor. A cry of utter desperation welling up just before the scene shifted, and then he was in another room, another place of loss where his life had changed forever.

Sobbing, holding the hand that was losing strength by the moment, raising his eyes to see the ravaged visage of his wife Lydia in her final moments. A skeleton's face on the pillows, gouged with a network of lines that hadn't been there a few days before. Before the poison had been somehow slipped to her, before the hours of convulsing agony, pain so deep and unreachable that her eyes had bugged out and her lips curled back in a snarl that had lasted for hours.

The torment was ending, and she'd been able to speak, telling Olech that the only way to save the children from the same fate was to pretend he'd never cared for them—or her. Ever the strategist, her pragmatism had never been more keen than the moment when she'd applied it to herself, her memory, and her survivors. Slipping away, the pain finally gone, and yet spending the last moments convincing him it was the only way.

"You know what you have to do, my darling. You *have* to. For them, for me. Do it for me."

Remembering his grief-stricken assent, kissing her hand until it had gone limp, and looking up again to find the wraith lying sightless and still. In the dream, however, that moment was slightly different. The death's-head turned toward him, and a rumbling voice like the roar of an underground river booming through a cavern spoke again.

"You have to do it."

CHAPTER THREE

"**D**ecided to sleep in this morning, young man?" First Sergeant Merrill Hemsley smiled at Lee Selkirk as he walked toward him. A low cloud of brown dust curled around Selkirk's boots as he moved, kicked up by the wheeled vehicle that had just dropped him at the firing range.

"My carefree days with you and your people are coming to a close, First Sergeant." Selkirk gave the older man a grin. "My boss is due to arrive any day now, so I have to clean up my act."

Calm commands rose from the firing line only a few yards away, as NCOs walking back and forth made sure everyone was ready to start shooting. A low wooden tower stood not far back from the prone shooters, and the gently rising terrain to their front was mostly open for a thousand yards in a mix of tan and brown. At set intervals, numbered boards stood up from the ground to indicate the boundaries of the lanes for each firing position.

Hemsley shook his head. "Sad state of affairs, when an adventurous man like you changes his habits just because his girlfriend is inbound."

"Girlfriend. Boss. Pretty much the same thing, in my experience."

"Mine too. That's why I married the Force." Hemsley turned to survey the line of prostrate figures just as the tower's speaker gave the command to open fire. Though recently retired from the Human Defense Force, Hemsley retained his rank and authority because he was the most senior soldier among the planet's motley group of colonists. The figures on the firing line wore all manner of garb, from fatigues of many designs to civilian work clothes. Both male and female, they sighted down the barrels of Scorpion rifles as the targets presented themselves.

Popping up from shallow holes at varying distances, the silhouettes of charging Sim soldiers would only be exposed for a few seconds. Slugs began dropping targets left and right, the rifles cracking and popping in a cycle that rose and fell as successive targets appeared and vanished. Selkirk noted that many of the silhouettes were still exposed when the allotted time for each of them ran out.

Hemsley folded muscular arms across his chest, disappointed by the marksmanship but unwilling to say so. "I suspect your boss is planning to meet with the Zone Guests before she deigns to visit us."

Selkirk recognized the derogatory nickname that most of the troops in the war zone used when referring to Zone Quest, the powerful mining outfit that was FC–7777's only other occupant. "Minister Mortas has always had a mind of her own. She might surprise you."

The last targets disappeared, and the range NCOs called out the cease-fire. The men and women on the firing line placed the Scorpions on notched stakes next to each position before coming to their feet. Although the Scorpion was designed to function in concert with tactical goggles, that day's exercise was being conducted with only the naked eye. Expectant faces looked out from under an assortment of cloth caps, waiting for the tabulation from the tower.

"I doubt very much that a first-timer in the zone— and a rich one at that—could surprise me too much."

"Position Number Twelve! Top score—perfect score!" The speaker crackled the words, and the standing figures all turned to see who had managed to knock down every one of the random targets. A few good sports hooted or clapped hands, but clearly the group didn't recognize the winner yet. It was one of the women, dressed in green canvas trousers, a tan work shirt, and a floppy brown hat.

"You sure about that, First Sergeant?" Selkirk asked, the grin broadening.

The shooter from Position Number Twelve doffed the hat, revealing blond hair that hung just below her ears and a brilliant smile. Confused expressions quickly changed to recognition of a face they'd seen many times on the Bounce, that of Ayliss Mortas, the new Veterans Auxiliary supervisor of their colony.

The firing line quickly converged on her, offering greetings and congratulations.

"So that's why you were late today. Slippery son of a bitch. How'd you sneak a civilian onto my range, Selkirk?"

"Oh don't be like that, First Sergeant—we're all civilians now, aren't we?"

First Sergeant Hemsley sat on the ground across from Ayliss, with a small campfire between them. "Yeah, there was a whole active-duty brigade here until your father shook things up. All-Tratian outfit, thick as thieves with the Guests, treated us like beggars." The day's training had ended, and all around them scores of other fires lit up the night.

"You don't seem to be beggars anymore." Ayliss remarked lightly, nodding at the field tray in her lap. When the sun went down, trucks from the veterans' underground settlement had brought out a hot meal along with a small supply of alcohol. "Zone Quest meeting your needs, now that the Tratians are gone?"

"Oh this? I wouldn't be much of a First Sergeant if I didn't know how to get my people a few luxuries." The flames danced across Hemsley's cheeks. "But you already know we're not on good terms with the Guests. Your boyfriend Selkirk's been sniffing around for two weeks now."

"I didn't see *everything*, First Sergeant." Selkirk, seated next to Ayliss, went back to consuming a piece of steak that he'd been eating with his hands.

"You came close. Almost got to my secret stash—before the Banshees caught you."

Though already aware that the colony included a small group of former Banshees, Ayliss felt a thrill at the mention of the elite all-female fighting units.

Selkirk gave Hemsley a look of innocence. "I was just taking a little walk, seeing where all those Sim tunnels went."

FC–7777 had been the site of a modest enemy colony before the humans had conquered it. The Sims had been mining an energy ore that the humans called Go-Three. Unlike the massive Zone Quest complex atop the nearby hill that almost qualified as a mountain, the Sims had integrated their efforts with the terrain. They'd tunneled into a ridge near the future site of the Zone Quest mine and constructed underground homes as they dug out the ore. Hemsley and his people now lived in those passageways.

"That's what the ladies told me. You're lucky your young man is so good-looking, Minister; the Banshees can get rough with men who misbehave. They usually end up with balls swollen the size of oranges."

"Oh, they're already the size of oranges." Ayliss bumped Selkirk with a shoulder, smiling broadly. "How many of the female colonists are former Banshees?"

The war over the galaxy's habitable planets had created an odd division in the Human Defense Force.

While men and women served in every branch at every rank, the combat troops sent to fight on the habitable planets were all male. The all-female Banshees fought in fully contained powered suits, and their ferocity was legendary.

"Only five Banshees, half a squad that opted to stay in the zone when their terms ended. I've got one 117 veterans all told, roughly split between the genders. Except for the Banshees, most of 'em never saw combat." The First Sergeant's expression grew grim. "But your father gave us this planet, and sent you out here to stop Zone Quest from mining it without our permission."

"Actually, he sent me to manage the establishment of this colony. Zone Quest is authorized to operate here as long as they provide you and your people with supplies and other support."

"You know they haven't been doing that. And that terminates any agreement."

"They told my father you've been consorting with a gang of space pirates."

"Pirates?" Hemsley snorted. "No self-respecting pirate outfit would be anywhere near this place. They're all focused on the construction zone and the planets with the big bases, where there's something worth stealing."

"But you have been getting your support from some unauthorized sources. Smugglers."

"We've been doing a little horse-trading with passing ship captains, sure. Like I said, I wouldn't be any good at my job if I didn't know how to procure a few things. But we're getting off track here. Your father gave this planet to discharged soldiers as a colony, and that means that Zone Quest either pays us for mining the place, or they leave. And I want to know what you're going to do about that."

Ayliss set her tray aside and brushed some dirt off her trousers. "Zone Quest is hosting a little ceremony tomorrow, welcoming me. You might want to attend."

"Oh, I know all about that. I've even seen that great big house they built for you. Only one that's bigger is Station Manager Rittle's."

"Lee, I'd like to express my thanks to those Banshees now. For not damaging your balls." Ayliss stood, and Selkirk rose with her. Hemsley and the others remained seated, but Ayliss spoke to them as she and Selkirk moved away. "You really should come to that ceremony tomorrow. I think you'll like it."

Hemsley came to his feet and walked over to Dom Blocker, who had been standing off to the side the entire meal. Ayliss's small security detachment had joined her at the range once her identity had been revealed.

"Your girl is going to have to do better than that."

"I'm sure the Minister will do whatever she deems appropriate."

"Those Zone Quest guys don't fool around, you know. Especially Rittle. He's tough, smart, and devious. She crosses him, she's going to need friends."

"Never had much to do with ZQ, in my part of the

war. Stole some good chow from them, but that was about it."

Some of the figures around the different fires began to sing just then. It was a popular love song with lyrics changed to match the war zone, and soon the other shadowy figures picked it up.

> Sammy man, Sammy man, just where are
>   you tonight?
> No one else has touched me in quite the way
>   you have.
> You thrilled me, near killed me, but always
>   fulfilled me,
> What would I be without you, sweet Sammy
>   the Sim?

"Most of these people never saw Sam up close, if they saw him at all." Hemsley shook his head. "I never liked that song."

"Me neither. Sam took way too many of my guys for me to joke about him."

> You taught me how to duck and dodge, to
>   shoot and move,
> To load, to pray, drag friends away, and
>   quickly too.
> Broke my heart, broke my bones, spilled my
>   tears and my blood
> How can I ever pay you back, Sammy the
>   Sim?

"Ya know, a long time ago I heard about this shit-hot platoon sergeant, crazy guy who was supposed to have given up a cushy job protecting rich people so he could come out to the zone and suck wind with the rest of us," Hemsley said.

Blocker moved closer, turning so he could see Ayliss framed against the other fires. "Sure sounds like a crazy guy to me, First Sergeant. Giving up all that for this shit."

"Heard he reupped out here, too. Finished two hitches, then got his old job back." The two soldiers exchanged grins, the tension of the conversation with Ayliss easing. "Now why would a smart guy like Olech Mortas rehire somebody he'd fired, after all these years?"

"That's easy. He's not half as smart as everybody thinks he is."

> *Can I say I miss you, just between you and*
> *me?*
> *I've lived, I've cried, and almost died, all*
> *thanks to you.*
> *I have a gift I never gave, but it's all yours*
> *Can't wait to see you again, dear Sammy the*
> *Sim.*

Ayliss and Selkirk stopped to chat with different groups as they passed among the campfires. The veterans were clearly intending to sleep out under the stars, and had already begun to arrange their bedrolls. After exchanging pleasantries for a few minutes, Selkirk steered Ayliss outside the illuminated ground so that they could approach the Banshees' fire.

"That's them there. The big blonde is named Deelia. She talked the others into accepting their discharges and seeking greener pastures."

"And the guy she's holding?"

"That's Tupelo, the one I told you about. Deelia's husband. He's supposed to have been one of the mechanics on the Banshees' armored suits. For a guy who just spent seven years as a suit jock, he doesn't seem to want to talk about it much."

"So you think he's something else."

"He's got Spartacan deserter written all over him." The Spartacan Scouts were an elite reconnaissance force made up of conscripts and worse. "The Banshees and the Spartacans have always been simpatico. His skills could be useful."

A careless boot scuffed the dirt in the darkness nearby, but before Selkirk could react, a lone figure walked up. Unkempt hair, boyish looks, and eyes that glowed with something more than firelight. Selkirk relaxed and put a hand on the man's arm.

"Hey there, Ewing. Coming back from a walk?"

"Oh, the journey's just starting, Selkirk. You know that." The tone was dry and detached. "Who's your lady friend?"

"This is Minister Mortas. Ayliss, this is the best communications man the Force ever cashiered, Christian Ewing."

"Hello there. It's nice to meet you." Ayliss extended a hand, and Ewing swayed slightly when he reached for it.

"I thought First Sergeant confiscated your smoking gear." Selkirk's comment caused Ewing to smile.

"He's got his stashes, I have mine. Besides, McRaney always has a little something extra for me when he visits."

Ayliss flashed a meaningful look at Selkirk. Depending on the source, McRaney was either a violent smuggler or an out-and-out pirate. Either way, proof that he was working with the veterans could get the colony's charter revoked. She decided to keep Ewing talking.

"So why did the Force get rid of its best commo man?"

"A question I've asked myself many times. It's not like I was the only guy in the fleet who enjoyed a bit of the herb. You know, I only started smoking to keep awake on radio watch. A night in space can last a long time . . . or maybe it never ends. Anyway, nobody cared until I started to ask if anybody else was hearing the music."

"Music?"

"Yeah. Music. Like nothing I'd ever heard. Couldn't tell if it was instrumental, or voices. Beautiful, amazing stuff. Didn't hear it all the time, but every now and then it was like they were performing just for me."

"And how's that? That they were doing it just for you?"

"Radio watch that late at night, this far out in space— who else was listening?" Ewing tilted his head back, studying the stars. In the distance, an ore transport blasted off from the spacedrome on top of Zone Quest's mountain. The dull rumbling seemed to drive a pulse through the orange fire of the blastoff, and its reflection gave Ewing's face a mournful look. "I miss that."

He patted Ayliss on the shoulder before walking off.

"Hey Minister, come on up here!" Lola, the lead Banshee, called over a bare shoulder, and Ayliss responded by jogging up the file. At daybreak, the five Banshees had shaken her from the sleeping bag she'd shared with Selkirk. Dressed in form-hugging running gear, they'd invited her to join them for morning PT. She'd enthusiastically accepted, and so far had found the running easy.

The small file had shuffled past the collection of burned-out fires and circles of bedrolls before heading toward the veterans' settlement and Zone Quest's facility. The open ground had quickly shifted to fields of dark rocks, the Go-Three that the humans and the Sims both wanted so badly, and they now ran past knee-high spikes of the stuff.

"That's a good man you have there, Minister." The dark-haired Banshee's name was Lola, and she'd been the group's leader in the war. She nodded at a spot several hundred yards away, where Selkirk's lone figure ran on a parallel course. He wore a small automatic weapon on a sling and kept it tight to his side as he loped along.

"He certainly is."

"Of course he's a sitting duck, exposed like that. So I bet that old bodyguard of yours has got people covering you from the high ground."

Modest cliffs rose just beyond Selkirk's jogging form, closer to the old Sim colony and the mining operation. Somewhere up there, Blocker was shifting the other bodyguards around to keep the runners covered.

"He's not so old, and he's a vet like you." Ayliss glided along easily. "Two tours in the zone, got just about every medal you can think of."

"I can't think of too many medals." That came from Tin, a short, pretty Banshee in the middle of the file.

"And why's that?"

"Because Banshees don't think much of medals!" The five veterans proclaimed, laughing as one for a moment. In the short time she'd spent with them Ayliss had heard several pet phrases like that one, many of them instilled during Banshee Basic.

The ground started to rise, with more of the black spikes appearing on either side of a dirt road cleared straight through them. Ayliss knew that any obvious changes to the landscape had been the work of military engineers or Zone Quest, as the Sims who'd lived there originally had concentrated on not altering the landscape.

Jogging over the rise, they now passed a field of jagged black rocks taller than a man. That was a sign of rich deposits, and one of the reasons the Sims had decided to live in this area.

"Did Hemsley pick this route for you?" Ayliss felt the first runnel of sweat down her back, enjoying the exertion. The terrain to their front rose dramatically only a few thousand yards away, into a jagged black mountain insulated by low Zone Quest buildings.

"He did suggest we run by the headquarters, yes." Lola flashed a challenging smirk at her. "Just showing Station Manager Rittle that we're friends with the new minister."

"Which of these mansions is mine?" The spiked slopes of the ore mountain had been cleared and leveled in numerous places, and the residences of the Zone Quest management team were easy to spot. White walls, broad balconies, and gun turrets.

"You didn't expect them to let you live inside their wire, did you, Minister?" Deelia, the muscular blonde, called out from the rear. "That really nice house there, the big one with the walkway going all the way around the second floor, that one's yours."

Ayliss looked more closely at the mining compound above them, noting for the first time the double anti-personnel fencing that surrounded most of it. "Now why would they fence off a place that would get blasted right off the slope ten seconds into a Sim attack?"

"Very good, Minister!" Lola smiled while taking them down a side road, away from the mountain. "Sounds like you know something about Sammy's habits."

"Just what I've been briefed, that's all." Ayliss saw a chance to hear about the Banshees' combat experience, and felt her pulse climb. "Nothing like what you must've learned."

"Oh, there's not that much to learn about Sam. He's just like any other guy."

"Except his dick doesn't work!" Tin and one of the others shouted at the same time. Although the physiology of male and female Sims included genitalia almost identical to that of humans, the Sims were unable to reproduce.

"That's probably why he never gets distracted. Sam's a focused guy, Minister. Goes for the throat every time." Lola gave her a sideways glance. "Don't be in such a rush to meet him."

Ayliss shifted into ministerial mode, disturbed to have been read so easily. "Got my hands full just meeting everybody here."

The file turned away from the hill, heading back toward the spike-covered ridge where the veterans had made their home. The dirt road twisted and turned, and the Banshees picked up the pace. Every now and then the bouncing figure of Selkirk would appear, shadowing them much more closely now, weaving his way through the black spear points.

"You gonna meet the Station Manager today?" Lola didn't seem to be breathing heavily at all.

"I imagine he'll be there when they give me the keys to that house."

"Give that fat fucker our regards."

"You should do that yourself." Ayliss made the words an invitation. "I invited First Sergeant Hemsley, but I don't think he'll attend. He's gonna miss something fun if he doesn't."

"You gonna shake things up your first day?"

"Come along and see." Ayliss looked over her shoulder at the rest of the women. "Now, are we going to actually get a workout here, or are we going to stroll the whole way?"

The sun was high in the sky when Station Manager Rittle took the rostrum. A temporary stage had been erected in front of Ayliss's new house, with Zone Quest bunting and a wide canopy overhead. Upper- and middle-management staff from the mining operation were seated in the shade, with Ayliss and Selkirk in the front row. Blocker and two of her guards, wearing body armor and holding short-barreled assault weapons, stood at the back. Gathered directly in front of the stand, but much lower because of the slope, was a well-scrubbed contingent of Zone Quest miners. Farther back, a loose collection of veterans—including the Banshees—stood in the sun.

"I greet the arrival of Colonial Administrator Mortas with great happiness, as I'm sure all of you do as well." Rittle wore a khaki full-body suit and dark glasses and, despite Lola's description, was only slightly overweight. "The personnel turnover on Quad Seven has gone on for too long, and I look forward to days of greater organization and increased cooperation."

The mining staff clapped politely, while the veterans exchanged subdued glances. Only a few hundred yards up the slope, the antipersonnel fence that enclosed the mining site stood out against the black rock.

"So, without further ado, I present this humble abode"—Rittle turned an open palm toward the building behind him—"to Minister Ayliss Mortas. May her stay with us be long."

More applause, this time joined by some of the veterans when Ayliss rose from her seat and approached the podium. Although her clothes were immaculate, she was wearing the same trousers, boots, and long shirt from the range the day before.

"Thank you very much, Station Manager, for your warm welcome and this wonderful structure. I'm happy to accept it in the name of the Veterans Auxiliary." Ayliss looked out over the audience, seeing First Sergeant Hemsley appear in the rear of the crowd. Over his shoulder she could make out the low ridge of dark points that stood over the veterans' subterranean home.

"Station Manager Rittle and I had an opportunity to tour the new building just before the ceremony, and we both agreed it was much too big for me and my staff." Seated behind her, Rittle's attentive face showed no reaction. "He then told me that the construction of a medical clinic for the veterans had been put on hold in order to build this edifice. You don't have to be the daughter of the Chairman of the Emergency Senate to pick up on an unstated message like that"—she paused, smiling, to accept the audience's modest laughter—"and so I'm pleased to announce that this will be the new colony hospital!"

The miners began to applaud, and then the veterans joined in. Confused expressions flashed across the managers on the stand, but that all ended when Rittle began clapping serenely.

Standing at the podium, Ayliss beamed at the audience while the applause continued. Olech and Reena had taught her that smile, and made her practice it numerous times. With the look of vapid joy locked into place, she sought out the figure of Hemsley in the very back.

Clapping his hands slowly, the top veteran fixed her with a look of wary examination.

"That was an interesting performance out there," Rittle remarked, looking over the balcony railing through dark lenses. Ayliss had just lunched with him and his most senior managers, but now they were able to converse alone. "That was nice of you, making it look like I already knew about your grand gesture."

Ayliss joined him at the railing. The Station Manager's house was two stories high, and the balcony ran all the way around it. The whole building was white, inside and out, with expensive furnishings brought from off-world. Exotic plants stood in ornate pots and green vines clung to the walls, an extravagance that Ayliss saw nowhere else in the complex.

"I imagine you expected me to do something along those lines. It's really much too large for my needs."

"It's not so much a question of need as it is of making a statement. When you're in charge, it's important to look the part."

"I would have thought that getting things done was a better indication of being in charge."

"Oh, that's a given. I've managed three stations so far, and they don't keep assigning them to you if you don't meet your quota."

"I wasn't talking about mining. I'm more concerned with Zone Quest's obligations to the discharged veterans."

Rittle turned toward her. "Those obligations go both ways, Minister. The colonists are supposed to maintain themselves in a condition of fighting readiness, in case it becomes necessary for them to defend the settlement."

"You're saying they haven't done that?"

"I'm saying they're not even close. Hemsley has refused to provide us with the most rudimentary information about the colonists' organization as a military force, and their other activities have gotten them banned from the station. It's hard to imagine them defending the place when we can't trust them to be inside the wire."

"What would those other activities be?"

"You sure you want to hear this, Minister? Once I bring these infractions to your attention, they become part of the record."

"I would have thought they became part of the record when they occurred, if they're as bad as they sound. What are you saying they've done?"

"Stolen Zone Quest assets, for one. You see the size of this place?" Rittle motioned with a flat hand toward the buildings, vehicle parks, and roads that sprawled along the slope to either side. "We used to house an entire Force brigade, but when it was reassigned, I didn't have sufficient guards to secure the place. The colonists stole everything that brigade left behind, as well as a significant amount of Zone Quest property in the form of rations, fuel, weapons, and ammunition."

"That's interesting. Hemsley told me he and the other veterans haven't received their standard allocation for any of those things, before or after that brigade departed."

"Really? He seems to run a lot of live-fire ranges, for someone who hasn't received his ammunition allocation."

"So you *have* been providing the veterans with the support that Zone Quest agreed to, in exchange for being allowed to mine parts of this planet."

"Of course not. I'm not going to give anything to people who've robbed me."

"But how are they supposed to maintain themselves in a condition of fighting readiness—to use your words—if you aren't living up to your end of the bargain?"

Rittle came to his full height and slowly removed the dark glasses. "I was hoping to avoid discussing this with you until you'd had a chance to settle in, but clearly you've been listening to some people who haven't been truthful.

"In addition to the items they stole from us, your colonists have been trafficking with an individual named McRaney, who is on the Human Defense Force's official list of pirates operating in this region of space."

Ayliss snorted, remembering Hemsley's response to that allegation. "If they're not getting the support they were promised, no one can fault them for pursuing it elsewhere."

"Our satellites have tracked several unauthorized ships landing not far from here and departing only minutes later. You might not be aware of this, but unreported contact with pirates or smugglers is a death-penalty offense." The glasses went back on, the face blank. "As soon as I have conclusive proof linking the colonists to those landings, I intend to report these crimes to HDF Command. As someone who's been in the zone for many years, I can assure that Command takes a dim view of anyone even remotely connected to such activity—no matter who their father might be."

"Regardless of who my father is, I can assure you that *I* take a dim view of anyone threatening me—or my veterans."

Blocker held his tongue until Ayliss's personal vehicle took them through the fencing. He'd been standing in earshot on the balcony, an impassive statue. Now he allowed his annoyance to show.

"That wasn't very diplomatic of you, Minister."

Looking out through the armored windshield, Ayliss answered serenely. "Then it's a good thing diplomacy wasn't what I was shooting for."

"And what, may I ask, *are* you shooting for?"

"That depends on a number of variables, Dom. I'll let you know if they start to line up."

"I doubt that your father recommended this approach."

"My mother would have. You told me yourself that when she didn't know if someone was a friend or an enemy, she assumed they were an enemy. I think that's wise."

"I said she couldn't *tell* a friend from an enemy. And she didn't try to find out. Lydia assumed everyone was a potential opponent, and she reacted accordingly. Your father was the exact opposite until she changed him. Way back then, watching those two, I swear I couldn't tell which one of them had been in combat." He looked out the window, forcing himself to shut up.

"Combat." Ayliss allowed herself a secret smile. "That's what it all is, isn't it?"

CHAPTER FOUR

"What's gotten into you, Olech?" Horace Corlipso asked the question while handing him a goblet of wine. "You didn't used to go racing all over the galaxy, disrupting things."

Warm sunlight streamed in through the chamber's transparent ceiling, floor, and outer wall. Wispy clouds passed close by while Horace's flying yacht slid through the air of Celestia.

"I only visited the construction zone. And they should have guessed I was coming." In addition to the far-off war zone, a smaller chunk of the galaxy had been designated the construction zone many years earlier. Defended by a fleet of warships, it was a vast stretch of space where enormous factory stations created the machines and tools of war. "After all, when I do get to leave Earth, I usually make the trip worthwhile."

"Still, you seem to have caught the leadership by surprise."

"All the more reason to replace them. If I can sneak up on them like that, imagine what a Sim raid force might do."

"I doubt the Sims could join a supply convoy and coast into the zone the same way."

"I brought an entire brigade of troops with me, with support personnel. Tripled the size of that convoy, and they waved us right through the cordon."

"So it was your intention to rotate the security assignment, regardless of what you found." Horace sat on the couch, close to his guest. Twenty years older than Olech and almost completely bald, he wore a flowing robe made of a rich, cream-colored fabric. "I call that disruption."

"I already knew what I was going to find—and you do, too. The construction zone has devolved into a circus. Half of the supplies are being diverted to non-military uses, and they're making more luxury items than weapons. Unauthorized vessels coming and going, all sorts of black market activity, and the Force units providing security were taking bribes to look the other way."

"A little graft here and there, Olech, nothing new. The units in the war zone are getting everything they need."

"I did find something unexpected. The highest level of Command in the war zone somehow managed to get *out* of the war zone. Generals Leslie and Osamplo, as well as Admiral Futterman, ensconced right there in the construction zone, and very comfortable. So far away from the war that they no longer had instantaneous communication with any of the units in their commands. Think about that. Directing combat operations with a time lag."

"A military headquarters on this side of the CHOP line?" Concern showed on the older man's face. The CHOP line was a line in name only, because of the extreme distances and constantly shifting nature of space, but it was a mechanically recognized boundary between the war zone and everywhere else.

"Exactly. Seems they forgot it was a death-penalty offense to cross the CHOP line while in command of war-zone forces."

"I assume you reminded them."

"I did—and you never saw such a gaggle of surprised faces. I gave them five days to get themselves and all their lackeys back to the war, and I'm sending the previous construction-zone security contingent with them. The army part, that is. Too risky to reassign the ships protecting the stations."

"I imagine they got the message. So this new brigade you put in place—how long before they start taking bribes and it all goes back the way it was?"

"I've been planning this move for a while. Recruited some highly reliable people. And I put a very unusual general officer in command out there."

"Really? Anyone I know?"

"Merkit, of all people."

"Now that *is* a surprise. I heard you sent him out to rebuild your son's brigade."

"Reena did that. And she wasn't nice about it." They exchanged knowing smiles. "But something happened to him out there. Apparently the Orphans turned him back into a soldier. Contacted me himself, when he was due to come back to Earth and resume his former duties. Said he wanted a combat assignment."

"And instead you made him the warden of a gigantic space jail run by the inmates."

"He's a gifted infighter, and quite tricky in his own way. The corporate types out there are going to have quite a challenge, slipping things past him."

"Unless they arrange some kind of an accident, of course. It's been known to happen."

"He has my full protection."

"That's what I'm talking about." Horace set his goblet on a low table. "You've really stirred things up lately, between this reorganization of the construction zone and the assignment of prized conquered planets to the Veterans Auxiliary. I'm hearing a lot of grumbling about you, and even a few veiled threats."

"I'm sure you stamped them right out."

"Of course. We're about to become relatives."

"But you disapprove of my actions."

"It's not disapproval, it's disquietude. The war will eventually end, and giving our allies their share of the new worlds will create a great deal of good will."

"We really should win the war before we start dividing up the spoils."

"But that won't work. According to that approach, every conquered planet would remain under military control on an indefinite basis. They could end up in anyone's hands. That is, unless the leader of our government decided to give some of them to the organization that employs his daughter."

"You do understand that we're not actually winning the war, right? Things have been quiet for a while, but there are still vast numbers of Sims out there."

"How strange. You see that as a negative."

"You don't?"

"No." Horace rose, looking down through the floor at a mottled brown smear that went for miles. "See that? One of our most productive mining regions, providing the minerals that are so vital to the conflict. And so little of it would be available, without the proper labor force."

"Slavery's not proper."

"We call it servitude. And, proper or not, it is necessary for the war effort. The only reason some people think it's not proper is because the servants are human. Just think how much more palatable it would be if they were something else."

"You can't be serious. The Sims kill humans on sight, always have. There's no way you could control them."

"Their leaders seem to do that quite easily. The Sims are an organized, hardworking species with great adaptability. And as for controlling them, let's just say that here on Celestia, we've become adept at identifying crucial motivations."

A low series of chimes rang out, and a far door slid back without a sound. A young woman entered, dressed in a sleeveless pink gown. Her blond hair was arranged in delicate ringlets, and Olech noted her beauty as she approached. The sunlight from so many directions went through the sheer material of her dress, showing that she wore nothing beneath it.

"Speaking of motivation, I'd like you to meet Emma." Horace beckoned, and the girl went to his side. He draped an arm across her shoulders and kissed the side of her head. "Enchanting, isn't she? She was living in the gutter when my people found her, filthy, abused, starving. I imagine you feel we should have left her there."

Olech stared in surprise. "It's been too long since my last visit. Is this where things are now—slaves outside the mines?"

"What are you suggesting? That servitude in exchange for survival is only acceptable if it supports the war?" Horace took the girl's hand, raised it, and turned her in a slow twirl. "Honestly, now. Would you send *this* to the mines?"

"I wouldn't send her anywhere. I'd take part of the planet's abundant profits and use them to help her. Not exploit her."

"I'm afraid our guest doesn't find you attractive, Emma. You may go now." The smooth skin of the girl's forehead wrinkled for just a moment, and fear entered her eyes. She switched immediately to a look of decadent cunning that Olech's political instincts told him was well rehearsed. Rising on tiptoe, she kissed Horace on the cheek while one of her palms glided deftly across his crotch. The older man watched her until the door slid shut.

"I was going to offer her to you. I guarantee it would have changed your opinion."

"I'm marrying your sister tomorrow."

"I suppose that's a good excuse." Horace picked up his goblet and walked to the side windows. "I'll tell poor Emma you were tired from the trip. The Step has that effect, sometimes."

"One of many." Olech joined him, looking down as the yacht approached the capital city of Fortuna Aeternam. "Tell me something, Horace. Do you dream in the Step?"

Olech's shuttle lifted off from Horace's yacht just as the sun was setting over the city. He studied the clouds from a portal near his desk, watching them go from a rosy pink to a blood red and feeling relief when the vista turned black. Leeger entered his office a few moments later, secured the hatch, and sat down.

"No extra devices from our visit, inside or outside," he reported, noting Olech's grave countenance.

"It's even worse than our people have been telling us. The slaves aren't just in the mines anymore. They've got slaves of every kind. Thousands of men and women dying all over the galaxy, and for this?"

"It's not surprising that they're crossing the line—

how do you punish someone for violating a secret agreement?"

"Horace finally laid his cards on the table. The Celestian leadership believes the Sims would make an excellent slave race, a labor force on the conquered planets."

"I'd call that ambitious, considering we can't communicate with the Sims and that they die if they spend too much time around us."

"Horace feels that's a plus. He believes there's a way to isolate captive Sims where they can be forced to work—tasks like mining, fuel extraction—by controlling their food supply. Rations delivered by robotics, no contact with humans at all."

"For that to work, they'd have to find a means of communication or a go-between." Leeger frowned. "I believe we might have discovered why so many alliance members wanted to hear Captain Nabulit's story about the alien."

"Fits, doesn't it? The only entity that can communicate with both humans and Sims. So if they're going to enslave the Sims, they'll need another alien just like the one Jan encountered."

"Does Horace know we're not winning the war?"

"That's the problem: the war's been going on for so long, at such a remove, that some people have concluded we've got the Sims stopped. Add in the notion that our technology will eventually give us a way to subdue them completely, and you can see why Horace and his friends have decided to focus on what happens after that."

"That would explain why they're so unhappy with your giving those planets to the Auxiliary."

"I gave them to the veterans, as the first colonies on new worlds to be populated by mankind. New worlds governed by our laws."

"The laws we're ignoring on the planet below us, just so we can get the minerals out of the ground."

"That decision was made long before I took office, and I went along with it because we need to win the war." Olech's eyes reached for the ceiling. "Am I the only one who understands that's the most important thing?"

"I doubt the slaves would agree with you on that." Leeger sensed he was agitating the Chairman. "What would you like me to do?"

"Horace introduced me to a slave girl named Emma. She's his current bed partner. Let's find out if she has family or friends who might like to leave Celestia."

"My people can do that." Leeger locked eyes with his boss. "I should remind you that Horace is the brother of the woman you're marrying, and one of the most influential people in the galaxy."

"Exactly why we need to explore the option."

"I'll get on it." Leeger rose and headed for the hatch.

"Hugh."

"Yes, sir."

"Have the SCOTS come see me." The acronym SCOTS applied to two different groups of Olech's advisors, a duplication meant to hide the existence of the smaller entity. The Select Committee on the Sims was made up of dozens of scientists, linguists, and other experts, but the Special Committee on the Step had only four members—all of whom were aboard.

"Can't that wait until after the wedding?"

"No. In fact, I'm almost certain I'll have to act right after the ceremony."

"**T**he surviving records of the probe's return are quite spotty regarding its location, and of course the planetary bodies of our solar system—as well as the system itself—have moved around considerably since then." Gerar Woomer, an astrophysicist of great renown and an expert on the Step, spoke to Olech in a small, dark room on the flagship *Aurora*. A hologram of Earth's sun and the planets in its orbit hung in the air between them, motionless. "With that said, I have finally calculated the coordinates you requested."

Woomer touched a finger to the hologram, creating a blinking red light in space relatively close to Earth. "For the purposes of the mission you have planned, this location should suffice. Following your guidance, I have plotted ten separate Step voyages, all starting from and returning to this point." Woomer's aged eyes took on a look of concern. "I must state again that your safety in this multi-Threshold voyage cannot be guaranteed."

"We've taken every precaution we can. There is no way to make it safer," Olech stated flatly. He and Reena had been holding hands tightly from the moment the hologram appeared.

"There is. Send someone else." Woomer turned

toward the room's remaining occupant. "Someone who is already sensitive to the kind of communication you hope to achieve."

"Mira? What do you think of that?" Reena whispered.

The fourth member of the Special Committee on the Step was a slight, gray-haired woman named Mira Teel. She was a prominent member of a large, loosely connected collection of people who maintained that the Step was more than a mode of transportation. Derisively nicknamed Step Worshipers, they considered the faster-than-light method of travel to be a means of communicating with superhuman entities.

"I'm more than happy to go in the Chairman's stead." Mira's voice was calm, measured. "Unfortunately, I fear that would not accomplish the goal of this journey."

"Mira's right. She's provided us with invaluable insights from her Step experiences, and the experiences of others, but for this to work, it has to be me."

Woomer sat down, leaving the hologram in place. "Speaking purely as a scientist, there is no proof that these Step 'experiences' are anything but a dream."

"Not everyone dreams in transit, Gerar." Mira spoke evenly. "In fact, it's only a small percentage. Of that small percentage, only a tiny fraction can remember the details of the dream. All of those dreams fall into one of two categories, either a 'memory' dream of a real event that actually occurred, or a real person from the dreamer's past communicating with them in a way they never did in life. Chairman Mortas's experiences in transit fall in the second category.

"I have long believed that the entities who gave us the Step meant to use it as a means of observing us and communicating with us. It makes no sense that they would give us the Step, then hide themselves."

"I've studied the panels that came back with that probe, and almost every one of them reveals a key element of Step technology. But two or three have never been fully explained." Reena's fingers whitened in Olech's grasp. "One of those seems to fit this theory exactly. It looks like a stick-figure human lying on a blanket, soaking in rays from the sun. I've never dreamt in the Step, not that I'm aware of, and yet from listening to the tapes of the people who have, I believe I know what that panel means.

"It's the explanation for why they gave us this gift in the first place. The rays in that picture are thoughts, or some kind of scan, and the figure on the blanket is a sleeping human."

"I've always dreamt in the Step, and my most recent dreams contained urgent commands to attempt this mission." Olech released Reena's hand and stood. "I want to thank you all for everything you've done. Many years ago, President Larkin tried to contact the beings who gave us the Step because he felt it was vital to winning the war against the Sims and whatever is making the Sims. I believe he was right in that intention, just misinformed in the way he chose to go about it."

"We're going to temporarily suspend the Step, so that this voyage will be the only one taking place." Olech touched the blinking light on the hologram.

"From this location, the *Aurora* will generate a series of Thresholds that will send me out to ten different warships. Each of those vessels, in turn, will send me back to the same spot.

"I believe that the significance of this location, combined with my sole presence on the craft making the journey, cannot be overlooked by whatever is using the Step to examine our thoughts. If they are indeed monitoring us in this way, I believe they will recognize this as an attempt to contact them. If we can find a way to communicate with these obviously higher beings, we may be able to use their knowledge to win the war.

"As far as I'm concerned, that's well worth the risk."

Woomer turned off the hologram, stood, and shook Olech's hand. "I'll be monitoring the whole process personally, Mr. Chairman. God speed."

Mira hugged him tightly, a blissful smile on her face. "You are going to reach out to a power that is far beyond human comprehension, dear Olech. Be of pure heart, and the entities will hear you."

The scientist and the mystic departed together, leaving Olech alone with his fiancée. They embraced for a long time, Reena's body wracked with silent sobs. She finally raised her brimming eyes to his.

"I can't believe you've managed to turn my wedding day into the second-hardest thing I'm ever going to do."

"What's the hardest?"

"Watching you climb into that capsule."

CHAPTER FIVE

"I was pleased with the company movement today. We made good, steady progress through some tough terrain. We have got to move more quietly, however; you have to glide through this stuff, not crash through it." Captain Dassa's low voice came through the speakers in Mortas's helmet. "Remember that Sam is out here somewhere, and we still don't know if he's been reinforced somehow. Fifty percent security through the night, but don't shoot up the first thing that makes a sound out there.

"Captain Pappas will now provide an important update from the social scene back home."

Stretched out on his stomach, Mortas winced behind his goggles. Sergeant Dak and the platoon's three squad leaders were facing him in a ring, flattened on the jungle dirt near the center of the platoon's night perimeter.

The battalion's intelligence officer spoke. "This one comes from the entertainment officer on the good ship *Dauntless*, orbiting over our heads. I'm sure you all sent your regrets at not being able to attend, but our very own Chairman of the Emergency Senate, Lieutenant Mortas's father Olech, has married his longtime companion Reena Corlipso in a ceremony on her home planet of Celestia."

The leadership of B Company's three separated platoons was quick to comment.

"Wait, I didn't get my invite. I really would have gone to that."

"She's nice-lookin', for an older girl."

"Why weren't you invited, Jan?" Mortas recognized the voice of Wyn Kitrick, the platoon leader of Third Platoon. "You get disinherited or something?"

"El-tee Mortas is the black sheep of the family—thought you knew that."

"That musta been some party."

Dassa let the merriment continue for a bit longer, then cut it off. "Okay, big day tomorrow. I want to be ready to move right at sunup, but in the meantime, let's not get too cozy. Sam is in the vicinity."

The different platoons signed off, leaving Mortas to address his platoon sergeant and three squad leaders. In the black-and-green world of his goggles, the armored men looked like bug-eyed turtles huddled on the floor of a green lake.

"I can't help thinking this feels a lot like every other training exercise we've been on." The turtles nodded, so he knew he wasn't alone. "Seven months out of action is a long time, so let's all remember this is for real. Sergeant Dak?'

"El-tee and I will be checking the lines during the night, so don't shoot us. Any questions?"

"Yeah," came the voice of Sergeant Frankel, who had already proven himself quite a wit. "Lieutenant, I only kissed up to you because I thought you were tight with your dad. I think you owe me an apology."

"Does it help that I sent a gift and said it was from the whole platoon?"

"Whatcha send, El-tee?" Sergeant Katinka, hulking even without the armor, asked in a gruff voice.

"A pair of old socks in a used ration bag."

"I'm not chipping in for that," said Sergeant Mecklinger, who had been with the platoon on Fractus. "And thanks for getting the whole platoon on your dad's shit list, sir."

"We were already on that list," Dak intoned. "I'll be by in a few minutes. That's it."

The turtles began to slide backward across the jungle floor, finally rising and heading off to their portions of the perimeter. Mortas rose to a crouch, but only moved a few feet to where Vossel, the platoon medic, was sitting with his back against his rucksack.

"Anything interesting?" Mortas asked as he sat down. The dirt beneath him was damp, and riven with thousands of threadlike roots common to that part of Verdur.

"No, sir." Vossel had been monitoring the surveillance imagery beamed down from the *Dauntless* while

Mortas and the others had been communicating with Captain Dassa. "Lots of little heat signatures, animals probably, staying well clear of us."

Mortas flipped the view in his goggles to the feed from the *Dauntless*. Stretched across roughly a mile, three rings of whitened dots stood out against the night jungle. Despite the heavy canopy of tall trees and thick foliage, the heat signatures of individual soldiers showed the defensive perimeters of B Company's three platoons. Targets for protective fires were marked all around them, and he narrowed the view to a tight focus on his own position.

First Platoon's perimeter was more of an oval than a circle because of the undulating nature of the ground, but he was satisfied that it was a good arrangement. The Orphans had spent so many weeks in training that setting up for the night was second nature. His three machine guns were positioned where they could provide the most protection, and the three squads had filled in around them. His grenade-launcher men, known as "chonks" because of the sound their weapons made, had already targeted any low ground the Sims might use to approach without being seen.

"You take your stink pill yet, sir?" Dak's voice came through his earpieces even though the platoon sergeant was out checking the lines.

"Of course. Can't you tell?" Mortas wrinkled his nose, repelled by the chemical aroma rising from his pores. The stink pill was a multipurpose drug that anyone new to the Verdurian jungle had to take every day. A single mission's exposure was enough to build up an immunity, but in the meantime, much of the platoon reeked of an odor that reminded Mortas of rubbing alcohol.

"Make sure you take it, sir," Vossel murmured. Though teenaged in appearance, he was a veteran Orphan medic respected throughout the company. "Some of the garbage that's around us will have you puking so bad, you'll feel like you're turning inside out."

Mortas returned to the overhead imagery and widened the view again. The three platoon perimeters disappeared, and three glowing shapes emerged several miles to the north. The monitoring stations stood on top of high ground, surrounded by antipersonnel wire and constantly watched by satellites in geosynchronous orbit. From west to east, they were code-named Almighty, Broadleaf, and Cordvine. Broadleaf, in the middle, was a Human Defense Force retransmission site, while Cordvine was a planetary monitoring station. Almighty, farthest to the west and separated from the other two stations by a wide stretch of lower terrain, belonged to Victory Provisions. Originally established to study potential food sources in Verdur's riotous garden, Almighty's more recent activities were a mystery.

In order to avoid detection, B Company had been inserted by shuttle several miles south of their current location. The day's movement had been intended to get them close to the region where the Sims were believed to be operating. Now they would begin patrolling in earnest, attempting to locate the enemy that had somehow learned to hide from the surveillance satellites overhead.

"Remember, we're looking for any indications that Sam's been around. As soon as you see anything— footprints, trash, holes—stop right there and let me know," Dassa's voice whispered through the headsets of every man in B Company just as the darkness was lifting. "Slow and easy, nice and quiet. You see Sam, don't shoot him up unless you have to. Use orbital weaponry to engage, and they might think they got spotted by aerial reconnaissance. Let's go."

"Move out," Mortas murmured, the platoon already arranged to search their assigned sector. The three squads were separated by roughly one hundred yards, with the middle squad slightly advanced. The terrain was so restrictive that the men would be moving in long files, the three elements parallel to each other. Mortas was in the center of the middle squad, and Dak was in the same position in the squad farthest to the west. Patrolling in a northerly direction and separated by close to a mile, the three platoons were arranged west to east as First, Second, and Third Platoons.

The jungle world had changed overnight and was now cloaked in a choking ground fog. Ghostly fronds and branches reached out from the whiteness, and the spongy terrain rolled up and down. The brightly colored birds that he'd seen roosting or flying the day before were nowhere in sight, and only a few of their desultory calls could be heard in the distance. Mortas kept flipping his goggles to the satellite view that allowed him to monitor the progress of his three squads.

His boots were still covered in mud from the previous day's march, and he quietly scraped the soles against an exposed root while walking up a slight rise. A vine hooked on his Scorpion rifle, and he reflexively pushed against it, thinking it would break. Strong as a cord of wrapped wire, it ran along the barrel with a loud scraping sound. Mortas stopped immediately, mindful of the near silence all around him, and eased the vine out of the way.

Topping the rise, he gauged his distance from the man walking in front of him. It was important not to bunch up, individually or as a unit, because the Sims had been in this jungle for a long time and had become experts at ambushes. The movement formation he and the NCOs had selected for the day was intended to cover a wide area while also allowing for a quick response to enemy contact. The outthrust middle squad, as the point of the spear, was likely to encounter the Sims first. The two squads to either side would then be able to move up and flank their opponents while the middle squad was returning fire.

Moving through the thick vegetation, Mortas could only see the man walking several paces in front of him. He knew this soldier well, having personally brought him to the Orphans. His name was Prevost, and he'd been a Triage Tech on one of the transports supporting the brigade's disastrous mission on Fractus. Triage

Techs were highly unpopular because they prioritized the treatment of the wounded according to a barbaric set of Force regulations, but Prevost had won his place in the platoon when he'd proved to be a savant with the chonk. Merely competent with a Scorpion and useless with a machine gun, he could put a grenade round just about anywhere he was asked. Prevost suddenly stopped and dropped to a knee, and Mortas did the same without thinking. He took advantage of the halt to flip the goggle view and study the terrain to their front.

Boundaries designating each platoon's search area were superimposed on the vista, a combination of aerial imagery that was pretty much a sea of green and a rough map that showed the rise and fall of the ground. The map was only an estimate, but it showed no significant obstacles, and he wondered why they'd stopped.

The air was tight around them, and the climbing sun had already started to burn away the mist. Looking up, he was surprised to see the vine-choked branches of a tall, thin tree shaking as if touched by a light breeze. Vossel spoke from behind him.

"That's one of the ant trees we were telling you about, sir. The little bastards have hollowed it out, and there's so many of 'em that it shakes when they get moving around. Looks like the wind's blowing the thing when there isn't any."

"Thanks."

Katinka gave a warning from the front of the squad. "We should be hearing from the Vree Vrees pretty soon. We just found a not-banana grove."

Mortas looked around in expectation, having heard a lot about the loud creatures the troops called the Vree Vrees. Resembling a large, muscular cat with a prehensile tail, the Vree Vrees objected to the presence of humans. Their favorite food was a curved fruit that so many briefers had insisted was not, in fact, banana, that the men referred to it as not-banana.

Prevost slowly rose, and Mortas was doing the same when a shrill cry burst from the greenery to his front.

"Vreeeeeeee! Vreeeeeeee!" Though expecting the bellow, Mortas was startled all the same. It was quickly joined by a host of others, and then the trees around them became a kaleidoscopic view of swinging fur and gripping tails. One of them, black with gray stripes, leapt onto the trunk closest to Mortas and only a few feet above him. It fixed slitted eyes on his, and huffed loudly at him from tiny nostrils before clawing its way up into the foliage. The troupe of Vree Vrees howled angrily as they raced by, and then they were gone.

"If Sam's anywhere nearby, he knows he's got company." Dak cautioned the platoon. "Stay alert. Let's move."

They discovered the presence of Sims at midday. Despite other contacts with the Vree Vrees, there had been no indications of enemy presence. The heat had intensified and burned away the mist, but it had brought a different kind of fog with it, in that the entire unit's alertness had slipped considerably as fatigue set in.

Sweating all over, Mortas was thinking about his last messages from Ayliss. As his sister's departure for the war zone grew near, her questions had taken on a sinister tone. Her last missives had included inquiries about the enemy he had killed on both Roanum and Fractus, and she'd been rudely unmindful of his attempts to deflect them.

Mortas was pondering the possible meaning of that behavior when the sound mufflers in his helmet clamped down around his ears, several times. It was a silent warning sent to the entire platoon, and all three files dropped to the jungle floor in response. Mortas flipped one eyepiece to the aerial view of his zone while sighting down the Scorpion's barrel with the other eye. No heat signatures appeared other than those of his men, and nothing moved in the underbrush to his front.

"Lieutenant, we've found cart tracks." Sergeant Mecklinger, up ahead, spoke in a whisper.

"Coming up." Mortas rose and began weaving his way through the prone bodies facing east and west. "First Squad, Second Squad, establish security. No surprises."

Hunched over, he followed the fresh boot prints through the damp humus. Already the men from Second Squad were spreading out, shifting the file formation to a long oval. The machine-gun team walking with them began setting up to cover their rear, and to either side of them the two other squads assumed similar defensive positions. Stepping over hard, exposed roots, Mortas soon reached the spot where Mecklinger waited at the base of a towering tree. All around them, the jungle appeared to be an impenetrable wall, the trees and bushes and moss bleeding together with the brush on the jungle floor.

Kneeling, Mortas tried to distinguish the marks that had halted the platoon. The Sims were highly disciplined when it came to maintaining camouflage, and he was surprised to see the ruts in the dark soil only a few yards away.

"Those look new to you?" he asked.

The helmeted head shook, the goggles fixed to their front. "No. They're not fresh, but look how deep they are. Either they were moving something heavy, or this is a trail."

Mortas reported the sighting to Dassa while Mecklinger rearranged his squad. The machine-gun team came up to cover their front, replaced by riflemen and chonk gunners facing to their rear. The rest of the squad spread out to cover the trail, and a two-man team then went across to recon the brush on the other side.

"We've got tracks down here too." Frankel, to the east, marked the spot so that it appeared in goggles all over B Company. Mortas marked his own position, surprised to have forgotten that most elementary response but chalking it up to excitement. The two soldiers on the other side called back to say they'd seen and heard nothing, and Mecklinger pushed the front half of his perimeter across the trail.

With protection now in place, the veteran squad

leader motioned Mortas to follow him. They knelt next to the parallel ruts, noting how fresh the new growth inside them appeared.

"Two-wheelers, or more?" That came from Dak, with First Squad to the west. So far he hadn't encountered the trail, which suggested it changed direction not far from where they knelt.

"Hard to say. Wider bodies than two-wheelers, though." Sim infantry employed ingenious hand trucks with collapsible segments and removable wheels that could be lashed to their rucksacks when not in use. Most commonly dragged behind them in the two-wheel mode, they could be configured to haul heavy loads many miles depending on the terrain.

"What other signs are you seeing?" Dassa asked on the radio.

Studying the spongy ground, seeing dark soil and a pattern of interlacing ground vines, short grass, and tiny flowers, Mortas detected nothing but the ruts. "Nothing so far. No footprints."

"That's odd. Get a good look around, see what's going on there."

"Understood." In his mind, Mortas saw the three ovals of his separated squads and considered how best to do this. The trail indicated an enemy presence, but it didn't seem to have been used in some time. Bring the three squads together in a large perimeter around this spot, or leave them spread out where they could provide early warning of an enemy approach?

He didn't have to make the decision, however. A voice he recognized as Private Ithaca's, a Fractus vet in Mecklinger's squad, interrupted his thoughts.

"Hey, I found something."

A hand waved at Mortas from the brush on the other side of the trail, and he and Mecklinger moved to it. The canopy overhead was dense in this spot, and his goggles adjusted to the lack of light. Ithaca was on his stomach at the base of a thick tree, and he pointed up the trunk when they approached.

"What *is* that?" Mortas asked, staring at a rusting metal pipe jutting a few inches out of the tree's torso at eye level.

Mecklinger ran a finger across the open end of the pipe, which had been distended by the blows of whatever instrument had hammered it into place. He rubbed his fingers together, and then sniffed at whatever was on them.

"It's some kind of sap." The helmet turned a dirty face and goggles in his direction. "They're tapping the trees."

"You ever see this before?"

"No, sir. Pulled this mission three times, not counting this one, and I never saw anything like this." He sniffed at the discharge again. "I think ol' Sam has been out in the jungle a little too long. Poor guy has gone nuts on us."

"**A**ny idea what they could be using this for?" Captain Dassa directed this question at Captain Pappas. Both men and the company command element had joined Mortas's platoon in order to see the tree tapping for themselves. Alerted to the strange Sim appliances, the troops of First Platoon had discovered several more of the pipes buried in the same kind of tree. The cart path moved past the tapped trunks, suggesting it was used to take away the sap.

"Could be a lot of things. They've been out here a long time, living off the land and what they can scavenge." Detritus from the battle for the planet years earlier had slowly disappeared over time, and any downed resupply drones were usually picked clean within hours. "They could be making adhesives, sandals, or even tires for the carts."

Dassa's goggled face looked away, an idiosyncratic way of telling everyone that he had an incoming call. Kneeling in the brush with the command element and Sergeant Dak, Mortas took a moment to view the overhead imagery of the area. First Platoon was now formed in a defensive ring on both sides of the cart path, which swung north only a few hundred yards from the spot where they had first detected it. Both Second and Third Platoons had snugged up on them to the east, in preparation for First Platoon's sidestep to the west of the trail. Leery of the path, Dassa had decided to skirt the newfound supply lane on both sides. Extra targets had been plotted across the company's front, and the fire-control personnel on the *Dauntless* had been warned that the infantrymen might make contact with the enemy shortly.

Mortas slid the goggles lenses up so that he could look around with unaided eyes. Lush greenery pressed in from all sides, and he fought off a shiver at not being able to see more than a few yards. Every man in B Company stood out as a tiny dot on the imagery provided by the *Dauntless* and the satellites, despite the jungle canopy and the heat of the day. They were astride a main Sim supply line, and yet there were no heat signatures for their enemy anywhere.

"Okay, keep looking." Dassa ended the communication with the commanders of the two Force detachments guarding Broadleaf and Cordvine to the north. "They're reviewing the satellite feed for this spot from the last few weeks, but so far nothing shows up except animals passing through. There is no way that a bunch of Sammies, pushing carts up and down this trail, could have gone unnoticed by the scanners."

Dassa looked at Pappas. "I pulled this mission once before, over a year ago, but the only signs we found were footprints. Look at this thing. They had to do some major clearing, just to be able to move the carts. A lot of work."

"Exactly." Pappas nodded, a green-faced owl wearing body armor. "Whatever they're doing with this stuff, it's important. And it's somewhere up this path."

CHAPTER SIX

Ayliss was warm. Too warm, lying there in Selkirk's embrace. Naked, sated, exhausted from the work of the previous days, but still too warm.

She fought to make herself wake up, feeling a tiny furnace inside her, bucking like an engine running out of fuel. Even asleep, Ayliss knew her body and knew something was wrong. She was sick, in a way she'd never experienced before.

Her eyes wouldn't open, and her mind raced as she slowly ascended from the depths. She couldn't be sick. Not here. Not *now*.

Voices. Male and female. Close in the darkness. Selkirk's arm sliding out from under her, roughly, alarmed, then he was gone. Remarkably, a chill ran straight up her back where he had been, and her eyes finally opened.

Unsure of where she was, but then recognizing her

room in the house that she thought she'd given away. Confusion and anger mixing together when she remembered Hemsley refusing her request for modest lodgings inside the old Sim tunnels. Shuffling up the slope with her small retinue, feeling Blocker's unstated reproach for having sent their shuttle away prematurely. Setting up in the building she'd given to the veterans as a hospital, sited between the Zone Quest managers she'd intentionally alienated and the veterans she'd courted.

Her eyes came into focus in the dark room and she saw Blocker at the door, in whispered conversation with a robed Selkirk and a shorter figure in the hallway. Ayliss pushed herself up into a sitting position, her face flushed and her muscles weak. The small figure looked in at her, and spoke.

"Minister, you have to come right away. Trust me."

The voice belonged to Tin, the irreverent Banshee. Ayliss impatiently tugged the sheet loose from the bedclothes and walked to the group, trying to appear sleepy and not ill. Blocker was wearing Force torso armor and holding one of the short-barreled assault weapons, and Selkirk was wrapped in a skimpy robe that actually belonged to Ayliss, but it was Tin who held her attention.

The brunette's face was smudged in soot, and a dark bandana held her hair in place. She wore black fatigues and combat boots, and Ayliss detected a slight smell of smoke.

"What is it?" she asked, pressing into the group as

if trying to keep the conversation secret. Her weight rested against Blocker's armor, who turned concerned eyes in her direction before surreptitiously sliding an arm around her waist to hold her up.

"There's been an accident." Wary eyes jumping from Selkirk to Blocker to the walls of the building constructed by Zone Quest. "Hurry."

In spite of Blocker's protests, and his solicitous palm applied to her forehead that took Ayliss back to the age of five, the group was soon rolling down the slope in an armored mover. The mining complex blazed with light, and the roar of an engine could be heard from the small Zone Quest spacedrome on the mountain's top.

Ayliss had changed into a set of dark green fatigues festooned with the Auxiliary's patches, and she gritted her teeth while they rolled down the road toward the entrance to the Sim tunnels. Weak and dizzy, hot but not nauseous, she had no idea what she might have caught. Blocker had already diagnosed it as a NOA, an acronym she'd never heard before that stood for Non-Specific Outerspace Ailment.

"We have to get you into the ZQ infirmary as soon as we're done with this." Blocker had grumbled, still displeased by her handling of Rittle. "If they'll take us."

The main entrance to the tunnels was an arch cut into the stone right at the end of the road. A dozen armed veterans wearing torso armor stood in a loose group outside the gate, and they waved the mover to a stop. There was some argument about who was going to be allowed admittance, but Tin's insistence got them all through.

Selkirk had already described those parts of the underground warren that he'd been allowed to see, and so Ayliss wasn't surprised to find the main tunnel well lit and clean. The Sims had smoothed and painted the stone walls once the minerals were extracted, and the floor was flat and level. Selkirk and Tin preceded them through the entranceway, and Ayliss concentrated on walking normally inside the circle of her bodyguards.

The entrance tunnel had been dug perpendicular to the ridge itself, and so they reached the main transverse corridor in no time at all. More armed veterans were posted there, and Ayliss recognized one or two of them in the light. They stopped the visitors, instructing them to wait in tones that were not friendly.

Tin stayed with them, and Ayliss was finally able to see that the short Banshee's fatigues were indeed singed. The soot on her face was night camouflage, but fire had come very close to her in the last few hours. Swimming inside the fog of her illness, Ayliss still detected the agitation that filled the air.

Moments later Lola approached, also dressed for night maneuvers but not smelling of smoke. "Come with me, please."

They only went a few yards down the ridge's center core before Lola stopped them at a side room. Looking down the long passageway, Ayliss detected several more entrances and decided these were the quarters the Sims had made for themselves. There appeared to be a lot of them, and she wondered again why Hemsley had refused her small party a place to stay.

"Minister." The voice came from inside the room, male and menacing.

Ayliss forced herself to look calm and then passed between Selkirk and Tin. She only got to the doorway, as the room wasn't large, and three stretchers were laid on supports inside it. Two of the stretchers supported boot-clad bodies that were concealed beneath blankets, and the third was occupied by First Sergeant Hemsley. His shirt was off, revealing a pale torso half-covered in a gleaming salve coated over angry pink flesh. More of the salve was on the left side of his face, which was swollen and red.

"What happened, First Sergeant?"

Two medics stood on either side of him, one squeezing an intravenous fluid bag while the other dabbed at the worst of the burns. Hemsley swatted the second man away before speaking.

"Isn't it obvious? The Guests attacked us with one of their gunships. Killed two of my people, a driver, and"—Hemsley shrugged, and then winced—"aw, fuck it."

Using his unburned hand, the old veteran reached out and pulled back the top third of one of the blankets to reveal the blackened face of Deelia. Ayliss gasped before seeing that the discoloration was just more camouflage.

"She didn't burn. She got hit with a minicannon

round, dead center." The blanket flipped back into place. A thumb pumped at the other corpse. "Fuckin' gunship tore up the mover we were using, killed the driver.

"Now what are you going to do about this . . . Minister?"

Behind her, Blocker cleared his throat as if to speak, but Ayliss stopped him with a raised hand. Something wasn't right here. The burns on Hemsley and Tin, but not on the victims of the gunship attack. If a mover had been destroyed, it would likely have caught fire.

"You got those burns pulling something out of that mover. What was it carrying, and where were you?"

"Whole buncha miles away, out in the middle of nowhere, taking delivery of those supplies I mentioned, the ones we're supposed to get from the Guests that we have to buy from the smugglers." A hand waved at Deelia's body. "That's not exactly important right now."

Smugglers. Station Manager Rittle's promise that he was going to link the veterans to piracy.

"What were you hauling? What was so important you got this badly burned?"

Hemsley stared at her in defiance, but Lola spoke up. "Tell her, First Sergeant."

"All right. Seeing as you care more about a little contraband than dead veterans. We were receiving a shipment of antiaircraft rockets. Shoulder-fired."

"You moron!"

"Call me any names you like. They *murdered* two of my people. What are you going to do about that?"

Ayliss felt the heat swelling all the way through her

body now, as if she'd been the one near the fire. Anger rose over the realization that Hemsley had played right into Rittle's hands.

"Do you have any idea what you've done? You gave them the only thing they needed. Proof that you're consorting with pirates." Her eyes moved to Lola's, then Tin's, startled to see disapproval. She went on anyway. "Now they have everything they need to kick you off this planet—and me too."

"That's what you're focusing on? Right now, with these two murdered soldiers lying right in front of you?"

She was suddenly aware of the stares from the two medics. Dizzy, weak, and made more so by the suspicion that she'd just made an enormous mistake.

A hand gently came down on her shoulder, Blocker's. "We should leave, Minister."

Feeling her vision narrowing, in danger of swooning, but not willing to do it in front of these people. These people who'd ruined everything and somehow believed it was all her fault.

"All right. Let's go."

"We have to get you to Zone Quest's infirmary." Back at the mover, Blocker spoke almost in her ear because Ayliss appeared to be losing consciousness.

"No." A weak hand gripped his arm, the blue eyes opening with effort. "They'll never speak to me again if you do that."

"They'll never speak to you again if you die."

"Just sick, that's all. Put me to bed for the night, we'll see how I am in the morning."

"No. Help's available up the hill, and I'm taking you there." Blocker would have continued, but Selkirk leaned in close.

"ZQ's complex might not be the safest place tonight." He glanced at the veterans near the tunnel entrance. "There's going to be trouble."

"From this bunch?" Blocker shook his head. "The Guests have got defensive wire, searchlights, and two gunships."

"That's right. Only two gunships."

"Tempting target, if they can get somebody onto the airfield." Blocker's face wrinkled for a moment. "Nah. Even something that simple, they're not up to it."

"That dead Banshee in there? Tupelo's her husband, and I didn't see him anywhere. Unless I miss my guess, he's a Spartacan deserter. He's more than up to it."

"Lee?" Ayliss croaked at Selkirk.

He took her hand. "I'm right here, darling."

"Get me back in with them. Do it for me."

Selkirk's face broke into a broad, half-crazy grin. He kissed Ayliss's forehead and slid out of the vehicle. "Anything for you, baby."

"**G**et outta here, kid." Hemsley was on his feet, still bare-chested, when Selkirk came back down the tunnel escorted by two uncertain veterans. Armed men and women came and went on various errands, but Selkirk sensed there was great activity in other parts of the settlement.

"Let me talk to Tupelo."

"He's grieving."

"He's preparing."

Hemsley turned, and the lights reflected off the salve. "You see a lot, don't you?"

"What is he, a Spartacan Scout?"

"I never asked. Whatever it was, it was messy."

"Has he even got a plan?"

"A plan." Hemsley snorted. "He figured out the Guests' defenses the day he got here. He's had a plan for a long time."

"He's one man. There are two gunships."

"You making an offer?"

"No. Minister Mortas is."

On the far side of the mountain, two dark figures scurried up the slope. The Zone Quest compound had vibrated with activity for several hours after the attack on the veterans, but as the evening wore on without a response, things had gone back to normal. Lights atop the double fencing still shone, and armored men still kept a wary watch on the ridge that contained the Sim tunnels, but the rest of the perimeter had settled in for the night.

Even the spacedrome had finally gone quiet, both gunships landing and shutting down. Tupelo and Selkirk had put the time to good use, rehearsing their movements and preparing their materials. Now, dressed in black from head to toe, the two men waited in a fold of the ground almost a hundred yards short of the fence.

They knew their heat signatures would stand out against the cold rocks if they moved any closer, but Tupelo had provided the simplest of solutions. He'd spent many nights circling the fence line, noting patterns and looking for opportunities. Flattened against the hard rock, he squeezed Selkirk's arm to signal that their moment had arrived.

Forty yards above them, a segment of the hill began to move with a grating sound. Two sections of rock seemed to be separating, but Selkirk knew what to expect, and so he recognized it as the opening of a very large pipe. Not far on the other side of the glowing fences was a low building that refined the raw ore so that it took up less room on the transports. The process involved an extraordinary amount of heat, and the unwanted by-products had to go somewhere.

Selkirk looked away as soon as the darkness in the pipe began to lighten, already warned that the initial flow was almost blinding. The hand on his arm released its grip but stayed flat. The air above them took on a noxious aroma, and then the ground began to vibrate. Up the slope, the pipe's insides became as bright as daylight, and a white-yellow sludge came rushing out.

Tupelo's hand began to rise and fall, and Selkirk counted with it. One. Two. Three.

Looking up now, seeing the superheated muck sliding toward them. Eight. Nine. Ten.

Unable to gauge how fast the lethal discharge was moving, but now doubting Tupelo's assurance that the count went to twenty. Wanting to raise his head higher, needing to find some kind of reference, but warned not to do this back in the tunnel. The vibration stopped abruptly, exactly on twelve as predicted, the sign that the giant pumps forcing out the detritus had stopped. Selkirk now became aware of heat reaching for the top of his head, felt the camouflage paint on his face beginning to melt, then the hand on his arm clenched hard.

Rolling away from each other, just in time, and then he was up, running hard, trying not to trip over the loose rock and hardened furrows left behind by countless dumpings. Forcing himself, against all logic, to get in close to the steaming yellow creek that now rolled downhill, knowing it would hide him from the heat-seeking scanners on the wall. Seeing the pipe now, knowing that the material from which it was made was invulnerable to heat and therefore safe to walk on, even as the lava-like river inside dropped off to a narrow stream.

Reaching the pipe, racing inside hunched over just a bit, trying to imitate Tupelo's bowlegged stride. Sweat pouring down, acrid air in his mouth and nostrils, he looked down to see the fiery stream between his pounding boots and was amazed to realize he'd kept up the count. In one minute, hatches would slide shut over the venting portholes where the pipe rose from the ground well inside the wire. Thirty seconds after that, a foamy spray would blast down the pipe, cleansing it with deadly chemicals.

Concentrating on not slipping, watching the molten sludge between his feet, trying not to bump into Tupelo, Lee Selkirk counted down what just might be the last seconds of his life.

Dull starlight played over the flat flight line, and distant lights provided lots of shadow. During their rehearsals, Tupelo had assured Selkirk that the Zone Quest security people had such faith in their perimeter fence that they seldom patrolled the complex grounds. That night, with so many of their personnel focused on the veteran settlement down the hill, the flat expanse of the spacedrome was completely deserted.

Massive ore transports stood out against the small fleet of personnel shuttles, but the gunships were parked off by themselves. With narrow bodies and wing-like rocket pods on either side, they looked like massive mosquitoes. Shuffling along under the belly of one of the transports, Selkirk reached for the small package tied to his back. By prearrangement Tupelo went left and he went right, breaking from cover briefly before ducking under the armored gunships.

The device was simplicity itself, a block of concentrated explosive with a basic detonator attached. Sliding the bomb out of the canvas bag, Selkirk glanced around him on the empty tarmac, refusing to believe that it could be this easy. Pressing the malleable explosive onto the hull under the main fuel tank, feeling it stick, he poked his head out to see Tupelo doing the same thing with the other ship. A raised hand signaled he was ready, and then Selkirk pressed the bomb's only button. It vibrated once, to indicate it was armed and that the countdown had begun.

Searching the nearby buildings for any sign that they had been detected, Selkirk rushed back to the shadows under the transport ship. Tupelo hustled up to him and knelt.

"The next refinery dump is in one hour. It's quicker getting out than getting in because you'll be going downhill. Find a spot to hide near the pipe, and don't forget the count."

In the blue-gray light of the stars, Selkirk imagined he saw a quick smile on the scout's face. "What are you up to?"

"You think my Deelia was only worth two jumped-up shuttles? I'll give you time to get away, but that rat fuck Rittle dies tonight."

"You can't do that. They'll kill you before you get anywhere near him."

"I been all over this complex, and they never even knew I was here. When those detonators go off, Rittle will come outside. He's that kind of boss. And I'll be waiting."

"How you gonna get away?"

"I'll think of something." The Spartacan's eyes

shifted around, getting ready to leave him. "Thanks for the help."

A horrifying image popped into Selkirk's head, Ayliss lying sick and helpless in an unfortified building between the two armed camps. When the Spartacan deserter killed their chief, the mine's security detachment would open fire on the settlement.

"Wait." Selkirk grabbed his arm. "You do that, it's going to be a wipeout. They've got a *lot* more firepower than your people, even without the gunships."

"You think we haven't planned for this day? Think you saw everything we've got? Thought you were smarter than that."

"Either way, it's a bloodbath. Come back out with me, and we'll cook up something better. I promise you, Ayliss is on your side."

"Don't you get it?" The other man's voice rose, pain welling up in the words. "Deelia was the only thing I ever had. And they—"

A single shot barked at them, and Tupelo crashed forward into Selkirk. The scout's head dropped on his shoulder as if he'd been knocked unconscious, and Selkirk knew immediately that he was dead. Hot wetness ran down the inside of his shirt, and he shoved the body away while rolling in the opposite direction.

A second round impacted against the tarmac where he'd been kneeling, a spark flashing. The momentary light reminded him that the entire spacedrome would be illuminated in moments, and that he would need a distraction. Guessing the direction from which the rounds had come, Selkirk ducked around one of the transports' massive tires and then sprinted across the open.

More gunfire, probably more shooters, but only one of them any good. The snap just above his head of a passing round, then more sparks as the ricochets bounced off the runway. Running madly now, his vision bouncing, Selkirk raced toward the parked gunships. Voices shouting in the darkness, panicked questions, telling him that they'd been discovered by a single guard or a lone sniper. Lights coming on in the nearest buildings, not enough to show him, more shots and near misses, and then he was skidding under the first gunship.

Finding the bomb where he'd left it, bringing his straining eyes right up under it, fumbling for the button that controlled the timer. Pressing it, relieved to see the readout come to life, and quickly thumbing it down to fifteen seconds. Searchlights snapping on now, beams cutting the shadows, wondering if the one explosion would set off the other bomb, and then releasing the button and scrambling away from the reaching rays. Fifteen seconds.

Emerging from the cover of the gunship, running flat out, straight for the fence without any thought of how to get over it. Or under it. Sprinting, adrenaline pounding through his every muscle, believing that if he could just reach the barrier, he would run right through it. Leaping perfectly, hands clawing, climbing, seeing the spot where he could flip himself over the top, not feeling the bullets when they found him.

CHAPTER SEVEN

Olech had expected to be nervous at his second wedding ceremony, but was surprised to find that was not the case. Standing in front of the purely decorative altar of the Celestian state religion, he looked down the long aisle flanked by row after row of dignitaries and their families. He knew all of the important faces, and had worked with most of them for decades.

That was one reason why he'd expected to be uneasy. The packed hall, with him standing at its front, far from the door, reminded him far too much of the day that President Larkin had been killed. Believing that several of the perpetrators of that crime were present should have heightened his discomfort, but it did not.

Standing there, wearing stiff formal dress and the blood red ribbon of the Unwavering, Olech felt an incomprehensible sensation, an otherworldly feeling of not being there at all. His mind drifted lazily, taking him back to the day when he and Lydia had been married. Attended only by two college friends, it had been a quick ceremony with no frills. Neither of them had come from money, and neither of them had felt a need for a third party to place a stamp of affirmation on their relationship.

He'd been nervous that day, jobless, unsure of what the future might hold, and yet he'd been happy. Lydia had always steadied him in that fashion, and so he'd viewed the official act of their marriage as the start of a wondrously unknowable journey that was guaranteed to be good simply because they would be taking it together.

Even the recollection of the way that journey had been brutally cut short failed to bring him back to reality, and he didn't mind it. He would be embarking on a different voyage that very night, without the woman to whom he was about to be joined, and so his future was the very definition of unknowable.

Light music drifted toward him from the loft at the rear of the hall, and he now saw Reena standing there smiling. Her gown was gold—the Celestians' festive color of choice—and a shining tiara crowded with precious stones stood atop her red hair. The congregation stirred as more and more people became aware of her, and they all turned in their seats so that no one was looking at him anymore.

Horace Corlipso stepped into the doorway, wearing an all-white suit that looked cool and comfortable. The very picture of decorum, he offered his arm to his

sister just as the bridal march began to play. They pro-
cessed up the aisle, returning each row to its proper
posture, Reena wearing a smile that only Olech knew
was false. As they got closer, and he saw the effort it
was taking for her to maintain that happy countenance, Olech Mortas silently cursed himself and his
plan, for having robbed the woman he loved of the joy
that should have been hers on this day.

They finally reached him, and Horace gave Reena
a light kiss on the cheek before turning to face Olech.
The man who ran Celestia gave him an unsettling
wink as he took his hand, leaning in to speak.

"We're family now," he whispered, and when
he drew away it was with a flash of teeth that Olech
couldn't decide was happiness or triumph.

Horace disappeared from his view, and although
the head prelate of the Celestian state religion now
took his place before the altar, all Olech could see was
the face he loved most in the universe. The smile was
frozen in place, but a single tear rolled over each of
Reena's cheeks.

Hours later, after the excruciating banquet where he'd
been forced to make idle conversation with hundreds
of officials and emissaries from the alliance planets,
Olech finally reached the shuttle that would take him
and Reena back to the *Aurora*. His new wife was already inside, having maintained the façade so well that
she was now almost completely drained. Leeger had

assisted her aboard, leaving Olech to bid good-bye to Horace.

"Congratulations, Olech. Or should I say 'Brother'?" The enigmatic grin was back, and Olech was suddenly finding it hard to stomach.

"Let's just use first names, like before." He cautioned himself not to ruin the act at the last moment, but it was no use. The ceremony had awakened memories of his murdered wife, and those feelings joined with the climbing dread of the night's mission to burst the dam of his self-control. "The Unwavering, those of us who survived, have always called each other brother."

"You and I have been through the wars too, in a fashion." The smile faded.

"We've certainly seen our share of bloodshed, haven't we?"

"Sometimes it's necessary. You know that."

"Not sure what I know these days. Before I go, I had a question for you."

"All right."

"When Lydia was dying, she told me to push the kids away and act like I didn't care about what had happened."

"Lydia was a fine strategist, right to the end."

"You advised me to follow that strategy."

"I did. We had no idea who poisoned her, so it was a sound plan. Whoever they were, it took away their leverage."

"If that's the case, why did you let me marry your sister? Didn't that just turn her into a target?"

Horace eyed him warily. "I'm not sure that many of

Lydia's murderers are still alive. I've long believed that most of them died with Larkin."

"Larkin wasn't involved."

"I know that. He was a fool, but he was a good man. No, I meant that so many of our opponents died in that melee that it's likely her killers were among them."

"I do recall seeing your security team rushing into the room. Although I was hugging the floor, there seemed to be an awful lot of them—and they were doing most of the shooting," Olech said.

"My low opinion of certain people in that body was well known. In the middle of all that confusion, some of my personnel may have taken advantage of what they saw as an opportunity to rid me of those people." The smile came back to Horace's face. "You telling me you've got some suspicions of your own, Olech?"

"No. Not anymore." Olech took the other man's hand. "Brother."

Walking onto the shuttle, Olech finally admitted the truth that he'd been denying for so many years. His new brother-in-law had assassinated the Interplanetary President and much of the old Interplanetary Senate, all for his own ends. And Blocker was right; someone who could do that could easily murder the wife of a man he wanted to control.

Once the shuttle was free of Celestia's orbit, Olech summoned Leeger to his office. Time was short, and he needed to adjust his plans based on what he'd learned.

"What have you found out about the slave girl Emma?"

"Horace didn't rescue her from the gutter. Her family came to Celestia like so many others, believing there was a job waiting for them in paradise. It was the standard fraud, and pretty soon their debts were so extreme that they were all in danger of going to the mines. The girl was sold to keep that from happening."

"Have our operatives contact the family, see if they'd like to live somewhere else."

"Already done, and they are receptive. Pulling this off will not be easy."

"Can it be done?"

"Yes."

"Horace is a much greater threat than I believed, but he has an important role if I disappear tonight. Make sure you don't move until he's played his part."

"Is there any way I can talk you out of this?"

"No, Hugh. So many thousands lost, so many more still at risk, and here I sit, almost completely safe, calling myself their commander."

"You did your time, and you almost got killed for it. Everyone knows that."

"It's not a question of popularity, or opinion. I genuinely believe there is a good chance this will gain us the contact that could tip the scales in the war. I have to try."

"Very well. Regarding Horace, if you do disappear I will have to clear this with Reena."

"Of course you will. She'll be in charge. Horace will make sure of that."

Not many hours later, messages bearing the codes of the Chairman of the Emergency Senate began to beam and bounce all over the galaxy. The message itself was not terribly unusual, as the Step had been suspended in the past whenever an anomaly was detected or a ship disaster occurred. Those infrequent interruptions were always of brief duration, and there was no reason to expect that this one would be any different.

All across the solar systems of the settled planets, bouncing off the construction zone, then spreading out to the enormously separated systems of the war zone, Command echoed the order. The message then fragmented, rebounding from the bridges of Zone Quest freighters to craft both large and small, legitimate and otherwise. The disturbance caused by the Step was easily monitored, particularly when no one was supposed to be using it, and the penalty for disobeying such an order would be swift and final.

For a brief time, the galaxy returned to an earlier age when voyages between even neighboring star systems were multidecade endeavors, and longer journeys were out of the question, even with the latest propulsion methods. For the duration of the suspension, just about every spot in the galaxy occupied by humans became an isolated outpost.

The *Aurora* had emerged from the Step almost exactly in the same location (relative to Earth) where the reconfigured space probe had reappeared so many decades before, bearing the instructions for the incredible technology. Ten different ships of war, in ten distant locations across the galaxy, now received instructions to read special orders that had been issued with the highest security coding. Cleared to use the Step for one special mission where they would take a tiny craft delivered to their care and immediately send it back whence it came, never moving themselves, the ships immediately swung into action.

In a receiving bay in the *Aurora*'s belly, Olech came through the hatch dressed in a black pressure suit. Technicians manned consoles or stood ready to assist in the launch, and a small group of Olech's confidants waited near the hatch of an unusual spacecraft. The small ship was designed to withstand the forces involved in the sequence of twenty Steps. It had no crew and would carry only one passenger, who would be returned to that same spot if the mission went according to plan. If it did not go according to plan, the tiny vessel was outfitted with every kind of long-range beacon and a stock of food and water. Sealed inside a Transit Tube within the ship, Olech would complete the entire journey in exactly the same way that every human experienced the Step—completely unconscious.

Wearing a forced smile, he approached the small group. Leeger stood stiffly at the back, but both Mira Teel and Gerar Woomer stepped forward to meet him.

"God bless you, Chairman." Woomer tilted his head at the technicians manning the consoles. "Every monitoring device in space is focused on our efforts here. Your ship is outfitted with the most recent locating apparatus, and I've plotted the paths of your voyage personally. Enjoy the ride."

They shook hands, and Woomer moved away. Mira, serene as always, stepped up in his place. A pink shawl, stitched all over with Step Worshiper symbols, was draped over her frail shoulders. She went up on tiptoe, and he leaned forward so she could kiss his cheek.

"How I envy you." Her eyes overflowed with both kindness and joy. "For the first time in the history of the race, one of us will initiate contact with the entities. You are exactly the right man for this role, darling Olech. Have no fear. You are about to experience a miracle."

The last member of the group now approached. Reaching up, Reena Mortas took his face in both hands. They kissed awkwardly because of the suit, but for a long time nonetheless. The tears were gone now, and his wife gave him a wink when they broke the kiss.

"You owe me a wedding night, Mr. Mortas. Don't forget that."

"I've been thinking of nothing else. I'll be back before you know it."

The technicians moved in then, leading him to the ship and through the narrow hatch. The Transit Tube took up much of the spacecraft's interior, a spacious cylinder with a reclining seat. A helmet was lowered over his face and locked into position, and then he was assisted inside the container. The technicians were well rehearsed, complementing each other's movements as they sealed the Transit Tube and engaged the ship's instruments before withdrawing.

Alone then, looking up out of the helmet's face shield and through the tube's clear cover. Only seeing the walls and the blinking lights and the cabinets that contained the food and water he would need if he became stranded. Knowing that no amount of either one would sustain him if he could not be found. Remembering the rumors from his youth, of disasters in the Step where entire ships had simply vanished. Later, as a powerful Earth official, hearing the actual reports of freighters and even warships that had disappeared without a trace.

The clean air inside the helmet took on a sweet scent, the smell of the gas that would render him unconscious. A fluttering, gibbering hope blossomed that he would fall asleep quickly and awake to find the whole thing was a failure—with the exception that he had returned alive. Shoving that away, forcing his thoughts to review the logical thought process that had made this effort both sensible and, to his mind, necessary.

Feeling the engines engage, a dull throbbing through the cushioning beneath him, fearing for just a moment that the flight would start before he was sedated. Ordering himself to calm down, that he'd traveled this way hundreds of times before. His thoughts becoming scattered, flashing from Reena to Ayliss to Jan, then to the too many faces of the dead. They'd all perished while he had lived, the boy soldiers of the Unwavering, his dear wife Lydia, his bodyguard Faldonado, President Larkin, and, in a way, his very own son. He'd believed for a time that Jan had been killed on Fractus, and the grief and the shame had never left him.

More flashing lights. The engines coming to life, taking him forward into space, into darkness. Going now, ready or not.

Fighting a rising spur of panic, he tried to remember that first Step, when he'd been fifteen and a green volunteer, sealed in a tiny cylinder with all of the other teenagers, headed for what they knew was a losing battle. Recalling his iron resolve, his utter rejection of his own safety in the name of protecting humanity, his near certainty that he would not return. God, he'd been strong back then, or ignorant, or just a better man than the phony he was now.

A man who'd found himself surrounded by political hacks and climbers, slowly giving in more and more in the name of winning the war, turning a blind eye on the profiteering and the outright theft and the human misery on Celestia. Every day another compromise, another rationalization, until years of it had piled up, and he'd finally been forced to admit that it was no longer an act, that we become what we pretend to be, and that the brave young boy who'd shipped out to the war would have spit in his face if they'd ever met.

No. His eyes fluttered, the drugs finally taking effect, tears rolling down his face. *No, that's wrong. So many mistakes, so much lost, but my heart was always pure. Defend our people. Win the war. Look at me now, shit-scared again, but here by my own choice again, I do this willingly, for total strangers and the ones I love, because in the end that is all that is left, my love, I love you Reena, I love you Lydia, I love you Ayliss, I love you Jan. I love*

CHAPTER EIGHT

On his stomach in a patch of sickly weeds, Mortas was thinking about water. Night had fallen hours earlier, and the darkness magnified the gurgling of a small stream just on the other side of the trail he was watching. Although drinking the water straight from its source would have made him too sick to stand, Mortas still wanted it. He'd consumed most of the water in his canteens during the afternoon's long, hot movement, and he ran his tongue around the gummy paste that covered the inside of his mouth.

When the sun came up they would push patrols out, across the trail and the stream, and begin the process of rendering the water drinkable. All three platoons carried sophisticated equipment that would siphon the liquid straight from its source and, at the end of a long tube with several intermediate stages, pour the filtered results into waiting canteens. Purification pills would then be added to complete the job, and the local water would be safe to drink.

Unfortunately, the water source was on the other side of a trail running east to west that was even larger and more developed than the north–south path they'd been following. Moving through the bush while keeping the cart track in sight, they'd encountered more and more signs of Sim presence. The pipes hammered into the trees had become so common that they'd stopped calling them in, but a few hundred yards later they'd detected footprints in the jungle muck that couldn't have been more than a day old.

All three platoons, moving north at a slow, steady rate, had reported boot prints and oddly shaped impressions that were probably made by crude sandals. The surveillance satellites watching over the three sites to their north still showed none of the heat signatures associated with the Sims, and the *Dauntless* had confirmed there was no sign of the enemy anywhere. The heat and the vegetation had closed in on them, sending sweat running down their arms and fatigued paranoia into their minds. Every now and then, a covey of birds would explode into the air not far in front of the troops, further jangling their nerves.

First Platoon had just reached the east–west trail when Second Platoon discovered the bunker complex. Excited radio calls had passed back and forth, and Dassa had halted both First and Third Platoons in place, so they would be in position to help Second if their unseen foes materialized.

They hadn't. The bunkers were expertly camouflaged, but the complex was small and so it took no
time at all to determine that it was empty. Second had
swept on through, right up to the edge of the east–west
trail where the bunkers ended, then formed a defensive perimeter using the Sims' own positions. Markers had begun popping up on goggle maps across the
company, indicating that the abandoned positions had
formed a circular strongpoint just east of the junction
of the two paths.

The water table in that region was high, so the bunkers had only been dug down a few feet before walls
and ceilings had been constructed over them using
logs and dirt. In classic Sim fashion, the jungle around
the complex had been left undisturbed—which meant
that the rotting logs used to build the positions had
been brought from a considerable distance away.

Darkness had approached, and so Dassa called a
halt right there. The evidence of an organized enemy
presence, utterly undetected by the humans' battle-
tested overhead surveillance, had made most of the
company highly uneasy. Many of the veterans of the
debacle on Fractus darkly commented that this was
not the first time the orbital eyes had failed them, and
so Dassa had arranged the company in three defensive
positions covering the two trails.

Mortas moved most of his platoon several hundred yards back, assigning Sergeant Frankel's squad to
ambush the trail. Mortas had stayed with them while
Dak had supervised the arrangement of the other two

squads in a perimeter to which Frankel could fall back if pressed. Second Platoon remained in the enemy fighting positions, covering their part of the same trail, while Wyn Kitrick's Third Platoon had swung behind them to the south, covering the northbound path they'd followed most of the day.

Captain Pappas was quietly broadcasting a description of the enemy emplacement now occupied by Second Platoon. "Standard Sim fighting positions, well camouflaged with overhead cover capable of defeating our scanners. Defensive orientation concentrated to the north, with only a few positions covering the other cardinal directions. Indications that several standing structures were present, but have been dismantled and removed. These structures may have been fabricated from the fuselages of downed resupply drones and other materials left over from earlier fighting, all of which could have concealed the enemy from orbital and aerial surveillance."

Wiping a dirty hand across his face and feeling the stubble of his beard, Mortas flipped his goggle view to the surveillance feed. He saw the three glowing rings again, the platoons of B Company formed into defensive postures, and only the solitary flickerings of individual birds and animals moving around them. The heat signatures of the jungle creatures were too small to be Sims, leaving him to wonder just where the enemy had gone—and what they'd been doing there.

Pappas offered a clue. "A series of short trenches within the enemy perimeter have also been discovered. The soil inside these ditches shows signs of having been badly scorched, which is surprising given the water content of the ground. It is likely that this was caused by a flammable material generating extreme heat, but there is no other indication of what that might have been or what the enemy was doing. It is extremely unlikely that such a heat signature would have gone unnoticed by surveillance satellites, suggesting that the enemy erected some kind of shielding over the trenches while the burning was in progress.

"Possible reasons for this activity could involve rendering the sap collected by the enemy into a different substance, use unknown at this time. The danger represented by creating such a large heat signature suggests that the Sims considered this activity to be highly important."

Mortas's attention began to lapse, and he recognized that he was in danger of falling asleep. Returning to the imagery in his goggles, he toggled the view until it included the three monitoring stations to the north, their heat signatures standing out like roaring green furnaces against the blackness of the jungle.

He narrowed the view again, enjoying the sensation of plummeting straight toward the ground, until he could make out the individual dots around him. One of the platoon's machine-gun teams covered the trail to the west, and a scattered line of men formed the ambush. He identified himself and Vossel, set back from the trail, and then a pair of two-man teams several yards to his east and west. Despite the absence of the enemy and the fallback position occupied by the remainder of the platoon, the ambushing squad was still responsible for its own local security and had to make sure Sim infiltrators didn't sneak up on them from behind.

A slight breeze drifted through the dense foliage, making Mortas aware of his own stench. A mix of body odor and the sharp scent of that day's stink pill, it would have been revolting if it hadn't been helping in a small way to keep him awake.

The sound dampeners in his helmet snugged down hard without warning, and Mortas flattened against the dirt in a reflex born on Fractus. The dampeners detected large sound waves a fraction of a second before their arrival, protecting the wearer's hearing and providing a moment's warning that something big had just detonated nearby. A brief spasm of movement from several of the veterans waiting in ambush proved his reaction was not unique, but no blast followed.

Instead, a warning message came through. This one was straight from the *Dauntless*.

"Warning. Enemy movement detected." A robot voice chattered a preset message activated when the scanners got a hit. "One mile southwest of civilian monitoring station Almighty, moving northeast. Estimated size: platoon strength."

All around him, bodies switched the view on their goggles to see where almost forty enemy soldiers had appeared as if they'd materialized out of the ground. Sergeant Frankel spoke to his men. "Don't get distracted. Sam's a tricky bastard, and whatever he's showing the satellites is far away from here. Keep your eyes open and watch your assigned sectors."

Dassa echoed a similar command to the rest of B Company, and Mortas shifted the overhead view all the way around his platoon's split locations. The jungle showed no signs of the Sims, but that was hardly reassuring, given what was happening to their northwest.

The green-white dots of the Sims' heat signatures were in three parallel columns, with roughly one hundred yards between them. Eerily reminiscent of his platoon's movement formation that day but moving at a steady pace. Mortas focused on the three soldiers in the lead, marveling at the ease with which they were moving forward through the bush.

"Almighty, are you seeing this?" Dassa called the civilian security force defending the Victory Provisions station.

"Hard to miss 'em, isn't it?" a bored voice responded. "Don't get worked up, Army. We got somethin' for these assholes."

The dots shifted again, hustling northeast toward the Victory Provisions site. All across their silent jungle positions, the troops of B Company exchanged quizzical looks that conveyed their confusion about what the enemy was doing. Despite their rapid progress through the jungle, the Sims would soon encounter the steep slopes surrounding the civilian station. At the top of that elevation was an electrified antipersonnel fence and a trained security force. Almighty had its own armed satellite that could rain rockets down on any opposition and, in the unlikely event that those systems failed, the *Dauntless* was overhead with even more firepower.

"Rockets on the way. Rockets on the way," the bored voice announced. "Lemme show ya how it's done, Infantry."

The dampeners snugged down again, but the enemy target was so far away that Mortas didn't react. The night was dark enough where he might have glimpsed the incoming ordnance, but the trees and foliage made that impossible. A target designator popped up on the enemy concentration in his goggles, and a moment later the image flashed in a spasm of light. The first rocket was dead-on, and several more impacted right after that. The burst of white blotted out the dots that were the enemy, and chunks of burning material arched away into the jungle.

When the image returned to normal, several small fires marked the spot where the enemy platoon had been. To the west, a single white dot was zigzagging across the blackness, looking like a crazed firefly chasing a much smaller and more nimble insect. It sped up suddenly, charging forward at a fantastic speed before coming to a sudden halt. Mortas decided it was a lone Sim survivor, fleeing the strike, terror-stricken, and that he'd fallen down some kind of an embankment in the darkness.

One last rocket raced down, slamming into the spot where the single Sim lay, the sound of the blast a mere whisper when it reached them.

"Evenin', Sam. So glad you could drop by," the Victory Provisions man said in farewell. "Go back to sleep, Army. Didn't need ya—don't need ya."

Before anyone could respond, dampeners all over the jungle clamped down and the robot voice spoke again. "Urgent warning. Urgent warning. Major fire detected at Retransmission Station Broadleaf."

Mortas swung the goggle image from the rocket strike to the Force station that sat between Almighty and the planetary monitoring base Cordvine. Normally the building's rectangular silhouette glowed with heat, but now it pulsated on two sides as if the northern and eastern walls were a set of bellows.

A tiny speck of light, an ember thrown from a fireplace, burst into life on the northern slope, then disappeared. Mortas was just wondering what that might have been when a half dozen more of them blinked from the same area and the radio burst into chatter.

"This is Broadleaf! This is Broadleaf! We are under close attack! They're inside the wire!"

Adrenaline surged through Mortas as he increased the resolution. Dots began to emerge from the burning structure, men running into the lighted compound and abruptly stopping, dropping, and lying still. More flickers from the jungle, and now he was just able to make out the impacts against the wall of fire, a giant blacksmith's hammer pounding a redhot piece of steel. Boomers. Enemy rocket launchers. The sounds of the blasts finally reached them, along with the muttered chatter of enemy machine guns, and yet there were no Sim heat signatures from the firing positions.

Orphan voices came over the radio.

"How did they get in there?"

"Why can't we see them?"

"We have to get there, *now!*" Mortas recognized the voice of Lieutenant Wyn Kitrick, from Third Platoon. Kitrick had signed himself out of the hospital when the Orphans had gone to Fractus, but his unhealed wound had forced his evacuation before the bruising battle. Mortas knew the man carried a fair amount of guilt over that.

"Get up there?" Lieutenant Stout, leading Second Platoon, exclaimed. "Miles of bush, in darkness, then up a cliff face with Sam waiting on top? Not a chance."

"What, we gonna leave them to fight by themselves?" Kitrick again. "No. We gotta go help them."

"Everyone stop talking. You know better than that." Dassa's iron command stilled the panic. "Broadleaf, can you direct orbital fire onto the enemy?"

"Negative, Orphan! You gotta do it for me!" Terror jumped on the other end of the transmission, and the booming sound of the rockets came with it. "They're in the compound! Dozens of 'em! Hit everything outside the building! Bring it in as close as you can!"

"Understood. Hang tough, Broadleaf! Rockets on the way!"

Right next to Dassa somewhere in Second Platoon's perimeter, an expert in the application of support fires took over. His technical description was Aerial Support Systems Liaison, but across the infantry these men were warmly addressed by their acronym, ASSL.

"That's right, I need a mixture of high explosive and antipersonnel. Designating targets now." The ASSL's calm purr soothed Mortas's excitement, and he flipped his goggle imagery back to the area around his platoon. He saw nothing, the birds and animals having already cleared out, but the surprise appearance of the Sims at two locations left him wary.

"Stay alert, First." He spoke on the platoon net, imitating the ASSL's serenity. "Eyes and ears open."

Shifting back to Broadleaf, he now saw fire billowing in waves from the main structure. Even if they drove off the attack, the site would be a total loss. The ASSL spoke now, a warning that a tremendous amount of explosives was about to strike. Moments later, the entire site simply disappeared in a blinding cloud of light that grew, collapsed, then grew again. Ordnance impacted all around the main building, antipersonnel rounds bursting overhead to drive shrapnel downward into the enemy overrunning the station, while high explosives blasted the surrounding jungle.

The ground trembled when the shock wave reached them, dissipated by the miles but still felt in the torsos of the prone soldiers. A pulsating roar surged through the vegetation, the hollering of some mythical monster, and the echo lasted a long time. Staring into his goggles, Mortas saw that the lights along the perimeter fence were dead. Fires burned all over the north and east slopes, but the structure itself was no longer ablaze. Still generating heat from its center, it had somehow transformed into an oval shape. No more flickers of rocket fire showed from the cover of the trees, and no sounds of gunfire could be heard.

"Broadleaf, this is Orphan. Can you hear me?" Dassa called the site.

Silence.

"Broadleaf, this is Orphan. Can you hear me?"

Nothing came back.

"Broadleaf, this is Orphan. Contact us if you can. We are coming to you." Dassa addressed the entire company. "Saddle up, Orphans."

The decision to move did not sit well with some of the troops. B Company had accomplished many an arduous trek through difficult terrain before, but this was markedly different. The first few miles between their positions and Broadleaf ran over unmapped ground because so few Force units had operated that far away from the sites. The bush was thick and undisturbed, and their route was loaded with deadfall and unexpected ravines. Once they got close to the stations, they would be entering a zone that was infamous for Sim booby traps.

Finally, and worst of all, they were rushing through the darkness toward a target that had already been hit by an enemy who had somehow managed to blind the humans' orbital scanners.

"Second Platoon will head straight for Broadleaf,

and the command element will travel with them."
Dassa named the game even as Mortas was calling the
remaining two squads of his platoon forward to link
up with Frankel's squad. "Third Platoon will follow
the route I am marking now"—military symbols appeared in goggles all over the jungle, indicating a
movement corridor that would shield Second Platoon's
eastern flank—"Wyn, I leave it up to your discretion to
deviate from that lane as you see fit.

"First Platoon will follow this route"—a shorter
journey, one that would put Mortas and his people just
short of the ridge where the stations sat, protecting
Second Platoon's western flank—"again, deviating as
necessary. We have to move fast, but not so fast that we
run into something, especially each other.

"Sam may have come up with a trick for avoiding
our sensors, but remember we have fire supremacy. So
if you bump into Sam, form a perimeter where you are
and bring the rockets down. Let's go."

Sergeant Dak appeared next to Mortas just as Dassa
finished speaking.

"Platoon's ready to move, sir."

"What formation should we use? We have to be
able to react if we run into something."

"This bush, in this darkness, I say three squads in
column. Spreading out when we can."

"What are you thinking?"

"It's a real problem. I know we have to get up there,
but this is gonna take forever."

"What would you do?" Mortas had already drawn

most of the same conclusions, but didn't have an answer to his own question.

"The Sims who hit Broadleaf aren't waiting up there, not with the shit we can drop on them. They made their attack and ran off. The CO should have the *Dauntless* fly a Marine security force right onto the site. Or find a clearing, and have them shuttle Second Platoon up there that way."

Mortas was considering just how to suggest this option to Dassa when the company commander's voice came over the headphones. "Marines from the *Dauntless* are going to be inserted onto Broadleaf by shuttle. We will continue the move as planned, but we'll hold up when the shuttles come in. I want to be able to move around the ridge to pursue the enemy, or to engage him if he appears on this side.

"Keep on the move, but don't rush. Let's go."

Dak drifted back to Mecklinger's squad in the rear, while Mortas moved up to Sergeant Frankel's squad in the lead. The platoon was in a tight perimeter, most of the men kneeling with weapons ready. Frankel was at the edge of the trail, having sent two men to scout out the far side, and Mortas knelt near him.

"Comin' back." The dark green world inside his goggles showed the open ground of the trail, but not much else. The trees, brush, and vines closed in all around them, and Mortas wondered how they would be able to push through the vegetation without sounding like a troop of elephants. Two dots of light appeared in the distance, slowly elongating until they were recognizable as men carrying rifles. The scouts knelt on the other side of the trail, and Frankel sent the first half of his squad across.

The forms, hunched inside their torso armor and helmets, shuffled quickly to the other side and spread out. Already organizing themselves in patrol formation, getting as much separation as the terrain allowed. Frankel signaled to the rest of his men, and they hustled across in a loose group.

Mortas and Vossel followed, the damp soil making a sucking sound against their boots.

Hours later, Mortas was astounded to see how little ground they'd covered. The lead squad had to push through the worst of the brush when there was no way to go around. It was noisy, exhausting, and time-consuming work, and he'd already rotated all three squads through the point position. Vines hung up on everything from rifle barrels to canteens, and ages of collected deadfall created barriers that were taller than a man. Unyielding branches scraped along helmets and torso armor with a metallic screech that was almost a yell, and men tripping over unseen roots and rocks fell with a loud crash.

Walking inside the tight arrowhead of the lead squad, Mortas soon found himself concentrating on his every footfall instead of directing the platoon. His canteens were now empty, and his mouth felt like it was made of cotton. There was no time for rest breaks, so the only chance he got to switch to the overhead imagery was when the lead squad had to stop to deal with yet another obstacle.

Still miles to their north, the main building of Broadleaf Station was little more than a smoking ruin. Second Platoon, heading for it, was moving no faster than First, but Wyn Kitrick's Third seemed to have acquired wings. Every time he checked, Mortas was surprised to see the eastern flank platoon getting farther and farther away from Second. They were following their assigned lane, but even so a yawning gap was beginning to form between them and the rest of B Company.

A rushing sound broke the darkness overhead, and Mortas dropped to a knee along with the rest of the platoon. A muttering engine announced the presence of a reconnaissance drone, but that was little comfort. Captain Pappas came up on the radio.

"Hey ASSL, we're still not sure the enemy knows we're here. Who called for that recon 'bot?"

"Wasn't me." A pause. "The scientists at Cordvine are getting anxious. They made their security platoon send that up."

"Tell them to keep the thing away from us," Dassa ordered. "They can scout all they want to the north and east—Sam's probably expecting that."

The wet ground began to moisten his knee through his fatigues, but Mortas was reluctant to move. With the platoon stopped, the jungle had returned to the stillness that had surrounded their earlier position.

Exhaustion flowed through his muscles, and he reflexively reached for a canteen before remembering for the hundredth time that he had no more water. Most of the platoon was empty, and now they'd moved away from the water source they'd planned to use.

His eyes fluttered and tried to close, so Mortas put a hand on his bent knee and pushed himself up into a standing position. Vossel, crouched by a narrow tree, stood up next. All around them men began to rise, some tapping buddies who'd fallen asleep during the brief stop.

"Let's get going." Mortas had barely gotten the words out when the helmet buffers all over B Company clenched down tight and a robotic voice announced, "Imminent rocket impact. Imminent rocket impact. Seek shelter. Seek—"

The men had already thrown themselves back down, and Mortas felt moisture from the waist down when he joined them. To the east, a momentary flash of intense light burst through breaks in the overhead foliage. Seconds later, the rumble of a heavy explosion rolled over them.

"Who called for that?" the company ASSL demanded. "Where was our warning?"

"Uh, uh, sorry Orphan," a nervous voice answered. "We detected movement at the base of the slope and wanted to blast them before they got away."

"Who is this?"

"Oh, it's Cordvine. Sorry. We thought you were far enough away."

"I don't care what you *thought*. You call for fire, you make damn sure everybody knows you did it."

"Won't happen again—wait, we've got another activation! They're out there, I tell you!"

"An activation? You threw a rocket at a *ground sensor*?"

"What else have we got? The scanners didn't pick up the Sammies who hit Broadleaf, and by the time we see them they'll be—hold on, we've got more movement! Get your heads down, Orphans, I'm calling it in!"

"Negative, Cordvine, negative! We have a platoon moving in your direction!"

"I see your platoon on the screen, and they're nowhere near the activation! I'm doing it!"

Mortas spoke to his men. "Everybody get ready, more rockets on the way. Some dipshit at the monitoring station is shooting at shadows."

"Can't we call the *Dauntless* and cancel the mission?" asked an anonymous First Platoon soldier.

"It's not coming from the *Dauntless*. They've got their own armed satellite." Dak spoke calmly, the transmission so crisp that he could have been lying right next to Mortas. A moment later he was, throwing himself down next to the lieutenant. "Hey, El-tee. I got bored walking in the back."

"Rockets inbound. Rockets inbound," the ASSL called out in a businesslike voice, and Mortas decided he'd received advance warning from the *Dauntless*. "They're not too close, but ya never know."

To the east of the company's three separated platoons, more flashes of light and a series of concussions. In his goggles, Mortas saw the rounds impacting just off the tip of the ridge that was home to Cordvine and what was left of Broadleaf. The ASSL began arguing with the frightened man calling in the fire, and a hand tapped Mortas on the elbow. He turned to see Dak looking at him.

"None of that stuff is anywhere near us, but it's making a lot of good noise. How about we take advantage of that, and really cover some ground?"

"Tell me exactly what you're seeing." Dassa sounded fatigued, and with good reason. The commander of the *Dauntless* had diverted the Marine force to Cordvine instead of landing it at Broadleaf. Having finally reached the base of the tall ridge without encountering any enemy booby traps, Dassa and Second Platoon had immediately started the climb.

"Got heat signatures, not far to my front," Lieutenant Kitrick whispered from Third Platoon's defensive position, east of the spot where Second Platoon was beginning its climb. "Nothing on the overheads, but those are definitely Sims."

Mortas, crouched in the jungle west of Dassa, played with the images in his goggles. The fire at Broadleaf was finally out, and there were no indications that anyone up there was alive. He could identify the snaking column of Second Platoon, working its way up the slope, as well as the tight circle of Third Platoon. As Kitrick had said, overhead imagery was showing no heat signatures other than the humans'.

Dassa came back on, winded. "*Dauntless* isn't picking anything up. Are they coming toward you?"

"Negative. They're passing to my front, heading north. I can see the movement through the breaks in the trees."

"You want rockets?" The ASSL, climbing with Dassa, sounded equally tired. "I've got a good spot on you, and I can walk them in."

"No way. They're too close. I'm going to move up and engage with direct fire."

"No you're not. They'll hear you coming, and we still don't know why we can't pick them up on the sensors. Stay in position."

"After what they did to Broadleaf? They're right in front of me!"

"Don't you get it?" Annoyance crept into Dassa's voice. "What they did to Broadleaf is exactly why I don't want you to move. We didn't see them coming or going, and you're not rushing into what could be a trap."

The darkness all around First Platoon's perimeter was intensified by the looming, forested ridgeline immediately to their north. Mortas had arranged the squads and their machine guns well short of the slope, but it was so tall that it blocked out the stars. Birds and insects had begun clicking and chirping shortly after the tired soldiers had hunkered down in a defensive ring, and it was easy to imagine they were alone out there.

But Kitrick was seeing enemy movement that was not showing up on the scanners. Mortas flipped the goggles back to night vision and carefully scanned the wall of foliage to his west. Nothing.

Behind him, the night erupted in a series of sharp explosions that Mortas recognized as chonk rounds. The grenade-launcher fire was followed immediately by the steady booming of Force machine guns, then Scorpion fire joined in.

"They've seen us! We're engaging!" Kitrick shouted, his transmission bringing the battle right into Mortas's helmet. "Approximately an enemy squad one hundred yards to our east!"

"Hold your position, Kitrick! That is an order!" Dassa shouted, anger in the words. Mortas was baffled for just a moment, but then realized that the volley of chonk rounds had been too well coordinated to be a reaction to the enemy discovering Kitrick's position. Chomping at the bit, smarting over having missed the fight on Fractus, the veteran lieutenant had created an excuse to chase the enemy passing his position.

The sounds of a few Sim rifles came across the night sky when Third Platoon's fire slackened. Flipping to overhead imagery, Mortas now saw that Kitrick's entire platoon was on the move, two hundred yards from where they'd been, three squads identifiable as oval clusters of men pushing through the brush.

Mortas was straining to see any indication of the enemy when an enormous explosion detonated to the east, right where Kitrick's men would be.

CHAPTER NINE

Ayliss was adrift in an ocean of cold water, but there was nothing she could do about it. Too weak even to force herself into full consciousness, she felt her body descending into oblivion for unknown lengths of time before rising toward the surface without quite getting there. Her brain was packed with cotton, and the bucking engine in her core had turned into a blast furnace.

She couldn't tell if she was dreaming or not, but fragments of what had to be reality kept coming to her. Hands swabbing her face with damp sponges, followed by scattered phrases of encouragement and sympathy. An enormous paw on her forehead, and a voice she remembered from decades before. "Don't die on me, little bear."

Floating downward again, shocked to have forgotten the name from her childhood, when the huge man had been Big Bear and she had been Little Bear. Remembering the night of her mother's funeral, when she'd finally been returned to her home, finally away from the minders and handlers and toadies who only wanted to use her to get to her father. The enormous hands and the broad chest, holding her while she'd cried for the loss of both her parents, her mother because she was dead and her father because he seemed not to care at all.

Tears flowed from her eyes, and she moaned in anguish.

"It's all right, Little Bear. Big Bear is here."

Walking down the corridor, still in the body armor he'd been wearing all day and all night, Blocker forced himself to ignore his fatigue. An hour earlier, sitting with Ayliss, he'd heard the gunfire and explosions up on the hill. Suspecting that Selkirk was somehow involved, and believing that yet another of their limited options had been taken off the table. Ayliss had refused to enter the mining compound before losing consciousness, and whatever destruction had taken place there since then suggested that they were no longer welcome. Hemsley's tunnel settlement was barred to them as well unless Selkirk had made amends with the veterans, so they were stuck right where they were. If open warfare broke out, Blocker and his party were directly in the line of fire.

His small security detail was positioned at key points all over the building, armed and armored, but they wouldn't last long once the heavy weapons on the mining perimeter came into play. Something about that sneaky Hemsley told Blocker that the veterans had more than rifles at their disposal, and he stopped himself from considering what would happen in such a cross fire.

Most of the building was dark, but a dull glow emanated from the room where the strange commo guy from the settlement, Ewing, had set up shop. He'd walked up the slope on his own while they'd been getting Ayliss settled, and volunteered to help with their communications. Blocker initially told him to get lost, but had relented when the self-confessed drug user explained his unexpected offer of help.

"First Sergeant doesn't let me man the radios anymore. It's the only thing I was ever good at, and I'm not doing it."

Shorthanded, Blocker had relented. He'd been amazed when Ewing not only proved reliable on radio watch, but also boosted the power of their signals through a complicated relay involving Zone Quest's orbital satellites. When asked if ZQ knew about this piggybacking, Ewing had merely grinned.

"Hi, Blocker." Ewing removed a set of headphones. "I tried to request a ship like you asked, but the Step's been suspended."

Blocker lowered himself into a chair. "You know those never last very long."

"This one might. I just received the all-points announcement that the Step will be unavailable for at least a day. That went out over the Bounce, so they're not trying to keep it quiet. Command has been ordered to plan for a suspension that could last indefinitely."

"They give any reason?"

"No, so I asked around. The chatter says there's a major search under way in a couple of different sectors. Maybe somebody important went missing."

Blocker exhaled with a loud sigh, leaning forward and rubbing his eyes. A Step suspension of that magnitude could only mean Chairman Mortas, and only hours earlier they'd received the news that Olech and Reena had been married on Celestia. If Ayliss's father disappeared, their position on this planet was even more perilous than he'd thought.

"At least things can't get a lot worse." The old soldier in him regretted the words as soon as they came out, so he changed the subject. "You're doing a good job here. Just why did Hemsley ban you from using the settlement radios?"

A mischievous smirk flashed across Ewing's features. In the room's bright light he looked almost skeletal, his fatigues too large and his skin too pale. "I kept tapping into the deep-space feeds, all the echoes from the places man has never visited. You ever tune in to that?"

"No. I imagine you gotta be high to appreciate something like that."

"Not as much as you'd think." Ewing winked at him. "You remind me of First Sergeant. You actually give a shit about your people."

"You take the job, you take the responsibility."

"That's what I mean. Hemsley's not classified as a colonist. He reached retirement, and he was just waiting for transport home when they temporarily put him in charge of our group. We were a bunch of odds and ends, and Command didn't know where to put us, so they had him counting our heads every day at the transient personnel center. That's all he was expected to do, but he took the time to find out about every one of us, what we'd done in the Force, where we were from, all that stuff.

"So one day this captain comes by and says we're all getting sent to this planet where ZQ would probably give us jobs, and First Sergeant tells him that's not what we agreed to when we elected to become colonists. So the captain asks him why he cares, points out that First Sergeant is retiring, and that he'll be going home as soon as we're gone. And you know what Hemsley does right then? He says he's postponing his retirement until he sees us settled someplace."

Ewing smiled at the memory. "Can you imagine anybody doing something like that for a grab bag full of strangers? And that was long before Chairman Mortas made his big announcement about giving the colonists control of the planets."

Shocked by the story and astounded that he hadn't known it, Blocker was about to ask a question when a communications bud in one of his ears hissed at him. It was one of the roof guards.

"Lone individual approaching from the settlement. Looks like that Banshee that was here earlier."

Blocker stood, knowing what the news would be but hoping he was wrong. Trying to find a reason why a lone veteran would be visiting, and why Selkirk had not yet returned.

Moving quickly down the corridor again, telling the guards to let the messenger through, and seeing Tin when he got to the first floor. Still wearing the black fatigues and the dark bandana, the story easy to read in eyes that poked out from fresh black camouflage paint. The Banshee shook her head minutely when he came up to her, and he could have uttered her words before she did.

"I'm sorry. We're all sorry. Selkirk went into the compound with one of our people, and they got nailed just before the gunships went up. God knows how he made it over the wire, but we've got the body in the tunnel."

Confused by the words, startled to be so hurt by a report he'd received or issued so many times before, of a good man dead, and wondering how he was going to break it to Ayliss when she recovered. If she recovered. Lessons from past experiences kicked in, reminding him to make sure.

"You're certain it's Selkirk?"

"Yes. He's dead."

Ayliss's illness reached its peak a short time later. Her infrequent moments of lucidity had become fewer and fewer until she'd lapsed into complete delirium, filling her mind with memories, dreams, and outright hallucinations.

She started out back at Unity, in a briefing room with her father and Reena. The daily classes had usually combined tutorials on the players she might face in her new role with lessons Olech and Reena had learned over the years. At first Ayliss had found the encounters unbearably dull, and had only managed to stay focused because they represented one more step toward the chaotic environment she longed to enter.

"You keep telling me to make sure everyone leaves a negotiation or even a confrontation with something, to keep them on our side. If that's been your approach, how come you seem to end up killing so many people?"

Olech and Reena had exchanged glances, having noticed Ayliss's fixation on those times when they'd had to exercise deadly force.

"Because, as you already know from your own experience, there are some people who can't be reasoned with." Reena had given her a significant look. "You can debate them, you can befriend them, you can even try to placate them, but in the end they'll prove they're not interested in anything but being a problem."

Olech had joined in. "And then you're not only justified in removing them—you're a fool not to."

"But what if they haven't done anything that justifies killing them? Something small . . . like going back on an agreement?" Ayliss had raised her eyebrows at her father, and he'd understood her true question.

"Blocker's been telling you about your mother again, I see."

"He just wants me to get the full story. Warts and all."

"All right. What did he tell you?"

"He said that President Larkin tried to enlist your support when you were a junior senator, and that you agreed to go along until mother saw a way to turn the whole thing to your advantage."

Olech and Reena exchanged glances, and Ayliss was pleased to have discovered a part of his political past with which Reena was unfamiliar.

"Larkin wanted to take the Force promotion system out of the hands of the Interplanetary Senate. He recognized that some of the senior officers in the war zone were making tactical decisions based on the politics of their home worlds and not on military exigencies. I'd seen that at firsthand and knew it to be true, so I agreed to help him."

"But mother talked you out of it."

"Larkin didn't understand the role the corporations were already beginning to play in the war zone. Outfits like Zone Quest had strong allies in the Senate, and it was important for them to secure access to resource-rich planets as they were captured. Having sympathetic commanders in the right places was a good way to do that."

"So you agreed to help President Larkin, then switched sides when it was time to vote."

"He never forgave me for that. But your mother was right. He wasn't going to get what he wanted, and by changing my vote I landed some very important friends."

Her body surrounded with cold packs, Ayliss

twitched on the bed. Blocker continued swabbing her face.

Ayliss's fever dream jumped just then, to a high platform outside a secret research facility on a planet called Echo. Ayliss experienced a thrill upon recognizing the location and the individual who'd gone out on that platform alone with her. Python, the man who had almost trapped her in a scandal that would have ruined her along with Olech.

But the hallucination was different from the reality. Large and strong, Python was laughing at her even as she saw how close he stood to the low railing. He spoke mocking words that he'd never uttered in real life.

"Look at you. So smart, so sly, think you're as sharp as your mother was, and what's happened? Poisoned just like she was, going to die just like she did, and going to miss all the fun. Just like she did."

Fear and rage blended together at the goading, and she rushed forward with her hands out. Reliving the moment, that supremely marvelous moment, when she'd sent him tumbling over the high railing, his pants around his ankles. Seeing the expression of surprise and terror, feeling his weight shifting past the point of no return, her entire body singing with adrenaline as she shoved him over. Almost following him, but catching the railing and then watching, awestruck and ecstatic, as he fell away and slammed into the turf far, far below. A rush of excitement and relief and discovery had blasted through her brain.

Her fever broke at that moment, peaking and falling away just as the sensation of joyous conquest had slowly receded within her when she'd finished off the stricken Python with a rock.

"**H**ello, Blocker. How is the Minister?"

Station Manager Rittle looked out at him from a console in the communications room. As Blocker had noted at their first meeting, it was impossible to read the man. Blocker put up his guard before responding.

"She's on the mend. It seems it was just a NOA."

Rittle nodded, two old space hands speaking the same language. "I'm pleased to hear that. I would have visited personally, but the attack on our compound has left my security staff a little uneasy."

"I heard an explosion, but was tending to the Minister. I thought you'd had an accident with an ammunition store."

"The destruction of two gunships makes a lot more noise than that. And it was no accident."

"What can I do for you, Rittle?"

"You strike me as a reasonable man, Blocker."

"That I am. Unless, of course, the Minister's safety is concerned. Then I'm the most unreasonable man you'd ever meet."

"That wasn't an attempt to co-opt you. I have some new information that I need to share with you and the Minister."

Blocker concentrated on keeping his face bland, loosening the muscles with a will. Selkirk's body was in the tunnels, but the dead sapper who'd accompanied him had not made it out. He was presumed dead, but if he'd been taken alive Rittle would be able to force a confession out of him. Even if found dead, the man's background was shady at best and could be used against them.

"I'm listening."

"You already heard the Step has been suspended?"

"Yes."

"The suspension is for an indefinite period. Very few people know what I'm going to tell you now; I've only received this information because it puts the entire station in jeopardy. I'm sharing it with you because of the Minister."

Blocker now fought to keep a look of consternation off his face. "Go on."

"Shortly after his wedding on Celestia, Chairman Mortas disappeared in the Step. No one seems to know where he was headed or who was with him, except that his new wife was not along for the ride." Long associated with the machinations of the powerful, Blocker saw the same calculus running through his own head as had run through Rittle's. With Olech missing or dead, Reena Corlipso—Reena Mortas—was in an excellent position to assume his mantle. "The Step will remain suspended until search-and-rescue operations are terminated. Hopefully that will be soon, with Chairman Mortas found alive, but they could go on for days or even weeks."

An image of the planetary systems closest to Quad

Seven appeared in Blocker's mind. None of them close enough to bring assistance without the Step. "I appreciate your telling me this."

"There's more. Numerous Sim commerce raiders inhabit this part of space, along with human marauders like Hemsley's friend McRaney. They're not a problem as long as we can summon immediate help, but without the Step this station has been left wide open. I don't need to tell you that the enemy wasn't happy to see this planet's Go-Three supply fall into our hands. Once they detect the absence of Threshold signatures, they're going to figure out something is wrong."

"There must be Force warships in the vicinity that could be diverted."

"Yes and no. We're not the only place asking for protection, and some of those other places contain high-ranking officers. Most of the ships within range are being directed to assume defensive patrolling around more important targets."

"Like high-level headquarters." Blocker allowed himself to smile.

"Like high-level headquarters. Zone Quest is creating a series of safe havens in space, and Command has allocated several cruisers to defend them. Our safe haven is many days' flight away, and so I've been instructed to evacuate the complex and take all of my ships there until the Step is available again. I think the Minister and your party should go with us."

"And what about the veterans?"

"There's not enough room for them and, after their

attack on my station, I'd be foolish to let them on board any of my vessels. They've been insisting this planet is theirs, so now we'll see if they mean it."

"If you leave them behind with only the weapons they have, and the Sims do come, they're all dead."

"I have my instructions, and I am not taking any of those people on my ships."

Blocker's mind whirled for an instant, but he pushed it back into focus. With Ayliss still sick, he was in charge of their group and could easily get them to safety by accepting Rittle's offer. He'd been trying to summon a ship when the Step had been suspended, and Rittle's assessment of their vulnerability was accurate.

But if they did flee with Rittle's people, Hemsley's veterans would never forgive them. A healthy Ayliss would never agree to leave, and there was a chance that the Step suspension could be lifted shortly. If they abandoned the veterans and the Step was reopened without any Sims threatening the colony, Ayliss would never be able to return. Not liking the conclusion at all, Blocker spoke for his ward anyway.

"We won't be going with you. Please extend the Minister's thanks to the Zone Quest authority who directed you to make the offer."

"I wasn't directed to do that. And you're a fool to stay."

"I wasn't finished. I speak for the Minister when I say that if you leave under these circumstances . . . don't bother coming back."

"We'll return as soon as the Step is functioning again, and we'll bring help."

"You don't understand. Your presence here was authorized before this colony came into being. If you leave and come back, you'll have to negotiate a contract for mineral extraction with the planet's owners."

"We're lifting off in one hour. I'd reconsider your decision if I were you."

"The decision's made. We're staying."

CHAPTER TEN

"**M**ed-Extractor inbound." The warning sounded in helmets all over the jungle, and the troops in First and Third Platoons tightened up their joint perimeter. Mortas had moved First Platoon to the spot where one of Kitrick's squads had been torn up by a massive booby trap concealed inside a hollow tree. Three men had been killed and three others wounded, one badly enough to justify the use of the extractor.

For many miles around them, the engines of flying reconnaissance robots made a chug-chug sound as they flew just above the treetops. Drone gunships made lazy circles in the dawn light, all of it a diversion for the vessel that would speed the most seriously wounded man to treatment. The commotion had driven off most of the jungle birds, but every now and then a group of Vree Vrees would howl in the distance.

"Rockets inbound." Up at Broadleaf, the company

ASSL had arranged for a bombardment of likely locations where the phantom Sim force of the night before could have gone to ground.

"Get ready with the tree cutters." Mortas hugged the wet dirt of the jungle floor a mile away from the spot where the booby trap had gone off. Assuming the enemy knew the location well, Mortas had moved both platoons. Although the bulk of his unit was still intact, Kitrick was practically catatonic with grief over the cost of his disobedience.

"Suckered me. All this time in the zone, and I fell for it. CO told me not to, but I knew better," he'd muttered to Mortas when the junior lieutenant had finally reached the small clearing blasted out of the jungle by the trap. His men had been caring for the wounded and the dead, but Kitrick seemed unaware anyone was near until Mortas knelt beside him. "Jan. Good to see you. Fuckin' Fractus, half my platoon lost, and I wasn't even *there*. They made me leave. *Made* me. And now look what I did."

Vossel had given Kitrick a shot to calm him, and he was half-asleep on the ground next to Mortas. Flipping his goggles to overhead imagery, Mortas detected the blinking marker of the Extractor drawing near. He'd placed the two-platoon perimeter near a massive tree that could have been hundreds of years old, with exposed roots as tall as a man. Special explosives, dubbed tree cutters, had been emplaced all over the behemoth's base at Dak's suggestion.

"Done this before. Ya try to blow down a few small

trees to make room for the Extractor, and none of them fall. So much other growth wrapped around 'em, holds 'em up. Ya need to take down a big one like this bastard here, it's like the main pole in a big tent. Everything around it comes down too."

The readout in his goggles told Mortas that the diversionary rockets were about to impact. "Okay, cutters. Blow it."

Warnings buzzed in all the helmets, and the sound dampeners clamped down hard. Mortas reached out and gently placed a flat hand on the back of Kitrick's helmet, worried he might look up at the wrong moment. Then he pressed his cheek into the wet humus, smelling the decay even over the stench given off by the stink pills. For miles around, dull booms cracked through the still air as the rockets impacted.

"Fire in the hole! Fire in the hole! Fire in the hole!" yelled Dak, and then he detonated the charges on the tree.

A dull rumble vibrated the plates of Mortas's torso armor, and he was just thinking that he'd heard much louder explosions in other places when the main charges went off. To drop a tree that size required an enormous amount of force, directed at specific points, and the cumulative blast was like a hurricane wind. The ground seemed to leap under him, and Mortas cringed when the shock wave ripped across the jungle. Branches fell all around, and rotted trees collapsed as if melting. The vegetation for hundreds of yards was slapped and shot with flying debris, the greenery jumping and bouncing.

At last it was done, and Mortas looked up to a scene he barely recognized. The small clearing was covered in debris, from severed branches to a confetti-like rain of leaves. Man-sized clods of dark earth stood up, wrenched from the ground by the root systems of the trees that had been pulled down when the big one went.

As for that, a brilliant window of light had been cut in the jungle overhead. The giant tree had torn down the concealing foliage, and now men began moving in preparation for the Extractor. A pile of Third Platoon troops nearby dissolved and scrambled in different directions, revealing the wounded man whose body they'd been shielding with their own. Elsewhere, armored and helmeted forms in mud-smeared camouflage grabbed up the detritus from the blast and dragged it out of the way.

Moments later, guided in by a homing beacon and its own sensors, the Extractor sailed out of the sky and through the hole in the foliage. It moved at incredible rates of speed, so one moment it was a dot in the sky and the next it was on the ground, a gust of wind following it. Three times the size of a coffin and shaped like a sailboat hull, it could operate in planetary atmosphere as well as in space. When medical shuttles couldn't reach a wounded man, the Extractor was the best answer.

Heat blasted off of its sides, and steam rose all around the vessel as its top lifted off automatically. Inside, a cushioned space shaped like a human was surrounded by gauges and medical instruments that could deliver medicine, stop bleeding, and perform a full-body scan long before the stricken individual reached medical help.

Vossel and Third Platoon's medic gently lifted the wounded man from his stretcher and began strapping him into position. Other soldiers brought up his rucksack and weapon for evacuation, the backpack stripped of important items and the rifle too damaged to keep.

"Stand back," Vossel ordered, and the nearby soldiers moved away while still watching with concern. The medic activated a switch inside the Extractor, and the lid slowly lowered and locked shut. The entire vessel began to tremble, and Mortas gave the warning that it was about to lift off.

"Extractor outbound."

The box gave off a low hum and slowly levitated a yard off the ground. Turning in place, it pointed its prow toward the open space in the jungle.

"Rockets inbound." The signal came at the last moment, as distant crumps sounded where the missiles were landing. The hovering vessel stopped vibrating, and launched into the sky as if shot from a bow.

"Casualty evacuated," Mortas reported to Dassa. Anticipating the company commander's order, men all over the perimeter were preparing to move. They would have to carry the three bodies and assist the two other wounded men to the top of the ridge for shuttle evacuation.

"Good job. I've marked the route that we used, but stay alert. Sam's sneaking around out here, and we've had enough surprises. The company is forming a new perimeter at Broadleaf."

The main building at Broadleaf looked like it had been stomped on by a giant, then set on fire. Its roof had fallen in, and what was left of its white walls were blackened. Smaller outlying buildings had been badly damaged by the rocket barrage intended to save their inhabitants, and all for naught. Mortas had seen reconnaissance imagery of the site, a multistructure military station with extensive antennae inside a double fence of antipersonnel wire. The antennae were either completely gone, blown down the side of the ridge, or lying twisted where they had once stood. Dassa had cut through the fence when he and Second Platoon had reached the summit early that morning, but that breach was nothing when compared to the enormous breaks on the northern side of the ridge. Entire sections of fencing were simply missing, and it was hard to tell if that work had been accomplished by the Sim attackers or human support fire.

Shuttles had been coming and going for some time, taking the dead from Broadleaf up to the *Dauntless* and bringing in technicians to inspect the damage. They also carried supplies for B Company, and so First Platoon was finally able to refill its canteens. Second Platoon and the Marine platoon from the Dauntless manned a perimeter against another sneak attack, allowing First and Third Platoons to conduct resupply.

Having savored his first drink of water in many desiccated hours, Mortas poured a green powder into one of his canteens before refilling it. It was a fruit-flavored mix, loaded with vitamins and caffeine, and most of the Orphans considered it a necessity on long missions. An armed drone cruised over the clearing just then, a comforting sight after the events of the previous evening. The noise all over the clearing was an additional relief. The Sims on Verdur had run out of mortar ammunition years earlier, and the troops knew there was little chance that they would be able to lob anything up onto the heights. As a result, work parties swarmed all over the plateau.

Standing under the trees near the edge of the hilltop, Mortas overheard two soldiers who were breaking down crates of rations. One was from Third Platoon, and the other was a veteran machine gunner from Katinka's squad named Catalano.

"Hurry up and wait, same old stuff," the soldier from Third Platoon remarked in a bored fashion. "Rush over there, then saunter over here. It's like that whole alien scare eight months ago, the one your el-tee bumped into. One second the Force is on high alert, everybody getting scanned to make sure we're human, and then what? Not another word about it."

Screwing the cover back on and shaking the container vigorously, Mortas saw Captain Dassa speaking with Lieutenant Kitrick off to the side. Both officers had shed their helmets and goggles, which was an infantry signal that a private conversation was taking place.

Catalano, sitting in the shade and clipping the bands on a ration case, replied to the Third Platoon man's observation. "You already know why those bad-ass shape-shifters haven't come into the war."

"Don't even try that."

"It's true. He said he did it himself." Catalano glanced at Mortas. "That first alien musta been a scout of some kind. My lieutenant gave her some of that first-class First Platoon lovin', and she telepathically told the others all about it. If those chickenshits at Glory Main hadn't killed her, we'd have a bunch of shape-shifter allies right now—war'd be over."

Looking around, Mortas observed a curious gathering beneath a makeshift awning that had been rigged up on the remains of one of the fallen antennae. The camouflage fabric rippled over the heads of several seated soldiers, all muddy from the jungle, all working intently with handhelds. Captain Pappas, the battalion's intelligence officer, sat at their center with his own device, apparently directing the work. Fingers stabbed repeatedly at buttons while others ran across screens, and Mortas decided they were reviewing stored tapes of some kind.

"Pappas thinks he's come across some interesting footage from the past few months of satellite imagery." Dassa's words startled Mortas, who turned to find the company commander standing next to him. "I gave him part of my command group and a couple of the more tech-savvy troops to help him sort through it."

Mortas nodded, his mind so full of questions from

the last few hours that he didn't know which one to ask first. Remembering Dassa's just-concluded conversation with his fellow platoon leader, he decided to start there.

"Wyn was really torn up about what happened. He knows he made a mistake."

"We talked. Don't worry about him."

"He feels guilty about being evacuated from Fractus just before things got rough. And he was really close to Noonan." Captain Noonan had been B Company's aggressive commander before Dassa. He'd been killed, along with his entire command group, fighting a much larger number of Sims.

"Oh, that's not it. Wyn thinks he should have been given command of B Company after Fractus. He has a right to feel that way a little bit, considering how many open slots there were at the time. It doesn't help that I'm so much younger than he is, or that you and I are old buddies."

"Did you tell him I broke your arm once?"

"Everybody knows that. Let's find a seat." Mortas followed him to the side of what had once been a storage building, switching off his own radio as they walked. Sitting down, he lifted his helmet from his head and unstrapped the hard frame of his goggles.

"We've got some major developments to deal with, Jan. The Step has been indefinitely suspended, for reasons unknown. All over the war zone, Command is reshuffling the ships as best it can." Dassa shrugged slightly. "Normal propulsion doesn't stack up to the distances out here at all, so without the Step everybody's pretty much stuck where they are. The *Dauntless* is staying with us, so we've got her firepower and, if necessary, we can be evacuated by shuttle.

"Right now I don't see a need for that. Cordvine is asking to have its personnel taken up to the ship, but I think that's because of what happened to Broadleaf. Whether they stay or go, part of the company is going to have to secure their station. Luckily, Almighty isn't interested in leaving, or working with us. So that makes things a little simpler."

"We going after the Sims who did this, sir?"

Dassa's dark eyes drifted off toward the ruins of the main building, where ship technicians were sorting through the wreckage. "To the best of our ability, yes."

"Sir?"

"We have a minor supply issue, Jan. Unbeknownst to me, a long time ago somebody developed a protocol for handling the infantry-specific items for this mission. Just in case the cruiser assigned to support the infantry had to go somewhere in a hurry, they always transferred those supplies to Broadleaf. Makes sense, in a way, because Broadleaf was a Force station and they could just as easily send the drones to us as could a ship in orbit."

Mortas felt an uneasy feeling creeping into his innards. "So all those infantry-specific items were here when Broadleaf got hit."

"Exactly. You must have attended one of those prep schools for gifted students." They shared a smile. "Yes, everything the *Dauntless* sent down appears to have been destroyed in the attack. A lot of it can be made up from ship's stores, but there's one item that we can't do without—those tiny batteries that go in our goggles. And as of right now, the only goggle batteries we have are the ones we're already carrying."

Mortas looked at the dirt, running over the ramifications of this blunder. Without the goggles, B Company could only view overhead imagery using its handhelds. The devices gave off a dull glow in darkness, and it was ludicrous to think of infantrymen patrolling in the jungle using them to navigate the terrain. Most importantly, without the goggles, the Orphans would be unable to see in the dark. The range-finding and targeting capabilities the eyepieces shared with the Scorpion rifles, the chonks, and the machine guns would likewise be lost.

"How about the Marines? They must have a stockage for their goggles."

"Different goggles, different batteries."

"The security platoon at Cordvine?"

"They were issued the same goggles as the Marines—so they could get resupplied with batteries by any cruiser that was nearby."

"How about our friends at Almighty?"

"Their rigs are the next-generation stuff. Different batteries."

"So the tech-savvy humans are getting beat by the guys who are fighting with tree sap." Mortas laughed with genuine amusement, but then stopped. "Once our goggles are dead, we won't be able to see Sam's heat when he's nearby. If the aerial systems can't detect him from above, we're really in the shit, sir."

"That sums it up nicely. But you did bring up the only piece of good news I have. Come with me."

They rose, and walked across the clearing to a space in the shadow of two large trees. A morgue detail from the ship was photographing the remains of Broadleaf's complement that had not yet been evacuated. The bodies lay in a row on camouflaged tarpaulins, many of them missing limbs from the bombardment. Dassa walked past them, to a single corpse off to the side.

"Sam knew we'd bring in the rockets to run him off, so he chopped holes in the fence, set the main building on fire, did a little shooting, and then ran for it. But this one didn't get away."

They stood over the body, human in every respect except for its uniform. Tattered Sim fatigue pants were visible under the worn covering of a Sim combat smock, and the dead soldier's head was still protected by the flanged helmet of the Sim infantry. Mortas had seen this outfit up close on two other planets and immediately knew it had been modified.

Squatting, he noted dozens of finger-sized strips of metal that had been glued all over the shoulders, arms, back, and torso of the man's smock. His helmet was likewise adorned, and on one large piece Mortas made out what looked like part of a stenciled serial number in human numerals.

"Is that what I think it is?"

"It is." Dassa spoke with admiration. "Sam is the

most adaptable guy in the universe. They must have chopped up every downed drone, every crashed recon 'bot, and probably a few shuttle wrecks we didn't know about. Took the heat shielding and broke it up into little strips that they glued all over their helmets and their smocks. That's why we can't pick up their heat signatures from above. There's still plenty of it, but it's broken up, so it doesn't register."

Mortas lifted the smock and rubbed a thumb against the coarse black rosin holding the strips in place. "Well now we know what they were using the tree sap for."

Mortas awoke with effort. Someone was shaking his arm, and yet he was so completely asleep that it seemed like minutes before his eyes opened. The sky overhead was losing its light, and it took a moment before he remembered where he was. Dassa had ordered him to take a nap after discovering he'd been on the go for the previous two days and nights, and he'd curled up in his field blanket after briefing Dak on what he'd learned.

"You with us, Jan?" Captain Pappas was sitting next to him, the lenses of his goggles raised up under his helmet.

"Yes, sir." He moved his tongue around inside his mouth, surprised that the gummy paste was gone before remembering he'd drunk and eaten his fill before going to sleep. "What's going on?"

"Your platoon is going to take me out to that spot near Almighty where the Sim heat signatures showed up last night. They scaled the cliff here and wrecked this place without once showing up on the scanners, while at the same time half a platoon of them appeared bright as day at a different location."

"I thought we'd decided that was a diversion."

"It was. I bet there weren't more than three or four Sims over there, running some kind of torchlight show for us. But it sure looked real, especially the way they moved, and I need to see whatever might have survived the rockets."

"Begging your pardon, sir, but what could you find out that we don't already know?"

"Look here." Pappas took out his handheld and activated the screen. Mortas knew the entire company had moved into goggle-battery conservation before he took his nap, so he assumed there was a plentiful supply of power sources for the handhelds.

The screen was dark, with markers indicating the steep changes in elevation around the glowing rectangle of Almighty. Tiny heat signatures abounded in the blackness, the birds and animals that inhabited the forest going about their nocturnal business. A group of lights appeared, and Mortas was about to assume he was seeing a replay of the previous evening's bombardment when he noted that the cluster was in a different location and much smaller. The fireflies rambled across several hundred yards of jungle, then vanished.

Another clip started right after that, and the time stamp in the screen's corner told him that this footage was from eight months earlier. A long column of fireflies flickered into existence against the blackness, but they didn't seem to move at first. After close to a minute, the entire dotted line started lurching forward toward Almighty.

"Look at the signatures in the center. See how they keep their exact intervals? Nobody getting closer, nobody getting farther behind. Incredible discipline, right?"

"Incredible is the word. Nobody can walk through this crap without weaving left and right and getting hung up on every other vine. I'm guessing that line of troops was just a bunch of stationary heaters of some kind, with probably two live bodies at either end."

"Very good."

"On a prearranged schedule, the guy in the back extinguishes one of the heat sources while the guy in the front activates a new one. Looks like a whole column of moving Sims."

"I believe that half platoon we saw last night was a similar arrangement."

"Wait a second. Those clips you just showed me—nothing happened to them. No rockets, no gunships. How did the satellites miss that?"

"How indeed? I didn't, and all I did was filter the footage using the exact same protocols the scanners use. There was no way they could have missed this. Cordvine routinely bombards the jungle, just on a whim, and Broadleaf wasn't shy about dropping something on suspicious signatures like what we're seeing here. But not our friends at Almighty. They seem to have been exhibiting a very live-and-let-live attitude these past few months."

"They didn't the other night. They nailed that concentration, or diversion, as soon as it appeared."

"As soon as we called them about it, you mean."

Mortas remembered the snide comments from Almighty from the night before, and the station's hostility to Force units operating in the area. "You think something weird is going on over there?"

"That's not all." Pappas activated the handheld, showing a calm nighttime scene to the west of Almighty. Mortas was waiting for a set of lights to appear, more Sim deceptions, when a series of explosions burst in the jungle. The spasms of fire flashed into life, probably a dozen of them, and an area of at least one hundred square yards began to glow. The heat wasn't a fire, and it slowly spread before starting to cool.

"Now I'm completely baffled. I didn't see any indication of the enemy."

"Neither did I. And I have no idea what that glowing patch indicated." Pappas turned off the handheld. "But I intend to find out what our friends at Almighty have been up to."

"I can't say how long the Step is going to be suspended, but it can't be too long." Dassa's voice came though the earpieces in helmets all over B Company. Riding in the back of a shuttle headed for the jungle near Almighty, Mortas's platoon listened with occasional comments.

"One thing's sure, it'll come back online ten seconds after we don't need it anymore."

"Aw, don't be like that. Thing needs a good cleaning. Think how long everybody's been using it."

Dassa continued, broadcasting from what was left of Broadleaf. "We've got excellent communications, so every aerial support system is still available to us. By cutting back on goggle usage, we should be able to ride this out. But just in case we don't, the engineers on the *Dauntless* are working around the clock on a way to link the goggles into the batteries in our helmets."

"See? There's a good answer. A couple of exposed wires running between your eyes and your ears, and everything will be fine. Especially when it rains."

"Nah, they'll come up with some kind of waterproof adapter that weighs two hundred pounds."

Leaning back against his rucksack, Mortas studied a moving schematic on his handheld. Normally he would have tracked the flight on his goggles, but the batteries needed to be saved. Three shuttles were ferrying his platoon's three squads to a spot near Almighty, close to the location where the Sims had diverted the humans' attention the previous night. Landing zones on that part of Verdur were hard to come by, so rocket fire had blasted an open space for them over a period of hours. Harassment fire had continued through the day, striking the jungle in numerous places, and every so often a rocket would impact in the steadily growing clearing where they would land. At least in theory, the technique lessened the chances that the enemy would recognize that a landing zone was being created.

The three shuttles were coming in from different directions, having lifted off from Broadleaf as part of the back-and-forth with the *Dauntless*. Instead of going into orbit, they'd flown many miles away before dropping down to treetop level and heading for the clearing. Mortas monitored the progress of all three birds, fearing one of them might get shot down, and was ready to divert to the crash site.

Dassa continued. "I'm in communication with Major Hatton, and he's working up a plan to move the rest of the battalion here using normal propulsion. It will take days, but they'll bring everything we need. In the meantime, Major Hatton noticed something that we missed. If Sam only wanted to kill one station, he probably wouldn't have hit the one in the middle; he would have hit either Almighty or Cordvine.

"By removing Broadleaf, he's isolated the remaining two sites. I think that means he plans to knock off at least one more of them before reinforcements get here. Sam thinks he's put us completely on the defensive, but he's wrong. We're going to be ready, no matter where he pops up next.

"Second Platoon will secure Cordvine, while Third and I finish up at Broadleaf. First Platoon will patrol the jungle near Almighty, to gain intelligence and to respond to any moves against the station. We can reassemble the whole company using the shuttles if necessary, but we cannot simply go over to the defensive. Sam has figured out a way to avoid detection by our scanners, so we can't let him operate out there with impunity.

"Remember what they did to Broadleaf, and remember what they did to us. Now it's time for us to kill 'em back."

The handheld indicated that the three different craft were all approaching the landing zone, and Mortas switched it off. Stowing it in a pocket on his armor, his hand brushed against the sheath of a long, narrow commando knife tucked between two ammo pouches. It had belonged to Corporal Cranther, the Spartacan Scout who'd been marooned with him on Roanum, and it stirred a memory that was just out of reach. He reached for it mentally, sensing that it had some significance for the current mission, but it slipped away.

Something to do with shuttles, but there had been no shuttle flights on Roanum. Or water. Or food. Just lots and lots of walking. They'd escaped the planet by stealing a Wren shuttle from the Sims at their spacedrome, but that couldn't be it. The nagging memory seemed important, but he had to set it aside when the craft's rear ramp suddenly dropped, bringing him back to the present.

The twin rows of soldiers in camouflaged armor, wearing rucksacks that bulged with extra ammo, rations, and water, hustled down the ramp into the mangled greenery created by the rockets. Turning on his goggles in order to see the terrain around his location, Mortas grabbed his rifle and hurried after them.

"You seeing what I'm seeing?" Captain Pappas whispered from the center of a small clearing that had been blasted into the vegetation southwest of Almighty the night before.

Or it should have been a small clearing, cluttered with fallen branches and a few sagging trees held up by the profusion of growth around them. Instead, a hole ripped in the canopy above let in the last of the day's light to show an unexpected scene. A partially cleared area stood under the gap and extended for one hundred yards in every direction. Mortas's platoon was in a loose perimeter around that zone while Pappas tried to understand what it meant.

"They manicured the place. It's like they were trying to plant something and keep it hidden. Chopped out the trees and cleared the bushes in rows, leaving the rest in place." In the dying light, Mortas saw the intelligence officer hop up and scurry forward several yards, mindful that the platoon had not yet secured the dense overgrowth around the bizarre site. "I'm where the rockets hit, right now. Big crater, minor damage to the trees, no sign of whatever Sam was doing out here."

Dak spoke to Mortas from across the clearing. "Not a good place to spend the night. We gotta get going."

Mortas nodded without speaking. The platoon had moved to the site quickly after being dropped off by the shuttles, but the ground had fought them. Overloaded with what they needed to survive and bulling through vegetation that seemed to have been in place for millennia, they'd been astounded to find this oasis of order.

"Just need a few more minutes." Pappas rose again, running forward. His rucksack bounced against his armor, and it seemed to be an optical illusion that he was able to jog through the ground vegetation. Mortas glanced down at the handheld, having already selected a defensive position for the platoon. It wasn't too far away, but he'd picked it using only the elevation lines suggested by the overhead imagers. No human had ever set foot on that location, and so there was a chance it wouldn't be any good at all.

"Listen to your platoon sergeant, el-tee," a familiar voice purred in his ear. "We're locking down for the night, and you want to make sure we know where you are."

It was the same mocking fool from the previous evening, the radioman at Almighty.

"You know exactly where we are," he responded darkly. "We're right there on the screen, plain as day."

"Oh, I see you. Poor perimeter, three disjointed squads, and no idea where Sam is. You better get your shit together, if the boogeyman comes calling."

"We got plenty for the boogeyman—and anybody else who pisses us off." Dak spoke dismissively. "Now why don't you go get another cup of coffee and let the men work?"

"Sure, sure. Good idea. I wouldn't want to get drowsy and call something in on the wrong target tonight."

"No you wouldn't." Dak's answer was lost, as the disembodied voice had already terminated the link.

"We need to get moving," Mortas announced. Tapping the handheld, he emplaced a marker on the side of the cleared area closest to their destination. "First Squad, Second Squad, slide around to Third and form a temporary perimeter. Move out to our night position in five minutes."

Putting the device away, he touched Vossel's prone form with his boot. The medic was facing the other way, rifle ready, and simply came to a knee. Long weeks of field training had transformed the two of them into a pair of near-telepaths in the way they had come to understand each other's intentions. Mortas tilted his helmet toward the clearing, and the two men zigzagged through the undergrowth in a crouch.

They knelt when they reached Pappas, hidden by the shrubbery left in place by the Sims. The intelligence officer knelt as well, three rifles pointed outward. "See what they did here? They chopped out these lanes, five yards across and two hundred yards long. Look how they leveled the stumps with the ground, how they took it down to bare dirt most of the way."

Mortas remembered the images from the night before, the three columns of men headed for Almighty. "Sleds. Instead of firepots set in the ground, they mounted them on sleds or runners or Sim two-wheelers. Three guys dragging them forward at a nice slow pace, and it looks like half a platoon."

"Yep. Sam's tricks take time to set up, but they really work."

"Saw one of those Sammies running away after the first rocket," Vossel whispered. "Guess they took his Smock of Invisibility away from him."

"Or it got blown off," Mortas offered, haunted by the image of the desperately running figure, tripping, falling, and ultimately unable to outrun the rockets.

"I doubt they were wearing them at all. Defeats the purpose if you're trying to create a diversion," Pappas offered. His sigh came through the helmet speakers. "Let's get gone, Jan. We had direct hits on this spot the other night, and there's almost no sign they were even here. Somebody picked this place clean."

The new position was nothing to brag about. A modest finger of raised ground in the heavy forest, it wasn't large enough for the entire platoon. Mortas played with the idea of ringing it evenly, but that lost the advantage of the higher elevation, and so he put Katinka's squad on the berm facing north and ran the other two squads down the incline so that the platoon was arranged in a rough triangle.

"Getting sentimental on us, Lieutenant?" Dak whispered, once he'd checked the positioning of the three machine guns and the grenade launchers. Mortas had been coordinating defensive fires with the ASSL on Broadleaf, his back against a fallen tree trunk, and was caught off guard.

"What's that?"

"You got us formed in the shape of a heart. Thought you were going to break out some marking powder and write 'Jan plus Betty' in the middle."

The absurd suggestion made him laugh, and Mortas cut his mike until it subsided. B Company's ASSL finished marking his last target, and when it popped up on the handheld, Mortas acknowledged it and signed off. Dak sat down next to him.

"One of my platoon leaders in Third Corps, he did that once. Then he took a snapshot of the imagery and sent it to his girl back on . . . somewhere, I forget where he was from."

"Bet the censors ripped him for that."

"Actually, not. You see, unless you been out here, things like that picture don't look like what they are. Buncha headquarters pussies, riding out the war giving everybody shit, what would they know about an overhead image of an infantry perimeter at night?"

"Where you from, Sergeant Dak?"

"So you finally got around to me. Been pestering every new man, and didn't bother asking your right arm." Dak gave a short laugh. "Tratia, sir."

"I heard Tratians join the Force to get a break from all the discipline."

"They do have a lot of rules there, don't they? But yeah, in a way that is why I joined. I never liked school, there was always so much better stuff going on right outside the window, and after a while I just stopped going. My father didn't understand, but he was a guy who bought into all the laws and the rules. To be honest, I think it worked for him.

"I got into fighting for a while, but then I started stealing anything that moved—not for the money, I'm not a thief—and boy did I get into some great chases with the enforcement types. The police, some of them liked the way I drove, and they kept warning me, 'You're gonna end up in the Force. Magistrate's gonna send your ass to the war.' And stuff like that.

"One night, I came home and my dad was waiting. Time for the showdown, I guess. Told me I was gonna straighten up, go back to school, all that garbage. And then he says, 'You live under my roof, you obey my rules' which he really shouldn't have done."

"Why's that?"

"I took him up on it. I remembered what the police had been saying, and I enlisted the next day. Don't ever use that 'My roof, my rules' line on your kids, Lieutenant, if you and Betty ever have any. Of such moments, recruits are made." They both chuckled quietly. "Listen, sir. I checked the water situation, and we need to purify some of the local stuff."

"We topped off just a few hours ago."

"The move was tougher than we expected. By this time tomorrow we'll be empty, and if we call in for resupply Sam's gonna know where we are. I've put a small patrol together, all experienced jungle men, and

I'll lead them. We'll slip back to that one stream we crossed getting here and strain out some gallons real quiet."

"How long's that going to take?"

"All night. It's just as well that we stay put there; always dangerous to come back into the lines and besides, we'd be humping full collapsibles. Better you bring the platoon to us at first light."

"We're going to burn up some goggle batteries doing it that way."

"Oh yeah, that reminds me." Mortas felt Dak's hand on his arm, and two goggle batteries were pressed into his palm. "We're in better shape than it seemed. The veterans always carry extra batteries. If we exercise a little discipline, these should last a couple of days."

Mortas looked down at the tiny cylinders, unable to see them. "Captain Dassa asked for an exact report of how many of these we had."

"Oh, you know better than to expect the boys to answer a question like that truthfully. They would have confiscated the extras and given 'em to the knuckleheads who didn't plan ahead—no offense, sir, I'm not calling you a knucklehead. But in the future, always bring a couple spares of your own."

Dak stood and moved off through the gloom without making a sound.

The shortcomings of the platoon's position became obvious when it was Mortas's turn to sleep. He'd sat

radio watch for the first few hours, periodically getting up to quietly check the perimeter, then rolled up
in his field blanket. The slope was steeper than he'd
thought, and no matter how he arranged himself he
kept sliding downhill. Every few minutes, a new rock
or bur or root would find some exposed bone to press
against, and gravity increased the pressure until he
had to move.

Finally giving up, he groggily pushed his way out of
the thin quilt. A ghostly fog had seeped in while he was
asleep, and it made the prone figures of the platoon look
like primordial beasts with armored exoskeletons. The
jungle was quiet, though, and he turned on his goggles
long enough to check the overhead imagery. Now that
they knew how the Sims had been avoiding detection,
every flicker of heat on the screen could mean enemy
movement. Apart from a few jungle creatures walking, crawling, or flying off in the distance, everything
seemed all right.

He turned off the goggles and slid the lenses up
inside his helmet. Looking around, he spotted the
boots and legs of Captain Pappas sticking out from
under a camouflaged tarpaulin usually used for ex-
pedient shelters. Vossel, on radio watch, was sitting
cross-legged next to Pappas and appeared to be watching him closely. Having used the same technique on
many field problems, Mortas knew that Pappas was
viewing something on his handheld and needed to
keep the screen's light from being observed.

"I'm coming in, sir," Mortas whispered above the

form, and a muffled voice told him to wait a moment. He heard a switch being turned off, and then crawled under. Pappas's body odor was trapped inside the tarp, and Mortas made a weak waving gesture in front of his nose.

"Hey, I wouldn't go pointing any fingers if I were you, Jan." Pappas switched the handheld back on once Vossel indicated that they were covered again. "You're the one taking the stink pills."

The screen brightened, and Mortas pushed a wet blade of grass out of his way. Pappas was reviewing the footage of the attack on Broadleaf, with the resolution taken as far down as it would go. He was focused on the northern edge of the ridge, where the Sim attack had originated.

"Dassa sent patrols out to examine the northern slope, and you wouldn't believe what they found. The Sims had chopped at least three sets of steps out of the side of that hill, and reinforced them with cut branches. Sam must have been crawling right up to Broadleaf's wire night after night, and they never knew it."

"Can't hunker down inside a base like that. You gotta run defensive patrols all the time, just to keep the bad guys from setting up shop on your doorstep."

"There's more. At the bottom of the hill, they found two sections of fencing attached to a stack of heavy logs all tied together. The Sims had the logs secured just a little bit downhill, and they attached them to the fence using these ropes made from woven vines. When they released the trunks, it pulled the fence down."

"Is that what you're looking at now?"

"No. I've got the intelligence section on the *Dauntless* helping me. Sims wearing that heat shielding are hidden inside this footage, so if we can recalibrate the sensors to pick that up, we'll be back in business. We've already got new readings for the unshielded Sims dragging those firepots, just because we got out here and examined the ground where they pulled that diversion. They shouldn't be able to get away with that again."

Mortas stared at the screen, watching the fire start at Broadleaf and remembering the altered combat smock on the dead Sim. "Hey sir, how come they wore the special smocks onto Broadleaf? They had to figure they'd take casualties, and Sam's been showing good discipline hiding things from us. Why didn't they have the assault force take off their smocks?"

Pappas reached up with a grimy hand and wiped perspiration from his upper lip. "Keep this to yourself. The consensus is that Broadleaf was in real trouble, but that they might have made it if they hadn't called in rockets on themselves. The fire probably didn't collapse the building; the skipper of the *Dauntless* thinks our ordnance did that.

"Sam knows that our own weapons are sometimes our biggest enemy. He wanted to panic the guys inside Broadleaf—so the assault team wore the smocks to muddy the situation as much as possible."

"How many of them do you think we're up against?"

"Impossible to say, but based on all the work they've done out here, just in the parts of the jungle we've seen, it's at least a hundred. Which bears out the earlier suspicion that Sam somehow got reinforced. We haven't seen any new equipment yet, which makes me think it's another group of holdouts who somehow linked up with the gang that's been messing with the stations for years."

"Big planet, no doubt there were more of them elsewhere."

"Sure. But what brought them here? How do you find the only piece of civilization in the middle of a giant wilderness?"

The answer fell into place for Mortas with a mental thud, and he realized it was the solution to the puzzle that had been plaguing him all day. The sensation of an important piece of information, something familiar to him, flitting around just beyond his recognition.

"Sir, is there any way to check the flight patterns around the stations, going back a long time?"

"Of course. The satellites send out a continuous feed of everything they detect, and it's all archived. What are you getting at?"

"When I was marooned on Roanum, we were hoping to see aircraft of any kind. If we did, we figured it might show us the way to habitation."

"I understand. But all the drones, resupply or gunship, stick pretty close to the stations. A gang of remnants a hundred miles away wouldn't be able to see them."

"That's why I think you should check the flight paths. Our friends at Almighty aren't happy to have us in the area, and nobody really knows what they're doing here. What if they were sending drones way *way* out, then bringing them back low over the jungle so they'd be seen?"

"That would probably bring Sam here, and he would have found his buddies. But why would Almighty do that?"

"Why weren't they dropping rockets on Sam's light shows all these months? Maybe they wanted him to come calling."

CHAPTER ELEVEN

Ayliss awoke slowly, even though the entire building was shaking and the air outside was filled with the roars of straining engines. The membranes inside her nose and mouth were dry, and her stomach was queasy, but she knew where she was and that she'd been ill. She sat up, surprised to find that she felt extremely rested. Daylight glowed in the corridor and throughout her room, which seemed loaded with medical gear. An empty chair was next to the bed, and she remembered Blocker swabbing her face with a wet towel.

Somewhere far above there was a low boom, which she recognized as an ore transport breaking through the planet atmosphere. The air in the room was warm, and she pushed the bedclothes aside before standing on bare feet. A loose medical gown covered her, and Ayliss didn't bother to look for something more substantial before walking into the corridor. Though her body felt strong, her brain was pleasantly fuzzy as she went down the empty hallway. More engines kicked into life on top of the mountain, and she felt the tremors through the soles of her feet. Something big was happening, but she felt no need to hurry.

Emerging on the high porch that ran around the building, Ayliss squinted in the sunlight. She took in the familiar structures nearby, and the pressed brown dirt where the road led to the veterans' underground settlement. She'd ridden down that track just before falling ill, and her face reddened with the memory of how badly she'd mishandled the angry meeting with Hemsley. Seeing again the burn marks on his torso, and the bodies of the two dead veterans. Deelia had been one of them, and the Banshees had been disappointed by Ayliss's response.

She'd asked Lee to smooth things over. No, that wasn't true—or at least not the complete truth. She'd begged him to do something to get her back in the veterans' good graces, calling on his love to fix what she'd broken. He'd agreed, and now the alarm began to pass through her. Where was he?

"Minister." It was Blocker, standing behind her, speaking just loud enough to be heard over the launches. Too many liftoffs, but what did it mean?

Ayliss turned, about to ask, and saw the grief on the big man's face. She'd seen it only once before, when he'd told her that her mother was gravely ill. She remembered pretending not to understand, hoping that if she couldn't comprehend the news that it wasn't true. A child's reaction, and she was no longer a child.

"It's Lee, isn't it?"

"I'm so very sorry, Ayliss. Lee infiltrated the space-drome with that Spartacan deserter, Tupelo. They blew up both of Rittle's gunships, but then they got spotted. Lee made it out, but he was too badly wounded." Blocker cleared his throat. "He's gone."

Sorrow should have risen inside her, but it did not. Anger, her lifelong companion, rose instead, roaring all around her, scourging her, demanding revenge. Another loved one had been taken from her, and someone was to blame. Rittle. He'd set this whole thing in motion, when his gunships had attacked Hemsley's people. Her rage told Ayliss the rest, that the station manager had poisoned her—just enough to get her out of the way.

She raised a finger at the sky. "Is that why they're leaving? They're running away?"

Blocker appeared confused for a moment, but he mastered it quickly. "No, Minister, that's something very different—although they are running away. The Step's been suspended indefinitely, and Rittle believes the station could be attacked by the Sims. He offered to take us with them, but I said you'd refused."

The anger bellowed in her head, echoing with the blind resentment that Rittle was already beyond her reach. It began to redirect itself at the man standing before her, the one tasked with her safety, the one who was supposed to care so much about her, but then a larger question forced itself to the front.

"Why is the Step suspended?"

"I've confirmed this with Minister Corlipso by secure transmission, but it originally came from Rittle. Your father has disappeared, and they're looking for him now. The suspension will last as long as the search does."

The anger subsided, replaced by cold analysis. Ayliss looked up at the sky, tilting her head slightly so that the tear that threatened to overflow her eyelid was contained. "He told me he was going to attempt something using the Step, something dangerous. Did Rittle seem to know anything about that?"

"No. He only said that your father had disappeared after his wedding, and that Minister Corlipso was not traveling with him."

"That was the plan." Ayliss closed her eyes, forcing her mind to focus on their current situation. "All right. You did the right thing, refusing Rittle's offer. I need to get cleaned up, and then we're going to go see Hemsley."

"I refused Rittle's offer because I didn't want to put you in his hands. That's the only reason I didn't take you to the station infirmary as soon as you got sick. But without the Step, this whole place is wide open to Sim raiders. We need to consider other means of getting away from here."

Sims. The enemy that had lurked in the shadows for her entire life. Their decades-long aggression had shaped most of the decisions that had cost her so much, and now they were coming. The anger blossomed, eager, expectant. Ayliss stared up at Blocker. "We're not going anywhere."

"Check everything, and I mean *everything*. It'll be just like those bastards to booby-trap something that'll blow up the whole station." Hemsley, his face shiny with burn salve, spoke into a radio handset as Ayliss and Blocker approached. Several of the veterans' trucks were lined up in front of the tunnel entrance, obviously primed to loot the now-empty mining station.

"And what if we accidentally trip this booby trap?" a male voice asked, trepidation clear even over the handset.

"We'll write your folks a very nice note. Get going; we don't know how much time we have."

Hemsley handed the microphone to the truck's driver before turning to face the new arrivals. "My condolences, Minister. Your Selkirk was a good man."

"Thank you, and thank you for bringing him back."

"The Banshees did that. They were covering him and Tupelo from outside the wire, and they say he went right up and over the fence despite his injuries. Quite impressive. The whole settlement knows what he did for us."

Ayliss glanced at the parked vehicles, as if looking for a way to change the subject. "You're not wasting any time."

"None to waste. We've cut through the fencing

near the spacedrome, and right now I've got my people checking the place for explosives. We have to strip everything of value, get it onto the vehicles, and then get away from this place. We've had safe locations identified for some time, and stocked them with supplies in case we had to spread out." He allowed himself a short laugh. "Honestly, we thought we'd be fighting the Guests, but apparently they decided to live up to their name. This part of space is loaded with Sim raid ships, and they're going to come here unless the Step is restored right away. We're trying to contact McRaney, to see if he can give us early warning."

"He'll want something for that."

"Thank you, Minister. I never would have guessed that."

"You're going to pay him off in Go-Three."

"I doubt there's going to be any left up there. Rittle had four transports on station, and they didn't lift off empty."

"I'm not talking about his ore. I'm talking about yours."

"We're not miners, Minister. There was a little in the tunnels when we got here, but that's gone."

"There's a lot more down there, mined by the previous owners. You've been using it to buy supplies and weapons. Otherwise, McRaney wouldn't have anything to do with you."

"Ever think we might be friends? I been out here a long time."

"You refused to give me and my party lodging, and

you kept Lee out of certain tunnels because they're loaded with Go-Three. You're planning to buy some help with what's left—admit it."

"All right, that's all true. What of it?"

Ayliss gave Blocker a meaningful look, and he walked off several paces. Understanding, Hemsley limped to the back of the truck while Ayliss followed.

Ayliss spoke first. "You can use the ore to pay for help, or you can offer McRaney something better. A steady gig, a legal one, hauling Go-Three."

"I'd have to have the rights, if I was to make an offer like that."

"You do. Zone Quest has left, and that means this entire planet belongs to the colony."

"Begging your pardon, Minister, but somebody higher in your chain of command might disagree with that once the emergency's passed."

"They can disagree all they want, but if you fight for this place, it's going to make quite a story on the Bounce. Hard for them to take it away from you once that happens."

"Fight with what? We've managed to lay in a good supply of weapons, but this isn't a mustered-out infantry battalion. Most of my people were technicians who didn't know one end of a Scorpion from the other before I got to training them. Honestly, even now they don't know much more than that."

"We've got the Banshees, and a good number of combat vets—not to mention the senior leadership of you and Blocker."

"Blocker's gonna insist on staying right with you."

"Not if you remind him that he's a combat leader of recent experience, and that there are veterans of this war who need him in that capacity."

"I don't know what you're trying to do here, Minister, but I can't make my people fight. Even with the promise of winning the colony."

"You won't have to. Put me in front of them, and I'll sell it."

Hemsley gave her the same look she'd seen at her installation ceremony, a mix of appraisal and suspicion. "Just what *are* you up to, Minister?"

Her feet moved more slowly, the farther Ayliss got down the tunnel. Veterans were rushing everywhere, moving all the things she hadn't been allowed to see in the days before. Rifles, explosives, and a multitude of ammunition crates went by as she walked.

"He's in here, Minister." Lola spoke from one of the arched openings. She and the remaining Banshees were dressed in black fatigues, and had silently formed up around Ayliss before leading her toward the room.

Her joints still ached from her sickness, but her mind was clear and that was why it was taking her so long to reach the doorway. A whirlwind of emotions should have been swirling in her head: grief, guilt, loss, resentment, and of course anger. And yet nothing was there. She'd convinced Hemsley to stand and fight, and at that moment all of her rage had subsided with almost nothing to replace it. She should have been ripped by the loss of her lover, and yet all she could feel was a low throb of excitement that an opponent was on its way.

Ayliss gritted her teeth hard and entered the room. It was almost identical to the other one where the bodies had been stretched out, but this time there was only one. A clean sheet covered the corpse. Pushing herself to walk to its head, then carefully raising the covers to reveal the pale, still face. She dropped the fabric onto his chest, unwilling to see what she had caused, but her palm rested there anyway.

"He went right over the fence like it wasn't even there," Lola murmured. "We were already returning fire, and he ran straight for us. For a moment there I thought I was wrong, that he hadn't been hit at all, the way he was moving."

Ayliss reached out blindly with her other hand, finding the hard muscle of the Banshee's shoulder and grabbing onto it. Lola's hand came up in response.

"He told us to tell you he loved you, then he was gone."

Ayliss squeezed her eyes shut as if fighting back the tears, and lowered her head while wondering where her emotions had gone. Looking down at the corpse, she saw the slightest discoloration on the sheet, a tiny dot of brown that had to be blood. Still wondering where her feelings were, she pulled the sheet back up to cover Selkirk's face.

She gave Lola's shoulder an extra squeeze, and let go of it. Looking at the solemn faces of the other Banshees, Ayliss spoke.

"There's a fight coming, and I'd like to be with you when it gets here."

"The tunnel system was far more complex than Command or ZQ realized." Hemsley was at the wheel of a small, motorized cart that was taking Ayliss and Blocker down a long, wide tunnel. Phosphorescent minerals had been pressed into the walls, and the surprisingly good light was augmented by electric fixtures spaced along the way. "Sam dug here first because it was such a major vein. Everybody seemed to think it was just Sam and his thing for camouflage, but that wasn't it."

The cart came to a three-way fork, and Hemsley drove them straight down the middle. "Every single branch eventually comes out at a concealed opening, and every one of those openings will put you in good terrain for escape. Ravines, hills, and lots of Go-Three spikes. If you have to abandon a tunnel, run hard for the end and you'll have a good chance.

"But that's not our plan." The tunnel went uphill for a short distance, and Hemsley stopped the cart when it leveled off in a circular dead end. The first sergeant climbed out with pain and approached what appeared to be a gable formed out of rock. "Sam arranged his firing ports so that they complemented the terrain."

Reaching up in the narrow outcropping, he gripped something in the shadows and brought his arm down.

Light spread within the firing slot, and Ayliss saw the cord that Hemsley had pulled to open a two-sided camouflage covering. Hemsley limped back out of the way and gestured with an open palm. "Take a look."

Ayliss and Blocker stepped into the aisle hewn from the rock, and saw that they were halfway up the next ridge from the one where they'd started. Black spearheads jutted out of the dirt in several directions, but the most imposing sight was the small valley formed by the twisting high ground. It turned sharply in front of them, and the spined walls of rock rose high on both sides of the chasm.

"That's right. Any airship chasing somebody down this canyon has to slow up to make this or leave the canyon. No matter which one they choose, they'll have to slow down to make the turn, or to keep whatever they're chasing in sight. We've got five spots just like this one, all positioned to use the ground to give a perfect ass-end shot at whatever's in the air. And now, with that last shipment from McRaney, we have the missiles to pull it off."

"What if you do have to leave the tunnels?" asked Blocker.

"We've got food, ammo, and radio equipment cached in several different spots out in the rough country. The plan is to break up into groups so small that a Sam raider won't bother chasing us."

"How can we help?" Ayliss asked.

"As you can see, I'm having a little trouble getting

around. I can't be everywhere I need to be, and I could use a seasoned platoon sergeant to run the back half of this."

Blocker shook his head. "I stay with the Minister."

"I'm not hiding from this fight. I'm a really good shot with a Scorpion, and the Banshees said they can use me." Ayliss gave Blocker an earnest look. "You've got skills these people need."

"She's right. My gang is more rear-echelon than anything else, and they've never fought as a group before. Green troops need seasoned leaders."

Blocker shook his head slowly, then nodded. "We're going to need a very simple plan. If the Sims do show up, they're going to head for the station first. A few missile teams on top of the mountain could really hurt them just as they get here. Put me in charge of that."

He looked at Ayliss, sensing her excitement. "And you and your Banshees are going to be back here. That's not negotiable."

That night, the veterans gathered again. It was very different from the night Ayliss had spent with them under the stars, as they were underground in what appeared to be a communal hall dug by the Sims. The mining station had been stripped of every usable item, yielding a number of different vehicles which were now hidden at various locations.

Ayliss stood with Blocker and her security detail. Looking out across the throng, she was concerned to see so many expressions of fear and even rebellion. Veterans from the combat specialties circulated among the other colonists, adjusting body armor and giving out words of encouragement, but there was an air of disapproval.

The conversation was quiet, probably due to the level of unease, so it actually rose when Hemsley entered the hall. He walked stiffly, but hid his pain well as he headed for a low stone ledge that served as a stage. Stepping up where everyone could see him, he began to speak.

"You all know why we're here, and what we're up against. McRaney monitored a Sim raid ship headed this way, and before he had to run off, he said it would be here in the morning. My guess is that the Sims will search the station first. They're looking for Go-Three, and that's the most likely place for it. There isn't any up there, so there's a slim chance they'll just leave after that. Probably blow the station up, but who cares about that shithole anyway?"

The laughter was subdued, so he continued.

"I don't believe in placing a lot of hope in a slim chance. I think any Sim raider worth his salt will know all about the tunnels, so after they're done with the station, they'll come down here for a look. We've rehearsed this many times—for a different opponent—and so we are prepared. I say we're ready for them."

"First Sergeant, why don't we just get out of here? They're not taking the planet back; they're just after the ore. Why not get out of their way?" This came from a balding veteran, obviously uncomfortable in his armor. A large number of voices murmured agreement.

"That's simple. What have we been saying as long as we've been together? This place is ours. It's our future, and the future of our families. Zone Quest ran off before there was any sign of trouble, so if there was ever a chance for us to claim this as our own, this is it. We've got a good plan, plenty of the right weapons, and some of the best people I've ever been privileged to meet. There is no reason for us to let these assholes just come in here and take our stuff."

"The Step won't be suspended for much longer. There's no reason to fight when we can safely ride this out, just by getting out of the way."

A surge of approval ran through the crowd, and Hemsley turned a blank face toward Ayliss. Without a moment's hesitation, she mounted the platform.

"That's a good point, but I think you missed something. The Step suspension is a lucky break for us, in that it made Zone Quest leave. They were here before this planet was assigned to the Veterans Auxiliary, but now that they're gone, we've got a tremendous opportunity."

"An opportunity to get killed!" a voice shouted from the back.

"It is that, but it's also an opportunity that you'll never get again. When Rittle told me he was leaving, he offered to take me and my party along." Ayliss pointed an open palm at her detail. "I turned him down because this is my post—and it's yours, too. I told him something else, and I'll say it to you as well. I told him that if he ran off, he shouldn't come back.

"By all laws of ownership, this planet is yours because Zone Quest bugged out. Quad Seven was given to you for your service, and the only reason the Guests were allowed to remain was that they were here before that decree. They're gone now, and so this place is yours if you defend it. I'm willing to do that with you, so who's with me?"

The room filled with the shouts of perhaps half of the assemblage, but a voice rose when the noise subsided.

"Command took this place from the Sims because it's loaded with Go ore. They sent two entire fleets, then they planted Zone Quest here. As soon as the Step is available again, they're gonna put the Guests back in business."

"No one back home knows what happened here then, and no one knows what's happening here now. But you got lucky again." Ayliss beamed at the faces before her. "I'm your minister, appointed by the Veterans Auxiliary, and I'm the daughter of the Chairman of the Emergency Senate. As soon as the Step is back in operation, I'm going to ask every Bounce war correspondent in this sector to come here. We'll show every settled world the footage of the wrecked Sim ships."

A growl rose from the throng, and they seemed to draw closer.

"And we'll show them the dead Sim bodies!"

A shout answered her, and was joined by others.

"And I promise you, I will make a statement in front of the cameras saying that this planet belongs to the veterans of the first settlement, that it belongs to their families and their descendants, and I'll tell them how you all fought to win that! Now who's with me?"

A few short hours later, Ayliss was loading magazines for her Scorpion rifle. Blocker had attempted to assign the rest of the security detail to her, but she'd squashed that with ease. Blocker would be commanding a large circle of two-man missile teams on top of the mountain, and those teams needed reliable marksmen for protection. Ayliss and the Banshees would be providing the same kind of support for the missile teams around the tunnel complex, so the security detail was now with Blocker's element.

Ayliss was now in one of the rocky rooms off of the main tunnel, prepping for battle with the Banshees. Her torso armor was laden with ammunition pouches and a single grenade that she'd been advised not to use, and she was dressed in the black fatigues worn by the others.

"Ayliss, come over here." Lola spoke softly, and Ayliss looked up to see the Banshee standing by a chair, holding an electric clipper. She obeyed silently, hiding the thrill that pulsed through her at the idea that she was passing yet another milestone on the way to using her weapon for real. The requisite haircut was quick, and when it was done, her longest lock was a half inch in length.

Tin stepped up, holding a spray can. "Time to add little style. Shut your eyes, close your mouth, and try not to breathe."

The wet gusts ran over her unprotected scalp, down her neck, and then all across her face. It dried almost immediately, and Tin was holding a small mirror in front of her eyes when they opened. The face that looked back at her was almost unrecognizable. Nearly bald, skin and hair completely black. Ayliss smiled with glee, and Tin returned the look.

Lola approached, her own face covered in the black paint. "Stand up, Ayliss."

The other Banshees finished blackening their faces, and then formed a tight circle around the two of them. Lola took on a somber expression, and gripped Ayliss by the shoulder with one hand. One of the Banshees took Ayliss's opposite hand and placed it on Lola, in a mirror image.

"Before the Banshees go into battle, there's a little ritual we do. You'll be fighting alongside us, so repeat after me." The eyes, amazingly white against the camouflage, stared deep into hers.

"I will kill for you, Ayliss."

"I will kill for you, Lola."

"I will die for you, Ayliss."

"I will die for you, Lola."

"Live for me, Ayliss."

"Live for me, Lola."

The Banshee leader pulled her in close, and unidentified hands clapped her roughly about the shoulders and back. The others began exchanging the vows, but Lola held Ayliss for a moment longer. "Do not hesitate. See a target, put it down. Then move. Got it?"

"Yes." Fighting hard to keep the joy out of her voice, and not accomplishing the task. Lola gripped her upper arms and stared at her again, misunderstanding.

"That's it. Keep that edge. Fight like there's no tomorrow."

CHAPTER TWELVE

On the *Aurora*, still in close proximity to Earth, Reena Mortas stood in the same launch bay where she'd last spoken with her husband. The scene was almost identical, with the technicians working the consoles, Woomer nearby mumbling into a headset, and Leeger looking on with growing concern.

But it wasn't the same scene, or even the same day. Olech had disappeared on the very first leg of the planned series, and no one could offer an explanation. So they'd done what they'd prepared to do and brought up the second tiny spacecraft, a duplicate of the one that had carried her husband away. Mira Teel had donned a specially designed pressure suit, promised Reena that she would find out what had happened, and they had launched the vessel the same way as before.

The *Aurora* had generated a Threshold, and Mira had flashed out of existence just long enough to complete the first leg of Olech's previous course. The Force warship waiting at the first destination had sent her back, and the vessel had been brought on board. The revived Mira had been baffled, maintaining this was the first time in thousands of Step voyages that she had felt no presence other than her own. She'd insisted on trying again, this time running the full ten laps, but Woomer had overridden the suggestion. The sole Step voyage made by the old woman had provided him with new data, and he wanted to run it through his models.

Hours had passed, with quizzical messages coming from every settled planet, Command, and many of the larger corporations. Olech's seal had been enough to quiet them, and they'd all been told to prepare for an extended suspension of the Step.

Though urged to return to Unity, Reena had refused. The apparatus of Olech's government ran smoothly in his absence, and she was in constant communication from the *Aurora*. Woomer's models had run their course, the data and the math and the physics had been reviewed numerous times, and finally the Step expert had confessed to being completely flummoxed.

So Mira had gone back into the suit and into the craft and into the void. The rapid-fire, multi-Threshold journey had taken hours, and howls of high-placed protest had accompanied the detection of Step usage. Reena had silenced the rancor with a terse message revealing the loss of an important governmental official, and the correct conclusion was instantly drawn. The tectonic rumor had raced across the galaxy: Olech Mortas, Chairman of the Emergency Senate, was missing.

Reena's composure had increased as the time dragged by and the tiny vessel completed each of the legs of its long journey nowhere, reappearing near the *Aurora* only to be shot right back out again. Now its run was complete, and it was brought aboard. Technicians carefully opened the craft, and gently revived its insensate occupant. Waiting, Reena experienced a wild titter of fantasy, imagining that the returned ship was Olech's.

Mira finally emerged, dressed in the pressure suit and sobbing openly. The technicians walked her in front of Reena, looking fearful. Woomer approached and stood next to them.

"What did you learn, Mira?" Reena asked.

The eyes were wounded, and the voice bordered on hysteria. "Nothing! Nothing! They've stopped communicating with us!"

The aged face shook in misery, and she turned to Woomer. "What have we done, Gerar? *What have we done?*"

Reena finished typing the last in a brief series of heavily encrypted messages flashing between the *Aurora* and Celestia. Despite the long lag time and the sterile wording, she could feel Horace's giddy elation. Although it sickened her, Horace's reaction was exactly as Olech had predicted, and so she already knew what to say. Even then the mechanisms across the settled worlds were swinging into action, a shadowy league of the powerful ensuring they stayed in control.

Of course this shouldn't have been a surprise, because a much younger Horace and a set of his cronies had already seized power once before. This time the effort would require almost no bloodshed, and when it was done, they believed they'd have a puppet where Olech Mortas had stood.

The hatch opened, and Leeger entered. His face was haggard, but he stood before her desk with almost military formality.

"It's all right, Hugh. Everything is proceeding according to Olech's contingency plan."

"That's why I'm here, Minister."

"All right. What is it?"

"I assume your brother has already suggested that you temporarily assume the Chairman's role, and that he's offered to help you?"

"As expected."

"The Chairman left me with a special order if he didn't come back, and I told him I would not obey it without gaining your approval first."

"That sounds ominous. What was that order?"

"The Chairman believed that your brother would pose a grave threat, once you were installed."

"He's always been a grave threat. But clearly my husband thinks I can't handle him—a matter I'll take up with him when he returns."

"Yes, ma'am. I do hope that's the case."

"So what did he want you to do about my brother?"

"There is a young woman, forced into slavery, who is currently . . . attending to Horace. Her family was tricked into going to Celestia with the promise of work and a future."

"I know the game."

"Yes, Minister. The woman in question has agreed to . . . help us . . . if we protect her family."

Reena's expression became even more serious, but she didn't respond.

"The Chairman felt it was a necessary step, once you'd been approved as his replacement," Leeger said.

"His temporary replacement."

"Yes, ma'am. Everything has been arranged, if you give the order."

Reena looked through him for several seconds, and Leeger stood stock-still.

"I'm going to have to give that some thought, Hugh."

"Yes, Minister."

"Let's get off this damned ship. Let's get back to Unity."

Gerar Woomer exhaled deeply as he settled into the chair. Several large monitors lined the console in front of him, but this was home to Woomer. Located inside a Force space station not far from Earth, the small, dark room was the nerve center of his Step research. Although he'd spent the last several days aboard the

Aurora, all of the data from Olech's voyage had been fed into his systems here.

A buzzer sounded, telling him he had a visitor. Woomer already knew who it was, and pressed the button unlocking the hatch with trepidation. Hearing the footfalls ringing on the metal floor, he looked at a picture set into the console. A young Force soldier, dressed in full armor and cradling a Scorpion rifle, grinned back at him.

Woomer tried to keep that image in his mind as he turned the chair.

"You've outdone yourself, Gerar." A hearty male voice rolled out of the shadows, followed by a tall man in a gray business suit. The visitor crossed the floor with confidence.

"I can't take all the credit, Timothy." Woomer stood, though his legs were shaking.

"Modesty. You would have gone much farther, if you had a better appreciation for your own talents."

"As far as you?"

"That might be stretching it. Horace always said he saw something in me very early on." Timothy Kumar was Woomer's equivalent in the Celestian government, though not his equal as a physicist. "Speaking of Horace, he sends his congratulations."

"I'd rather he send proof that my grandson is somewhere safe." Woomer pointed at the photo of a young soldier. "And a promise to keep him safe until his enlistment is over."

"Already done, old friend." Kumar clapped him on the shoulder, lightly. "You can trust us."

"Considering you threatened to arrange an 'accident' for the boy, I'll forget you said that last part."

"But you were the one who ended up arranging a little misfortune for someone else, weren't you?" Kumar moved closer to the monitors, studying the data.

"Only so far. I sabotaged the calculations for a much later point in Olech's voyage. I can't take all the credit."

"But he disappeared on the very first leg. Are you saying this was a genuine accident?"

"No. Far from it." Woomer punched a button on the control panel, sending one of the screens into a frenzy. Several lines jumped across the monitor, surging up and down, most of them climbing higher until Woomer stopped them. "See it?"

Kumar leaned forward, reviewing the graph. "It appears to be the standard energy readings of a Threshold creation."

"You don't see it."

"What, exactly?"

"Here." Woomer pointed at the bottom of the screen, where a small spike stood out. "Don't feel bad. It's almost undetectable in such close proximity to so much activity. It took me days to find it."

"But what is it?" Kumar allowed his annoyance to show.

"It's a Threshold. Requiring only a fraction of the

energy we use, and completely beyond our capabilities. It's tiny, and only appeared for an instant."

"That's not possible."

"It's there. The readings all check out. But that's not the point."

"Stop playing games."

"How I wish this was a game." Woomer sat down, looking exhausted. "Here's the point. That Threshold came into existence just as we were about to Step Olech's capsule on the first leg of his voyage. It preceded the event perfectly. And it took him."

"It *took* him?" Fear of Horace Corlipso entered Kumar's voice. "You mean he might still be alive?"

"This is bigger than all that. No human capability could have generated that focused a Threshold. Whatever created it timed its appearance to coincide with Olech's expected launch. They snatched him at exactly the right moment, which means they knew what he was planning to do."

"This is crazy. You've cracked under the strain."

"Look at the data. It's all there. The only way they could have timed this so perfectly was by knowing his plan." Woomer fixed Kumar with a look of scorn. "Don't you see? This means Mira and her friends are right. Whatever gave us the Step uses it to monitor our thoughts. They read Olech's mind during one of the earlier Step voyages. And they accepted his invitation before he even sent it."

CHAPTER THIRTEEN

"We're ready to move out," Mortas said to Dak on the radio. The platoon sergeant and his small patrol had successfully strained out twenty gallons of drinkable water during the night, and Mortas was about to bring the platoon to collect it.

"Negative, stay put. We're coming to you."

"You sure?" Mortas mentally calculated the weight of the collapsible containers Dak's veterans would be carrying. "That's a lot to haul."

"I'll explain when we get there. It's not far."

Word passed all around the perimeter, every man fully awake even as the new day's sun began filtering through the vegetation. Everything around them was damp, and an eerie ground fog had come in with the moisture. Mortas moved around the legs of the triangle, making sure everyone knew that the patrol was coming in, noting the dirt on the men's faces and clothing. The jungle on Verdur was famous for eating flesh and equipment, and already the platoon seemed to be part of the smelly decay.

Code phrases came and went through the helmet speakers, and then a hunched-over figure appeared to the west. The platoon had traveled in a northeasterly direction to reach the position the night before, so Dak had taken his patrol out on a different azimuth, to the east, before circling back to the stream. Following the maxim never to use the same route twice, he'd headed north that morning before turning east again and emerging from the undergrowth.

The patrol's point man was waved in, and Dak and the others followed silently. The water containers were eased to the ground with relief, and individuals began peeling off from the perimeter to refill their canteens. Dak knelt next to Mortas.

"Crazy thing happened last night. A group of the Vree Vrees came up to the stream to get a drink. I know they saw us, because the males backed up the rest of them and they all moved away."

"That's funny. I didn't hear them."

"That's what I mean. They didn't make a sound. It was like they'd come across a group of Sims. I've never seen that before."

Mortas was about to summon Captain Pappas when Dak leaned in close and sniffed.

"Yeah, I know I reek."

"No, that's not it. I should have noticed this already. My patrol was made up of men who've been here before. Nobody taking the stink pills. And the Vree Vrees didn't go crazy."

"It's the smell from the pills?"

"Gotta be. Every time I've been here, we always had new guys with us, stinking up the whole platoon. Newbies are always spread out with the old hands, and after a day in the bush everybody smells like a goat anyway. I never even considered this."

An hour later, the platoon's lead element signaled their arrival at the segment of jungle that Almighty had inexplicably struck with rockets weeks before. The front of the platoon had been reconfigured to contain only men who'd been to Verdur before, and hence lacked the stench of the stink pills. Traveling two hundred yards ahead of the rest of the platoon, they had jubilantly confirmed Dak's theory when a gang of Vree Vrees had scattered before them without screeching even once.

Mortas had transmitted the revelation to Dassa, who was both astounded and elated. Second Platoon was now manning the perimeter at Cordvine, but Dassa had elected to send Third Platoon down the ridge's northern slope. Kitrick had recovered from his error, and Third had already discovered an enemy cart trail that ran along the base of the escarpment below the remains of Broadleaf. The Sims had obviously grown quite comfortable working in the vicinity over the months, and the revelation about the Vree Vrees suggested a major opportunity. Some aggressive patrolling might uncover the enemy's main camp, without the warning usually provided by the jungle animals' howls.

"You gotta see this place, El-tee," Sergeant Katinka, leading the advance squad of Verdur veterans, radioed back to Mortas. "Whatever Almighty used here, it messed up the vegetation."

"Like a defoliant, you mean?" Mortas asked, sweating heavily inside his armor. Now that the lead element had reached the day's first objective, the rest of the platoon moved quickly to catch up with them.

"Negative. It's all discolored, like something's messing with the internal processes. Everything's still standing, and so far we haven't found any indications of rounds impacting here. Can't figure it out."

Code signals were exchanged at the head of the column, then Mortas pushed through a lush green wall of leaves and vines only to find himself surrounded by the fallow colors of a cornfield in winter. The trees in this region were sparse in number and dimension, but they were choked with bushes and creepers and appeared to still be alive. However, every leaf and stem that should have been a vibrant green was a sickly brown or yellow.

Mortas turned to Pappas while the platoon ringed the area. "What would have caused something like this?"

"Well, Almighty's a Victory Pro station, and Victory Pro's all about food. Maybe they thought Sam was growing something here and wanted to kill it."

"Naw, that's not it, sir." Ringer's voice came into his ears, speaking from the other side of the affected zone.

"I saw this kind of thing on Tratia when I worked with the sanitation department."

Mortas and Pappas exchanged glances, and when Ringer didn't continue, Pappas spoke. "So what is it?"

"It's knockout gas. We had these big protests in the park, and the police hit 'em with this stuff in a pretty heavy concentration. I didn't see it happen, but when they had us clean the place up the next day, all the greenery looked like this. Took months before it straightened out."

Mortas ran a hand over a long, drooping leaf. Despite the discoloration, it felt damp and normal. "Why would they hit a patch of the jungle with knockout gas? Would that stuff work on the Sims?"

"Yes—their respiratory systems are almost identical to ours. But according to that footage, there weren't any Sims here." Pappas looked skyward, his eyes fixed on a series of calculations that weren't adding up. "This mission is getting weirder by the minute."

The revelation regarding the stink pills paid off only a few hours later. Third Platoon, patrolling northwest of Broadleaf's ruins, surprised a pair of Sim soldiers who'd been pulling a two-wheeled cart along a well-worn path. One was killed and the other escaped into the brush, but the intelligence yielded by the incident was important.

"The dead one was wearing one of those heat-shielding smocks, and from what we saw of the other one, he was too." Dassa relayed his observations to First Platoon in the jungle and Second Platoon at Cordvine. "What a stench! Walking around in that thing in this heat. Anyway, his boots are pretty rotted, and it looks like he repaired them with that tree sap goop more than once.

"Now here's the good part. The two-wheeler was loaded with what looked like logs cut in three-foot sections. But the logs were hollow, and they're filled with a rubbery substance that's also smeared on the sides. Smells like the junk they used on the smocks and the boots, so I'm going to guess it's more of the tree sap."

"I think we figured out how they set Broadleaf on fire," Pappas stated.

"Agreed. The stuff can be made into an incendiary as well as an adhesive. We dug a chunk of the rubber out and lit it on fire, and it caught right away. Stack enough of these against just about any structure and set 'em off, you'll burn the place down."

Listening, Mortas imagined what the scene had looked like. Columns of Sims, invisible in their special smocks and loaded down with the incendiaries, clawing their way up the steps cut out of the slope that led to Broadleaf. All in darkness, pulling the fence down with the tree-trunk contraption and rushing up to stack the log-bombs against the walls of Broadleaf's biggest building. Setting off the conflagration before hurrying back down, leaving just enough troops to fire on anyone fleeing. Hoping that the humans would bring the rockets down and finish the job for them.

"All right." Mortas looked over at Pappas. "Let's get going."

"Just a second." Pappas held up a hand, receiving an incoming call that wasn't on the company radio net. All around them, the platoon waited in an oval defensive ring with the Verdur veterans up front. Mortas wanted to keep moving, encouraged that the new formation created by Dak's discovery had yielded the company's first kill.

"Captain, we need to move. Sam knows where Third Platoon is now, but he might not know about us yet. Those two Sims with the firebombs were headed west, and that could mean we're getting close to their camp."

"Actually, we're not close at all." Pappas slid the lenses back up, a broad smile on his dirty face. "I figured out where they are."

"The Vree Vrees love the not-bananas, and until this morning they shrieked their heads off every time they encountered a human." On the radio, Pappas was briefing Dassa on his latest find. "Remember that abandoned Sim camp we found two days ago? We passed through a grove of not-banana trees just short of that. I didn't notice it because those trees are everywhere."

"And the Vree Vrees hollered at us before running off."

"Yes. They were there because Sam has figured out how to use them as guard dogs. He sets up near a grove of not-bananas, then transplants more of them so that he's got Vree Vrees on all sides. Sam's always had a green thumb."

"Well what else do you do, when you're sitting in a jungle with no communications and no supplies?"

"Right. I thought of this after Sergeant Dak's visit with the Vree Vrees, and I asked the botanists on Cordvine to help me prove it. Their satellites monitor everything from rainfall to surface temperature, and they just sent me what I'm going to show you." Pappas transmitted an image into the goggles of B Company's leadership at their three separate locations. In front of Mortas's eyes, a diagram of the ridge and the surrounding area came to life. Slowly, red dots began to appear in the jungle near the high ground. Some were large, and others ran together almost in a red smear. A meter in the corner of the diagram started to run, indicating that he was seeing ecological change over the past year.

"The scientists at Cordvine have got specific identifiers for just about everything that grows out here, and when I asked them to filter out everything but the not-bananas, this is what remains. See that?" Pappas inserted a cursor over the image and directed it to the location of the abandoned Sim camp. "There was already a pretty large grove near there, and over time it expands until it's all the way around that spot."

The image continued to morph, dots disappearing in various places while others formed lines and barriers that elongated and spread. The jungle was still loaded with the plants, but when the motion stopped, there were two very large red ovals to the north and northwest of Almighty.

"*Got* you, motherfucker." B Company's ASSL, squatting in the jungle with Dassa miles away, hissed with glee. "Now we'll see who likes fire."

The Orphans crept through the jungle with the last of the day's sun. Second Platoon was still at Cordvine, but on high alert because an enormous concentration of rockets was about to land on the suspected enemy base. Third Platoon was northeast of Almighty, poised to move west as soon as the bombardment began, and First Platoon was west of the station, ready to launch a similar attack north.

"Remember, we still can't see Sam on the instruments. He may be home, in which case we'll just be counting the bodies, but if he isn't, he's gonna be mad as hell," Dassa had counseled Mortas on the radio a short time earlier. "Get yourself a jump-off point that's also a good defensive position, and wait for my order to advance."

Dak and the Verdur veterans had scouted ahead of the rest of the platoon, locating a good-sized creek. Mortas now brought up the rest of the platoon, arranging its machine guns and grenade launchers inside a tight circle with most of the firepower directed across the water. The platoon's supply of goggle batteries was nearly depleted, and so he and Dak had been forced to make some tough decisions. The leaders still had batteries, as did Vossel the medic, all the machine gunners, and most of the chonks. After that they'd paired the men off, one with functioning goggles and one without, but even those with power sources were now running out. The light was almost gone, and the dense growth around them was already cast in darkness. The water flowed with a gentle gurgle, and the opposite bank began as a low patch of deadfall and knee-high bushes before rising to a wooded finger.

The men facing the creek were belly-down in the brush, weapons ready. Mortas found a good spot just back of the line, next to a tree heavily wrapped in vein-like vines, which gave him an acceptable field of vision. When he went into the prone, Vossel took the other side.

"Not smelling much more than body odor, sir," the medic stated flatly.

"You surprised? I bet nobody in B Company is taking the stink pills anymore."

"Oh, I'm not surprised—but you and the other new guys may be. You haven't been here long enough to build up an immunity. A day from now, half of B Company's gonna come down with the screamin' shits."

Mortas tried not to laugh, excitement going through him in a gentle throb. Despite the loss of Broadleaf and the dead men in Third Platoon, the company had performed quite well. His platoon's discovery about the Vree Vrees had helped Pappas determine the enemy's location. Dassa had maneuvered the company with great competence, in spite of their surveillance systems' inability to see the enemy, and now they were going to deliver a blow from which the Sims might not recover.

He was just recognizing the possibility that they might retire the Verdur mission permanently, that very night, when his earpieces clenched and a rocket landed a mile to his north. The explosion was dampened by the foliage and the undulating terrain, but a brief crack of volcanic light passed through the jungle's dark curtain anyway. Birds shrieked in the darkness, and they were soon joined by the cries of the Vree Vrees. Mortas flipped his goggle lenses down and turned the device on, but the answer to his questions came on the radio.

"Dammit, Almighty! Can't you stick with a plan even once?" B Company's ASSL shouted, furious that the station had launched the strike prematurely.

Another rocket landed, still a good distance away, and Mortas spoke to his troops. "Party's starting a little early, but the plan's the same. Watch for Sam, and wait for the word."

North and west of their position, a volley of rockets landed on one of the two enemy strongholds. Quickly viewing the imagery, Mortas decided that Dassa had ordered the bombardment to commence now that Almighty had jumped the gun.

Rockets were raining down on the first target, and the jungle's shroud wasn't enough to contain the light. Spasmodic flashes of white and orange outlined the tangle of trees, vines, and bushes, reflecting off of the stream as if it were glass. The *Dauntless* and the two remaining stations' weapons satellite slammed rockets into both targets, the explosions coming one after the other like echoes.

Prone figures shifted about in front of Mortas, the men enjoying the huge aerial assault taking place a mile distant. More lightning strikes and claps of thunder, and Mortas was just thinking that it should be raining when a group of men in ponchos ran up and over the low ridge on the other side of the creek.

"Movement! Movement to the north!" one Orphan called out.

"There they are! Comin' right at us!"

The figures were running hard, now that they'd emerged from the thick vegetation and come down onto the flat. Dark robes billowed behind them, and many of them were hunched over with heavy loads. Mortas was counting them, amazed to get past twelve, when the entire line opened up.

The goggles kept the sudden light from blinding him, adjusting so that the scene was all clear and crisp. The prone figures fired like a line of troops on a training range, bright flashes from the muzzles of individual weapons while a stream of dashes shot out of the machine guns. Special chonk rounds, designed for close-in fighting, detonated in the soft soil and created even larger spasms of white.

The Sims never had a chance. More of them were coming over the slope when the line roared forth its devastating produce, and their forward momentum carried them into the deadly field. Bodies stopped abruptly in midstride, falling sideways or forward or flipping over backward. Raising his Scorpion, Mortas zeroed in on a Sim running in a zigzag, his tattered battle smock flapping behind him. He fired a three-round burst dead center, and the figure crumpled into the muck. A slug hit one of their packs just then, and it burst into flames. The man carrying it spun around madly, fighting with the straps, while riflemen attracted by the light blasted rounds into him. He dropped to his knees and then fell forward, the pack turning him into a pyre.

"It's the incendiaries! They're carrying the logs!" Pappas shouted. "Emile, we've made contact with a Sim force that was already on the move, carrying the incendiaries!"

Prevost, the Triage-Tech-turned-chonk savant, shouted for his fellow grenade-launcher men to adjust their aim, throwing rounds in a low trajectory into the woods beyond the rise. The eruptions of light showed the outlines of more figures running to the east, using the low ridge to get around the ambush.

"This is Almighty! They're passing between your positions and headed our way! We're shifting fires!"

"What are you seeing, Almighty?" demanded the ASSL. "There's nothing on the scanners!"

The rocket fire ended, and yet the scene in front of First Platoon was still illuminated. More than one of the packs had ignited, and from the look of the blaze, Mortas believed they'd burn all night. The machine guns and grenade launchers had stopped shooting, but one or two of the men kept firing at the enemy back-packs that had not yet caught fire.

"Cut that shit out!" Dak growled, and it stopped. "Mecklinger, they went by us closest to you, any idea how many?"

"Yes! Only a few of 'em, but they're headed some-place in a hurry."

"Almighty, I ask you again, what are you seeing?" The net went silent as all of B Company waited for the response to the ASSL's question.

"They're . . . they're coming through the jungle, our guys on the wire are picking up heat signatures." The voice was trembling. "There's a lot of them."

"Give me coordinates, and I'll help you kill them."

"Marking targets."

Mortas changed his goggles to the fire-support view, and for an instant the jungle looked exactly as he'd expected. Desultory fires burned from the rocket strikes on the suspected Sim camps, and he could easily make out the heat signatures of his platoon and Kitrick's. Almighty's heat blazed like a night game at an athletic stadium, and he was just starting to pick out the tiny dots of light from the fires to his front when Almighty's new target markers appeared in the miles of blackness that separated First Platoon from Third.

The small crosses, each with an identifying code number next to it, were almost a mile away from Al-mighty's perimeter. A rocket burst in the middle of the dark expanse, fired from Almighty's satellite.

"Almighty, how are you able to see these signatures at this distance?"

"Just fire the fucking mission, will you?" the voice shouted. "We've been working this terrain for a long time, and we know when Sam is on the move!"

Pappas threw himself down next to Mortas. "I knew it. They figured out how to detect Sam on their scanners, even with the invisibility smocks. They knew where he was all along, and didn't tell us—or Broadleaf."

Despite the warmth of the air and the heat from the pyres, Mortas felt his insides grow cold. Remembering the bodies from Third Platoon, the wounded man in the Extractor, and the remains at Broadleaf.

"Sergeant Dak."

"Yes, sir."

"Prepare to move."

"Where are we going?"

"Almighty."

"You got it. Mecklinger, your squad has the lead, then Katinka, then Frankel."

Mortas drew an electronic thimble from a pouch on his armor, and flipped the goggle view back to the company-operations graphic. Slipping the thimble onto his index finger, he called up a menu of military symbols that he began moving onto the overlay. While he was doing this, Dassa spoke.

"I see what you're doing, Jan. Push your route a little more to the east before you head north, then take up a blocking position . . . here. Let the rockets do the work." A symbol appeared on the schematic, on the southern slope of Almighty's hill. "Wyn."

"Yes, sir."

"We're headed south. *Fast.* ASSL's going to concentrate support fires where Almighty says they're seeing enemy, and we're going to block them to the north. If they try to slide around to the south, Jan will kill them."

"Got it. Moving out in three minutes."

The First Platoon troops at the creek were already sliding backward, shimmying away from the still-burning fires to avoid being illuminated. Frankel's people were slipping up behind Mortas when Mecklinger's squad announced it was moving. Making sure Vossel and Pappas were with him, Mortas followed Mecklinger's people at an interval.

The pace was quick, pushing through whatever was to their front. Behind them, the jungle stank from the revolting smell of burning flesh. Only moments after they got moving, the first rockets sailed down into the zone identified by Almighty, where a Sim assault force was allegedly struggling through the undergrowth. Much closer to the humans than the earlier bombardment, it slapped the ground so that the troops felt the vibration through their boots.

The night jungle changed into a madman's dream, with air-cracking explosions to the west that were heralded by enormous flashes of light. Less than a mile distant, ageless trees were blown down, crashing to the earth like mastodons suddenly felled by an unseen weapon. The close, damp air responded like a set of bellows, one moment blowing heated air over them and the next pulling it back in a cooling rush. Amazingly, the moist vegetation caught fire where the rounds were landing, and after a few minutes, the orange light through the vines was a permanent companion.

First Platoon snaked its way through the unknown terrain, each squad on its own axis but still close enough that they could support each other. Goggle lenses were slid up into helmets as the batteries failed or as the sweat from the wearer fogged them so badly that they couldn't see.

"Dak, I take back every curse I laid on you for Goggle Appreciation Night." Mecklinger grunted, pushing his way through the foliage.

"Don't let him off the hook like that! This is easy because of all the fires!"

"Yeah, if he'd laid on a barrage like this for us, it would have been just a walk in the woods!"

The chatter stopped suddenly, and Mortas saw why when the man in front of him dropped out of sight. Another salvo landed just then, closer, and in the madly shifting shadow he just saw the ravine before being forced to hop down into it. Erosion had chopped the wound through the dirt, and the soil was loose when his boots made contact, still far from the bottom. His feet sank into the yielding wall, and Mortas fell forward with his Scorpion outthrust. A bush with needlelike thorns was waiting for him, stinging his hands and face before he tumbled head over heels to the bottom of the gorge. The straps of his rucksack slipped forward over his upper arms as the backpack rode up his neck, then onto his helmet, driving his chin into his chest.

A small stream ran through the cut, and he felt the water on his neck when the rucksack stopped his forward motion, leaving him upside down with his legs in the air, bicycling at nothing. His arms were tangled in the rifle and the straps, and the water started seeping under his torso armor before he finally sagged over to one side. Unidentified hands were grabbing him, pulling him to his feet, the pack falling back into place just before he got to the other side of the gulley. The dirt was steep and riven with exposed roots, and he clawed at them for a handhold, the Scorpion swinging back and forth in his right hand while his boots fought for purchase. The light above was blocked in the chasm, and he had to fight his way up, constantly in danger of overbalancing and falling back the way he had come.

But he didn't, and the surging figures to either side didn't either. The bombardment continued in its fury, but the soldiers were possessed of the energy of the hunt. Not seeing the enemy but knowing he was out there, under the rocket fire, no doubt trying to evade it and quite probably coming right at them. The necessity to reach the block position spurred them on, but the sensation of being in a lethal race spoke to them viscerally. Veterans of other battles and hardened by the months of training, the Orphans now practically sprinted up the slope.

Small figures suddenly raced through the files, bouncing and grunting, Vree Vrees and other forest creatures madly fleeing the bombardment. Furry bodies collided with surging boots, and Orphans swatted at Vree Vrees that mistook them for trees. Mortas felt a thud on top of his helmet, a wet paw sliding down his cheek for the moment it took to find purchase, then the animal was gone.

The point men suddenly shifted the movement even farther to the east, taking the sweating mass on a curving path that followed the contour of the ground instead of pushing up it. Almighty was at the top of the hill, and the rockets were now landing so close to the platoon that they had to believe that the Sims were only hundreds of yards away.

Dassa called out on the radio. "Third Platoon is in contact! Third Platoon is in contact! Shift the rockets away from us! Drone fire only!"

Now directly behind one of his men, Mortas wanted to slide his goggle lenses down to see Dassa's location, but he knew that he'd be temporarily blinded if he did that. The rocket fire slacked off, and he was able to make out the sound of an enormous volume of rifle and machine-gun fire to the north, along with the low booms of detonating chonk rounds. It was maddening, and he was about to slip out of the column so he could stop and view the imagery when he heard Mecklinger's voice. "We're there! My squad will orient to the northwest. Katinka, bring your people in on my right, oriented north to south. Frankel, put yours on my left, oriented northwest to southeast, and hook in with Katinka. Lieutenant?"

"Yes!" Mortas stepped away from the flow of bodies, running into a narrow tree and grabbing onto it to keep from falling. A tide of insects streamed across his hand, and he pushed away in revulsion.

"We should get at least one more of the machine guns facing northwest and sweeping west. If they hit us, that's where they'll come from."

"I'm on it," Dak announced, and suddenly Mortas was standing by himself in the darkness while the armored men pushed through the vegetation and disappeared. Dropping to a knee, turning the goggles back on, and seeing that Dassa was still almost a mile away, with Third Platoon arranged in a narrow perimeter firing to the south. Overhead, he just made out the chug-chug sound of a drone before it unleashed a long burp of minigun fire along the front of Third's position. The rocket blasts were coming up the hill, avoiding Third Platoon, coming closer to Mortas's rapidly forming defensive triangle.

The explosions from the bombardment each blossomed on the screen for a few moments as a furious patch of light and then subsided, but the previously dark and empty jungle zone between the two platoons was now on fire. Blazes continued to burn from the spot where his platoon had ambushed the Sim bearer party almost to the fences of the glowing Almighty complex, and he suddenly saw what had happened.

The Sims had been preparing to assault Almighty the same way they'd hit Broadleaf, with different elements moving through the forest carrying the incendiaries they'd fashioned from the local flora. The rocket attack on their base camps had been a waste of time because they weren't there, and Almighty had known that. The mercenaries had kicked off the bombardment prematurely in the hopes of driving the Sims into First and Third Platoons, destroying their opponents without revealing that they had learned how to detect the enemy's presence long before Broadleaf had been destroyed.

But there were far more Sims than anyone had expected. There had to be, because the rocket fire on the enemy avenue of approach was so intense that it had to be killing them by the score. The flaming remnants of their firebomb devices, and the size of the force attacking Third Platoon, were testimony to their numbers.

"Pappas."

"Right here." A hand landed on his armor, and the intelligence officer dropped to the ground. On his goggles, Mortas could see that the platoon had sorted itself out into the triangle described by Mecklinger. The line of dots facing northwest slowly elongated while the other legs of the triangle shortened, as Dak and the other NCOs put more of the platoon's power facing the enemy's location.

"Why is Sam still coming up the hill? Why didn't he scatter the moment the rockets started landing?"

"I have no idea. Makes no sense. Acting like a pack of lemmings."

"Major Hatton was right about why they hit Broadleaf." Mortas spoke calmly, the pieces falling into place. "The target was Almighty all along. They wanted to make us split up between Almighty and Cordvine."

Rockets slammed down five hundred yards away, rocking the earth and throwing debris almost to the platoon's position. Almighty had cut the jungle back from its fencing years before, and although the resilient growth had reasserted itself, thankfully there were no large trees left to tumble nearby.

"They're at the wire! They're at the wire!" the voice from Almighty shrieked, and Mortas shivered at the memory of Broadleaf. "They're all over the place! Get up here and help us!"

"Calm down, Almighty!" Dassa shouted. "I will adjust the rockets onto them! Mark the targets!"

The absence of the company ASSL chilled Mortas even further, and he guessed the man was wounded or dead. The gunfire at Third Platoon's position was slacking off, so either they'd destroyed the Sims attacking them or the enemy had peeled off for Almighty.

"Don't do that! You'll collapse the buildings, just like on Broadleaf!"

"Sir, you hear what I'm hearing?" Dak asked tightly.

"Yes I do. Prepare to move." Mortas switched to the

company frequency. "Skipper, I can get up there if you call off the rockets."

"Already doing that," Dassa responded. "We got casualties here, but we're coming too! Don't run straight into them—stop when they're in sight and use your heavy weapons."

"Got it." Mortas rose, excitement and fear mingling. His eyes had adjusted to the goggles, so he saw the dark green world and the soldiers of his platoon. Katinka's squad moving up next to Mecklinger's and, farther down the slope, Frankel's people getting into position. A plan forming.

"Okay, here's the play. Echelon attack. Katinka, you're the lead. Hug the fence, and when you can deliver effective fire, stop right there and start shooting. Mecklinger, you'll be sweeping along the slope below Katinka, and Frankel, you'll be below Mecklinger. Swing around just enough so you can fire up the hill without walking into Katinka's fire. We'll pin Sam against the fence or tear him up as he tries to withdraw."

Katinka's troops began moving immediately, and Mortas hustled over the underbrush toward Mecklinger's men. "Dak, you go with Frankel. I'll be in the center. Make sure you don't get too far out in front."

"Yes, sir," Dak answered, an expectant timbre in his voice. "Okay, First, it's our turn. Let's finish these bastards once and for all."

The thin trees and bushes parted easily, but the gradient was tough and they were moving neither uphill nor down. The last of the rockets had detonated a minute before, but below them the jungle was ablaze.

"Almighty, we are coming up on your wire from the south." Mortas exhaled easily, grabbing the narrow trees for balance as he passed. "Do not shoot us up."

"They are taking down the wire, Orphan! Where the fuck are you?"

And then the slope opened up into an avenue of churned-up soil, devastated shrubbery, and broken rock. It was as if a meteor had landed at the top of the hill and tobogganed all the way down, leveling everything in its path. Small fires burned in the open, then Mortas saw the crumpled forms and knew they were the bodies of the Sims who had been carrying the firebombs.

A human machine gun began thumping away up the hill, then chonk rounds started to land as Katinka's people came within range.

Mecklinger's men rushed forward now, reaching the edge of the devastated zone and throwing themselves down. Mortas joined them, the gunfire from Katinka's position rising in intensity while more chonk rounds detonated up the hill. Crawling forward, he was unable to see because of the brush, and then it parted.

The lights from Almighty lit up the night sky, reflecting off the antipersonnel fence that was shaking as if caught in a high wind. The outer segment was already breached, and Mortas watched in amazement as Sim soldiers struggled to peel it back on either side of the hole. All pretense gone, knowing they'd been detected, the heavy smocks abandoned, laboring in fatigues that were little more than rags, many of them bare-chested.

The platoon opened up, easily felling the Sims still outside the wire in a roaring rain of gunfire and grenades before turning the weapons on the Sims inside the breach. Using the last of his goggle batteries, Mortas raised his Scorpion to see a small cluster of men, also in tatters, cutting away at the last obstacle between them and Almighty. Arms working improvised bolt cutters scissored the air while others hacked at the fencing with what looked like machetes. Just behind them, flinching as the first rounds passed over their heads, a tight knot of bearers knelt waiting with backpacks filled with the incendiaries.

Sighting in, Mortas saw the goggle's red dot settle on the back of one bearer's head. Scorpions began to crack all around him, and he breathed out slowly while gently squeezing the trigger. The rifle kicked against his armor, and the Sim slammed face forward into the dirt. Other Sims around him also fell, twisting, kicking, but then the whole group was moving, there was a gap in the fence, it was widening like a dam being ripped apart by torrents of water, and they were passing through.

"Katinka! Shift your fire between the fence and the main building! Don't let them cross it! Everybody else, up the hill!" He struggled to his feet, the mangled earth shifting under his boots, then he was running through the debris, lifting his knees high, athletic muscles propelling him over the ruined terrain. Katinka's machine gun started chattering again, and just beyond the broken fence he could see the explosions of the chonk rounds. A writhing body appeared on the ground, hands reaching for him, a Sim missing at least one of his legs, covered in dirt and blood, then he was past him, hurdling the branches of a young, uprooted tree, and then he was rushing through the wide break in the outer fence.

The ground there wasn't torn up, and he almost sprinted for through the triangular cut in the inner fence. Bobbing figures, not far ahead, were spinning, dropping, but still trying to reach the two-story structure at the top of the hill. Mortas ran straight into the cross-hatched barrier, feeling it give and then resist, and he caught it with one hand. The goggles dimmed, and he swept the lenses up into his helmet while kneeling and sticking the barrel through the fencing.

Other bodies came up on either side, then they were all firing, too close to miss, chopping down the last of the bedraggled soldiers who had survived the assault and almost reached its objective. They were no more than a dozen, every one of them clutching a pack of incendiaries, behaving as if there were no men to their right or behind them, scything them down. The last ones collapsed with a wail of despair that sounded like a large bird being mercilessly devoured, and then they were finally still.

"This is Mortas. We finished them. They're all

dead," he reported to Dassa, leaning heavily against the wire and feeling as if he would pass out.

"What were they doing?" Dak asked in astonishment, pushing through the hole with his Scorpion ready. Other Orphans followed him, and for a moment Mortas was at a loss as to what he should do next.

"Jan, did they make it through the fence?" Dassa asked, breathing heavily. Turning, Mortas saw Third Platoon struggling up the hill a few hundred yards back, carrying several wounded men.

"Yes, sir."

"Take your men up the hill, and surround Almighty. We're going to get some answers."

CHAPTER FOURTEEN

"**N**ice place you had here. Not sure I would have given it away." Lola sat in a corner of one of the many empty rooms in Ayliss's former abode. The corner windows on that side allowed them to look up at the abandoned mining station and down toward the tunnel's main entrance. One of the veterans' missile teams was set up in the next room, the building's roof sheltering them from enemy long-range observation. So far that seemed unnecessary, as the last report from McRaney had indicated no enemy ships anywhere nearby.

Somewhere up on the hill, Blocker was supervising missile teams hidden in a semicircle around the mining complex. Ayliss and the Banshees were providing security for teams around the tunnel made up of gunners whose skills Blocker had deemed questionable. At the center of the two half circles, the injured First Sergeant Hemsley was directing the whole show from a radio room inside the ridge.

"Turned out to be a pretty good hospital—even though I didn't expect to be the first patient." Ayliss's headset crackled, a message for the entire perimeter.

"Hey, everybody," Ewing's monotone purred from the tunnels. "I don't want to upset anyone, but I finally hacked into the Guest's satellite system. A large craft is burning through our atmosphere right now, and it looks like McRaney's."

"Shit! I should have known." Lola scrambled to her feet, snatching up her Scorpion. She gave Ayliss an exasperated look. "Get up! We're about to get fucked!"

She was out the door before Ayliss could rise, but the Banshee leader's next orders came over the radio. "Banshees, get on top of the tunnels! *Hurry!*"

Ayliss rushed out into the corridor, surprised to find it empty until she remembered the missile team. Turning through the door, she found Lola in a tight argument with the gunners.

"Don't you understand? McRaney knows the whole setup here. He knows the station's empty, that there's lots of Go-Three in the tunnel, and that we have missiles! He won't bring his ship anywhere near this place. They're gonna come in with smaller craft, and they're gonna land on top of the complex!"

"How do you know that?" The man standing in front of the Banshee had a large pink discoloration on his cheek. Ayliss had mentally dubbed him Birthmark, and he was clearly rattled by the sudden change. His partner stood near the window, where two of the shoulder-fired missiles were leaning against the wall.

"They want the Go-Three, so they can't blow the place up. But if they get on top, they can fight their way down inside, heaving satchel charges as they go. You two stay here, stay hidden, and when their landers take up a hover over the spikes, open fire."

"We'll be sitting ducks! They'll flatten this place!"

"You only have two missiles. Fire 'em both, and beat feet—just like we planned." Lola grabbed the man's arm. "Come on, now. You can be a hero for thirty seconds, can't you?"

"We can get killed in thirty seconds, too!"

"All right." Lola glared at the man as she slung the rifle across her back and walked to one of the launchers. She picked up the long tube by its pistol grip and put it over her shoulder. "One missile. But you better use it."

She didn't wait for a reply, pushing past Ayliss and heading down the corridor. Ayliss, trying to process everything she'd heard, followed. They hustled down the stairs and emerged into bright sunlight, then Lola was racing down the same road where they'd gone jogging just a few days earlier. Ayliss sprinted after her, and the radio spoke as they ran.

"Hey there, McRaney. Coming to help us?" Hemsley sounded cool and sarcastic, despite the way Ayliss's headset was jumping around.

"Oh, you saw us, huh? I knew I should have killed those satellites." The voice was deep and untroubled. "Listen, First Sergeant, it's nothing personal. They're gonna reinstitute the Step pretty soon, and the Sims just don't seem terribly interested in this place. I gotta make this work for me.

"We just want the Go-Three, so there's no reason for anybody to get hurt. You take your people out the ass end of that rabbit warren, head for those nice comfy hidey-holes, and come back in a couple of days. We promise not to break anything."

Ayliss's breath came in short gasps, her heart pumping hard. The armor and boots made her feel like she was running through a sauna that was somehow heaped with snow, and no matter what she did with the rifle, it slowed her down even more. Lola was getting away from her, despite the extra weight of the missile. The Banshee cradled the long tube against her chest with both arms, so Ayliss imitated the combat veteran's moves. The running was still tough, but at least the Scorpion wasn't taking her off balance or hitting her anymore.

"You know, a pirate should be a better liar than that," Hemsley answered.

"It's a good deal, and you should take it. I'm not lying."

"Sure you are. If all you wanted was the ore, you'd be telling me to have my people bring it out. You know there's a *lot* of it, and it would be too much like work for your lazy shitheads to have to move it. So I'm guessing you've got something else in mind."

"I don't know why Rittle thinks you're so stupid, Hemsley. Hey, it's just business, but he figures that the only way he can still work this claim is if Sam came by and killed you all."

Lola reached the base of the ridge and went straight up, dodging between the huge black spikes. Ayliss, fighting for air, felt she had to speak up. "This is Minister Mortas! This planet belongs to the colonists now. Zone Quest has no claim here."

"Hello, Minister. Please keep talking, it'll help us locate you. Rittle promised me a bonus if I could provide proof of your death. It seemed important to him."

The steep gradient made it impossible to respond, and the threat sounded real, so she decided it was probably best to shut up. Somewhere above and behind her, a dull roar that she recognized as the sound of engines began to grow. The radio flowed with wild questions and frightened protests.

"What the fuck is going on? I thought they were scouting for *us*!"

"Give 'em the ore! Who cares about a bunch of rocks?"

"Everybody shut up—they're monitoring us!"

Her head spinning with exertion, her lungs refusing to take in any more oxygen, Ayliss stumbled onto the top of the ridge. Black thorns pointed skyward all over, most of them taller than a human. She'd never been up there, and began looking around frantically for Lola.

"Everybody stay calm." Hemsley sounded bored. "The plan's the same, just with a different target. They won't bother with the station, so get ready for these pirate pussies to come right here. They ain't after the ore, they're after our skins. They kill us all, the planet goes to the Guests—that's why Rittle is paying them.

"So if you thought you had nothing to fight for, well now you do. It's kill-or-be-killed time, people. And I know which one of those I choose."

Ayliss tottered through the maze of black points, regaining her breath. The top of the ridge was a vast oval of a plateau, and she wondered for an instant if she was alone.

"Ayliss! Come to the center!" Lola ordered, and she began to run.

The engine noises were undeniable now, a high whine that she associated with the sport bikes she and a group of university friends had ridden once while on vacation. Flashes of red shot through her vision, and Ayliss stopped running because she had to. Leaning a hand against the black rock, surprised at how hot the sun had baked it, then turning to look at the station. The screeching sound suddenly coalesced, and two large objects crested the rocky hill. Long and narrow, with pointed prows and roaring engines aft.

"Those are landers! There's nowhere for them to set down up here, so when they take up a hover, wait 'til the troops come down on the ropes and light 'em up!" Lola's commands pounded into her brain, painting a picture that cleared her head instantly. An enemy in her gun sights. What she'd come out here for, what she longed for, and best of all, they were allied with the murdering assholes who'd taken Selkirk and had now put a bounty on her head.

"Hug the spikes, and they won't be able to pick up your heat signatures!" The words were distant now, unimportant. Ayliss's breathing settled down, and a blissful silence surrounded her as she rotated the Scorpion's selector switch to combat mode. The sun was warm on her neck, and a breeze filled with engine smells kissed her cheeks.

The landers split, heading to either side of the plateau, one a mere two hundred yards away. It was a thing of beauty, carried through the scorching atmosphere in the belly of a larger craft and therefore unblemished. Its bottom curved into something resembling a keel, and Ayliss made out the hatches for the landing gear just as doors slid upward all along its sides. She leaned against the nearest spike and raised the rifle.

"Take your time, shoot the one you're looking at, *then* move on to the next!"

Ayliss nodded, one with the Banshees scattered across the spiny mesa, joyously agreeing with the low voice that could have been Lola or Tin or one of the others. Lowering lines dropped all across the lander on both sides, and she put her eye to the sight. Its optics were simple, but the image that popped up showed the inside of the lander just over one of the madly jumping ropes. A figure stepped to the edge, wearing a strange helmet but stripped to the waist. She was amazed that he wore no body armor, and then the Scorpion jumped. The figure flinched as if startled, then fell back inside.

A rush of delight jetted into her brain, and Ayliss knew that if she didn't hit another thing that day, it would still be enough. Her entire body vibrated with the sensation and the tremors from the straining engines that were now traveling through the rock. Bodies came out the doors now, moving fast, knowing they were exposed, twisting to face the lander, then kicking away, rappel harnesses wrapping their waists and buttocks.

There seemed to be a lot of them, sliding down from both sides, but that was good, *God* it was good, there they were, and she could kill them now. They were dropping fast, experienced at this sort of assault, camouflage pants and boots pressed together, a guide hand on the rope above while the other one held the loose end of the line away so it would run through the snap link faster. Some armored, most not, and she turned the rifle to one of the latter, a huge man with the scalp-tight helmet she'd seen before, the sights lining up and this time she made herself feel it as she squeezed the trigger.

The man's body had been in an L shape, but the slug hit him dead center and he collapsed, hands releasing, body arching, the rope catching in the snap link, slowing his descent to a crawl. The sun flashing off of the headset, Ayliss seeing that it was some kind of light, and realizing it was meant to aid them once they entered the tunnel. The body beginning to spin, but by then she'd found another one and had shot him too.

This one wore a blockish backpack, which the slug hit instead of his body. He exploded, a brilliant burst of fire and light, but everything was serenely quiet and so the blast was a muffled crump that nonetheless killed the pirates to either side of him. Bodies reaching the spikes now, dropping out of sight, freeing themselves from the ropes, but there were still targets hanging under the lander. Their rappel rigs had fouled when the explosive went off, one of the satchel charges Lola had mentioned, and Ayliss took her time killing them.

Surprised that the magazine was empty, angry that one of them was still on the line, yet remembering Blocker had taught her to move after shooting. Dropping to a crouch, dodging between the rocks, tossing the empty magazine aside and dragging another one out of the pouches on her armor. The lander's engines screamed, its contents delivered and its pilot eager to get away, and then the sounds of the fight came to her.

Engines roaring overhead, rifles firing behind her, some of them far behind her, and then Lola's voice.

"Shoot the landers, damn you! We're doing our part—you do yours!" Ayliss remembered the missile crew back at the house, and laughed out loud that they had so obviously run off, laughing because they were missing it all. A fresh magazine slammed home, running bent over, her eyes searching the brief spaces between the spikes, the rifle a living, lusting thing in her hands.

And then one of them was ten yards in front of her, coming slow, torso armor and a stubby weapon that was probably a good choice for close-in fighting on ships and in tunnels and right here right now. Startled eyes and the same silly headlight rig and a few days' worth of beard, then her rifle was coming up, smooth, as if a reverse gravity were raising it, and before she got the sights to her eyes she gently brushed the trigger and shot him right in the throat, just above the armor. A snap shot, Blocker would have called that, he wasn't a big fan of them but taught her anyway, and of course she was a natural. The stubby weapon fell to the dirt and the hands came up, grabbing, surprisingly little blood showing, and he dropped to his knees and his face.

Two figures rushing at her, one firing while the other fumbled with a satchel charge, Ayliss realizing the pirate was going to waste the huge explosive on her as if it were a grenade. A round smashing into the spine behind her, fragments of rock stinging her cheek and driving dirt into her shooting eye, the Scorpion coming up blindly now, three rapid shots and the shooter bounced back off the rocks and disappeared. The one with the bomb ran straight into her, knocking her down, the deadly package already armed, dropping the canvas sack and running off.

Only to come flying right back, Scorpion rounds slapping his armor and finding his face, his head jerking back sharply as he fell. Ayliss rolling, tangling with the rifle and coming straight up against one of the rocks, her face cringing in expectation of the blast, then something was grabbing her. She thought the satchel charge had gone off and her body was being hurled around the black cone, her hands scraping against the surface; and then she was thrown down and the bomb went off.

Dirt and dust plumed around the spike, her arms were hung up in the Scorpion's sling, and she looked up to see what was crushing her to the ground. Lola's face was right over hers, covered in grime and blood, her eyes and mouth both round.

"I think I stopped part of that," she whispered, her head sagging onto Ayliss's shoulder.

Ayliss took the Banshee by her body armor and gently slid her off, fear mounting when she noticed how slack Lola's body had become. Struggling to free herself from the rifle, and then seeing the ugly holes blasted through Lola's armor. Dropping to her knees and holding the Banshee in her arms, she was surprised to feel breath on her cheek.

"I wasn't lying, back there." Lola coughed, and blood flecked her lips. "I will die for you, Ayliss."

Lola's eyes lost focus, and her body began heaving, her head bucking while Ayliss tried to keep her still. It subsided in moments, and when she laid Lola down, it was clear she was dead. A heavy aroma of explosive was all around them, and the scent fed her rage.

"I will kill for you, Lola," she told the dead face. "I will kill them *all*."

"**F**uck! Did you see that? They just blasted Lott and Kersey's position! How did they spot them?"

Ayliss didn't recognize the voice, but a long, low rumble came to her ears from the other side of the mining station, and she had to assume it was one of the missile teams. Blocker came up on the net, confirming this.

"Stop talking! They're monitoring us!"

McRaney answered, mocking. "Why are you telling them to shut up? It's a very reasonable question, and I'll answer it for you. When we sold you those missiles, we attached tracking devices to them. They started operating the moment you tested the systems, and I have a fix on every one of your positions. See?"

A harsh double crack broke the air on top of the tunnel, followed by a loud boom that Ayliss felt through her boots. A plume of smoke billowed up from somewhere out on the mountain's top.

"They know where we are! They've known for hours! I'm getting out of here!"

"Everybody move to your alternate positions!" Blocker ordered, and Ayliss heard the sound of a truck engine behind his words. "Drop the missile you've turned on but take the other one with you!"

"And do what? They're gonna spot us the moment we put the thing in action!"

"Oh, I forgot to mention that I can turn on the locators myself," McRaney commented. "If I were you, I'd drop every one of those and get away from them as fast as possible."

Another pair of whipcracks, much louder now, and another deep blast from on top of the hill. Ayliss stood on tiptoe, straining to see through the grove of spikes, but it was no good. She did get a look at the hospital, just in time to see Birthmark and his buddy run out. They came sprinting down the road, terror on their faces, and she remembered Lola telling them to stay put.

Ayliss raised the Scorpion, sighting in on the lead runner. They'd left the one missile behind, and were covering the ground with amazing speed. She was just about to squeeze the trigger when an image of Lola, running down that same hardpack with the other missile, came to mind.

Turning from the cone, she ran toward the center of the mesa, somehow knowing that was where Lola had left the other launcher. Passing a dead body, a pirate in the headset rig who was facedown in the dirt, she practically tripped over Tin. The smaller Banshee was sitting with her back against one of the spikes, her legs stretched out before her and one of the enemy satchel charges in her hands. Her Scorpion was on the ground next to one of her legs, and glancing at the weapon caused Ayliss to notice the bloody field dressing wrapped around Tin's thigh.

"Hey, Ayliss. Thought I was alone up here. I think we got 'em all, but I figured there'd be more, so I picked this up." Tin smiled warmly, patting the canvas bomb. "Only heard one of these go off, and there's been no yelling from below so I think they never even got near the entrances."

"Buncha pussies. We tore them *up*, didn't we?"

"Yes we did. Can you imagine what we would have done if we'd had our suits?" Ayliss pictured the armored pressure suits the Banshees normally wore into battle. "The round that hit me would have just bounced off. I wouldn't even have felt it."

A steady rumble reached them now, and they

both looked at the crest of the mining station's hill. A shadow passed over the rim, something big blocking out the sun, then the circular edge of McRaney's ship appeared. Dirty brown and streaked with black from entering the planet's atmosphere, the saucer-shaped vessel swiveled a twin-barreled cannon toward the ridge.

"Tin, Lola brought one of the missiles up here with her. Where did she put it?"

"Lola's dead, isn't she?"

"I'm sorry, Tin. It was that satchel charge you heard. She died pulling me out of the way."

"I didn't ask, because McRaney's listening . . . and because I didn't want to know. We were a supertight squad, Ayliss. You should have seen us out there, when we were really in the shit. One time, we hit this Sim supply dump, well it wasn't really a supply dump, it was kinda more like one of those . . ."

Ayliss squatted down, then slapped the blackened face. Tin's head snapped to the side and came back, blinking quickly. She raised a hand to her cheek and then grinned.

"Thank you, sister. I was drifting away there, wasn't I?"

"Tin, you're in shock, but I have to know where that missile is."

The wind smacked them both, a sudden gust that disappeared inside the one-two blasts of McRaney's forward cannon. The ground beneath them jumped, and voices began yelling on the net.

"We have to get out of here! They just blocked the entrance! The next one's going to bring the whole place down on us!"

"Stay where you are!" Hemsley bellowed, for the first time sounding excited. "You go out in the open, they'll run you down and kill you!"

A hand gripped Ayliss's arm, and Tin shouted, "There's a tiny clearing near the edge, right over there! Good firing position, that's where Lola left the launcher!"

Ayliss propped the Scorpion on the dirt and used it to help her stand. Before she could move, Tin called out to her.

"The moment you turn that on, they're gonna know where you are! Wait until they fire those guns again, then move really fast!"

Ayliss fixed her with a look of fearful resolve, then raced off through the cones. The open area Tin had described was only twenty yards away, but it was littered with broken rock thrown up by the last impact from the cannon. The missile was nowhere to be seen, and she began rushing desperately around each of the spikes, searching.

The world jumped and roared just then, tossing her a few inches in the air and dropping her roughly to the dirt. Ayliss's head spun with the concussion of the blast, then she was covering her head with her arms as rocks rained down on top of her and the boom of the guns passed over. When it ended, she looked up to see smoke rising from the center of the plateau, barely a hundred yards away.

"The roof's collapsing! They're going to bury us down here!"

"We're cut off! We're cut off! God help us, somebody come get us out of here!"

The cries from below drove her back to her feet, the Scorpion forgotten, and Ayliss tottered over to the nearest black cone. Debris was all around it, but then she saw the dark tube on its side. Leaning back against the spike, she picked up the launcher and tried to remember the sequence she'd been taught only the night before. Remembering Tin's words and stopping herself, dreading the next impact but knowing she had to endure it. Turning, shaking her head to clear the fog, and then shambling toward the cones on the edge of the plateau.

Seeing the brown ship fully now, brazenly sliding forward over the top of the station, two other cannon exposed on either side, ready to launch a salvo that was going to drop the entire ridge onto the people below her. Knowing she couldn't wait, putting the missile on her shoulder, blowing out hard breaths before taking in one last big one, and then hitting the button that would put the sights and the weapon itself into operation.

Nothing happened.

Astounded, she yanked the long tube off her shoulder and looked at the boxlike housing that held its electronics. Her jaw dropped when she saw the black fragment of rock buried in the weapon's guidance system. She could push that button until the end of time, and it would make no difference.

Exhausted, Ayliss sagged against the rock and let the useless weapon fall from her hands. Looking up to see the enormous brown disc, its horrible guns swiveling toward her, and making herself laugh just one more time.

Motion caught her eye at the building that had briefly been her home on this planet. A small figure that she knew was actually quite large, running out onto the balcony that wrapped the whole building, a length of pipe on his shoulder. It was hard to see him because of the ship's shadow, and she knew what was about to happen.

"Dom! Dom! It's going to *land on you*!"

"I sure hope so, Little Bear!" The words came out in gasps, Blocker obviously having run a great distance to get where he was. "Half these things didn't even *work*! Get your head down, darling!"

The missile fired, the blast of its superheated propellants darkening the white building behind Blocker. At such close range, the projectile impacted only a second later with a sharp crack that slapped her eardrums. The ugly brown disc shuddered all over, and the vibrations increased while its engines fought for control. It began to tilt toward the ground on one side, then its front started to rise, and the whole ship slid back toward the white building.

"No! No No! No!" Ayliss was shrieking and running, almost to the edge of the plateau, when the back of the craft contacted the side of the mountain. Metal screamed as the weight forced it to crumple, and it slipped even farther back and chopped into the structure.

It exploded in a fireball that lifted her like a small child being plucked up by a parent or a trusted guardian, and heaved her back among the rocks.

CHAPTER FIFTEEN

In a large, circular room far beneath Unity Plaza, Reena was receiving reports related to the Step's suspension. The Sims had been uncharacteristically slow in responding to the absence of their opponents' biggest advantage, but now they were exploiting it. The room was two stories tall, with wide screens suspended from a gantry that ran all the way around its black walls. On the screens, Sim raiders were chasing human ships in several parts of the war zone and one colony was under attack.

"The cruiser *Persephone* was being slowly corralled by a squadron of Sim recon vessels, and her captain Emergency Stepped them out of it," a Human Defense Force colonel explained while pointing at one of the monitors. "She's offered to defend her decision in front of a disciplinary board—or in front of you. Those were her own words."

In the time since Olech's disappearance, Reena had attained a mien that was almost robotic. Icily calm, she'd received the latest updates on the search for Olech's capsule—all negative—with the same equanimity as the news that the suspension would have to be lifted. Nodding to the colonel, she turned to Leeger.

"What will happen if I authorize emergency use of the Step?"

"Every local commander will use it to shift spacecraft as he or she sees fit. They'll come up with an excuse later. That's what I'd do."

"All right." Reena gave the colonel a brief, lifeless smile. "Thank you, that will be all."

Once the man had moved off, Reena waved Leeger in closer. "I need to send a secure message to General Merkit in the construction zone."

"Yes, Minister. And what are your plans regarding the Step?"

"I'm going to leave the suspension in place for a few more hours, to give Force commanders in the war zone time to plan. As long as we've created this situation, we should get something out of it. The Sims are already overextending themselves, and when the Step becomes available, we should be able to inflict some heavy damage."

"And Merkit is going to coordinate this?"

"Yes."

"It's not really his specialty, Minister."

"Oh, but it is."

Far away, in the part of space known as the construction zone, General Merkit strode down a wide corridor inside one of the region's largest space stations. Jointly owned by Zone Quest and the Human Defense Force, it had been visited by Olech Mortas before his ill-fated journey to Celestia.

"Wait here," Merkit ordered the twelve armed men who were his personal security detail. Olech himself had assigned them when he'd rotated the Force units defending the stations and factories of the construction zone. The leader of the detail, a hardened veteran of such assignments, positioned his men on either side of the passageway without a word. Initially skeptical of Merkit's survival instincts, he'd been astonished by the man's talent for sniffing out troublemakers among the corporate managers who were now his subordinates. Demotions and incarcerations had been handed out liberally, and the security man's instincts told him that the situation was in hand for the time being.

Merkit activated the palm-reading lock on the hatch to his front, which opened without a sound. Everything on this station worked perfectly, and the environment was downright luxurious. This was the place where Chairman Mortas had discovered the senior-most leaders of the Force in space, impossibly far from their commands in the war zone.

A beautiful brunette in a low-cut dress looked up in surprise when Merkit passed through the opening, rising from behind an ornate reception station.

"Excuse me, sir, but you aren't on the access roster for these spaces."

"I'm the general in command of this entire zone. I'm not on the access roster because I can go anywhere I want. Where are Generals Leslie and Osamplo, as well as Admiral Futterman?"

Flustered, the woman led him through two more hatches and down three more corridors before reluctantly pointing toward yet another hatch. Replicas of gas lanterns adorned the walls on either side, and the entrance had been dressed up to look like the wooden door of an ancient public house.

"Thank you, I'll take it from here." The woman was gone seconds later, and Merkit watched her flee. "All that, and the brains to know when to run off, too."

The hatch parted to reveal an oval room with several tiers. Two bars faced each other on the first tier, and several tables with chairs populated the levels that ran down to a broad section in the middle. Just one of the bars was open, and the room had only three occupants other than the bartender. Seated at a table in the dead center of the floor, they wore the uniforms of two general officers and one admiral in the Human Defense Force. Open bottles were in front of them, and three half-filled glasses.

"Merkit!" one of them, a general with rugged good looks who was just going gray, called out. "I wondered how long it would take you to ask why we hadn't rejoined our commands. You know, like Chairman Mortas told us."

The other general, a blond man with a bit of a tummy, gave Merkit a dismissive look. "Don't worry about us. Everything is packed, and we'll be leaving as soon as someone reinstitutes the Step."

The admiral, a much older man, ignored the new arrival completely.

"Gentlemen." Merkit greeted them in a breezy fashion before calling out to the bartender. "Another glass, please."

"Why you drinking with us, Merkit? Didn't you change sides?"

"I did. And that is exactly why I'm here." The bartender, a young civilian who had obviously heard about Merkit's recent activities, quickly covered the distance to the table and delivered the glass. He was gone a moment later, and Merkit poured himself a small one.

"So what happened to you?" General Osamplo, the pudgy blond, pointed at Merkit's midsection. "Did Olech starve you until you agreed to work for him?"

"No, I lost the weight reorganizing a chewed-up brigade on MC–1932. But you were all sitting out here when that happened, so I wouldn't expect you to know about it."

"What the hell do you want?" demanded the admiral.

"I come with an offer."

General Leslie's eyebrows rose. "Really? Last time we heard from the Chairman, he was yelling at the top of his lungs and not interested in our input at all."

"No one's asking for your input. The Step suspension will be lifted in eight hours. As I'm sure you're well aware"—Merkit gave a short laugh that might have been mistaken for a cough—"the Sims are launching raids in several different parts of the war zone. Minister Mortas feels this is an excellent opportunity for you gentlemen to create a plan for cutting them off and destroying them the instant the Step is available."

"You said this was an offer. What do we get for that?" General Osamplo leaned forward, his desires obvious.

"Oh, you can't stay here, if that's what you were hoping for. I'm sure you'll be able to use Force funds, and the always-available support from the corporations, to arrange for a new headquarters just as cozy as this one. But let's face it, gentlemen; you can't command troops if you're not in the same time zone with them.

"No, what you'll get is a major victory on your records. And Minister Mortas has promised to sing your praises on the Bounce." Merkit stood, his glass untouched. "Eight hours. Get to work, gentlemen. Kill the enemy. After all, it *is* your job."

He was at the top tier when the admiral called to him. "Merkit, twice you referred to the Chairman as Minister Mortas. Care to explain that?"

"u've all heard the rumors, and they're true.
⸺an is missing, that's why the Step was
⸺ v wife is directing operations from
⸺ the full support of her brother and
⸺adership of all the settled planets. This
⸺ it's a good one."

He started for the door but stopped after a few paces. "I didn't care for Reena myself at first, largely because she kicked my ass in a very public fashion. She's a good ally, gentlemen—and a dangerous opponent. You've got quite an opportunity here, so make the most of it."

CHAPTER SIXTEEN

"I'm not going to say it again. Every last one of you come out of that building, no weapons, with your hands in the air." Captain Dassa spoke from the edge of the flat ground at the top of Almighty's hill. First and Third Platoons had ringed the entire complex, ready to fire from the rim of the plateau.

"I'm not going to say it again, either! Get off our hill, or we will hit you with rockets!" An angry voice came over the radio, but Mortas thought he detected a tremor of fear.

"Fair enough. Go ahead."

"What?"

"Go ahead. Rocket us."

There was no response for many seconds, and on either side of Mortas soldiers from First Platoon slid back a little farther down the slope. Dassa had assigned them the half of the perimeter that controlled its open landing zone, while Kitrick's platoon covered the building. Finally, the voice came back.

"What did you do? Without that satellite, we're defenseless!"

"Defenseless? You mean like Broadleaf? You knew the Sims were building up to hit them, and you didn't warn them. They're all dead because of you. Seven of *my men* are dead, and a dozen more wounded, because of you. The *Dauntless* has severed your link with your satellite, and they're ready to blast it if there's any sign it's coming back to life. So come out. *Now*."

"Fuck *you*, Orphan! This place is a fortress, and we've got plenty of everything we need."

"All right. You can stay in there. I'm going to pull my guys back, then the *Dauntless* is going to level this place."

"You're crazy. You can't make that call."

"Actually, I can. I'm the senior-most combat specialties officer on this entire planet, and according to Force regulations, that makes me God. So I'm done talking to you. Come out right now, or you're dead."

The two-story white building loomed in front of Mortas's eyes. Most of the hill's trees had been taken down when it was built, and the night's fighting had cleared the promontory even more. An enormous blast door faced the site's landing zone, but apart from that it had few openings. Mortas, now deprived of the imagery in his goggles, tried to remember what it looked like from above. The exertion of the final battle and the stress of the previous days and nights were finally catching up with him, and the rising sun made him curiously lethargic.

"All right, you assholes. We're coming out. *Don't shoot*. You're gonna be toast when the corporation hears about this."

"Stop talking and come out."

The blast doors gave off a low hum in the early-morning air, and then they burped loudly before growling back on either side. All along the rim, Orphans inched forward on their stomachs and sighted down their weapons.

A bewildered man in an orange coverall emerged first, palms high, eyes frightened. He stopped just a few steps into the open, and no one followed him.

"Keep walking!" Dak hollered, and the man flinched as if he'd been punched. Raising his hands even higher, he trudged across the flat ground until he'd almost reached the edge.

"Lie down on your face and don't move!" a voice commanded from the other side of the clearing, and he obeyed with obvious relief.

"Let's go, in there! Walk out to your buddy, find a space, and get your faces in the dirt!"

A column of men slowly appeared, some in coveralls, others in fatigues, and a surprising number of them wearing lab jackets. Mortas counted close to fifty before they were all out and in the prone.

"Anybody else in there?" Dassa called to the prisoners. "If there is, and they cause trouble, you're all dead."

"Nobody's left inside! Tell your men to stop pointing those things at us!"

"Fuck you, asshole!" an unidentified Orphan shouted. "And shut the *fuck* up!"

"Wyn, take your people and clear the building," Dassa ordered. "Jan, have half your people cover the prisoners while the other half takes over Third's part of the defense." Men in armor and dirty fatigues quickly rushed up onto the flat, directing machine guns into the darkness of the open blast doors. Others approached the opening from either side, hugging the walls, and then they were entering in teams.

Mortas slid back down the embankment a few yards and began moving down the line. The warm dirt gave way beneath his boots, and he had to balance himself with his free hand. Mecklinger's squad had been assigned to cover the prisoners, and Frankel and Katinka were already spreading their men out to re-form the ring around the complex. It was doubtful that enough Sims were left alive to make another attack, but with the Victory Provisions people neutralized, it was time to turn at least some of the soldiers outward.

He met Dak on the other side of the building, having made only minor adjustments to the positions selected by the squad leaders. A happy thought had occurred to him while he'd been doing this, and he grabbed Dak's armor.

"No casualties in First. None."

"This is a new experience for me." Dak grinned from beneath a layer of grime. "We should do it this way more often."

"Beats the hell out of Fractus, doesn't it?"

"Fractus? *Fuck* Fractus."

Mortas was hustling back to his original spot when Kitrick spoke on the radio. "All clear, sir. The place goes down into the hill for several levels. Damnedest stuff I've ever seen. You and Captain Pappas need to look at this."

"**Y**ou are not going to believe what we've found out." Hours later, Pappas was seated at a console in the main operations room inside Almighty. Marines from the *Dauntless* had just taken the last of the prisoners away on shuttles, and Mortas had entered the building for the first time. Most of Third Platoon was back out on the perimeter, but there was little concern about a possible attack. Pappas and intelligence people from the *Dauntless* had found the system that allowed the occupants of Almighty to see the Sims even when they'd been wearing the special smocks. According to that imagery, a tiny clutch of the surviving enemy was steadily marching out of the area.

"Your idea that Almighty had been using drones to attract more Sims turned out to be accurate." Hitting a few buttons, Pappas played a time-lapse schematic that showed numerous flights going out from Almighty for hundreds of miles and then looping back, day after day. "They wanted to bring Sam here in large numbers."

"Son of a bitch," Dak said.

"It gets worse." Pappas switched the screen to actual footage of Almighty and the surrounding jungle.

Roughly a mile away from the hill, a small white cloud erupted from the greenery. A black object shot straight up out of the jungle, then neatly sailed down toward Almighty's roof. Seemingly at the last second, a round hatch opened to receive the object.

"What was *that*?" Mortas asked, his mind still numb with fatigue.

"The whole point of this installation," Dassa responded. He'd removed his helmet and goggles, leaving ruts in his cheeks and the outline of the eyepieces in the dirt. "The lower levels are some kind of crazy laboratory. That thing we just saw was a capsule. They'd sown the area with mantraps, and when a Sim got grabbed, it shot him up in the air and delivered him to a cage downstairs.

"They'd electrified the floors and, judging from the footage they didn't manage to destroy, they were trying to find out if Sam can be taught to perform basic tasks. They'd show the prisoner a video of a human in the same cage, moving colored blocks from one spot to another, then they'd shock him until he did the same thing."

"I knew there was something really wrong with those guys, just from the short time we were guarding them." Dak shook his head. "Half-crazy looks, some of 'em giggling, the rest looking like they were headed for a firing squad."

"Let's hope so," Pappas answered. "These sick bastards kept really good records of the whole operation. Those drone flights attracted several hundred Sim leftovers. Once Sam saw enough of his buddies take the ride to Almighty, he got serious. Started gluing the heat-shield material onto the smocks, but our Victory pro friends stayed ahead of them. They applied a special filter to their sensors, and it let them track Sam wherever he went.

"That's why they hit that one jungle patch with knockout gas. Sam was avoiding the mantraps, and they needed some new subjects. Our sensors couldn't pick up the signatures, but theirs could. And they never shared that with Broadleaf or Cordvine."

"But what were they hoping to accomplish?"

"I believe somebody somewhere has decided the Sims could be an excellent labor force."

The group went silent for a few moments, then Dak spoke. "These cells down below. Any occupants?"

"Two, but somebody shot them before we came in here."

"Anything else?" asked Mortas. "Please tell me that's all."

"There is one more thing, a recent data feed sent to them with heavy encryption." Pappas looked at Dassa. The company commander spoke.

"Sergeant Dak, no offense, but I'd rather you didn't see what we've found."

Mortas frowned in confusion, but answered as if he understood. "Whatever it is, if I'm allowed to see it, my platoon sergeant should as well."

"All right." Pappas punched some more buttons, and a tape began to play. Mortas recognized it immediately, having lived through it less than a year earlier.

It was the room on Glory Main where he and the alien had been locked in the transparent tubes. The lights were flashing, and the alarms were going off, and the nude form of Captain Amelia Trent was being burned with chemicals in order to force the alien to reveal its true shape. In the tube across from her Mortas saw his own collapsed form, screaming while fire burned up the swarm of tiny black moths into which the alien had burst during its final moments. Although he'd seen the video before, he believed it was being kept a secret.

"What the hell is *that* doing here?" he asked, more befuddled than angry.

"Near as we can tell, it was sent to every Victory Provisions station in the war zone. We haven't decoded the orders that came with it yet, but I think someone is trying to find another one of the aliens you met." Pappas looked up at him. "If their plan is to turn the Sims into a slave labor force, a shape-shifter who can communicate with them would be a big help."

Mortas stepped out into the daylight with gratitude. Shuttles were landing and lifting off with regularity, and large stacks of supplies were starting to form. Dirty soldiers were moving the crates and boxes away from the landing zone, and after so many days and nights beneath the jungle canopy, the direct sunlight was brightening their spirits.

"Looks like we'll be getting some nice, clean water," Dak offered from his side.

"That sounds good." Mortas ran a hand through his hair, reluctant to put the helmet back on. "You know, I was feeling pretty happy about this mission until I went in there. Now I feel . . . dirty, somehow."

"Oh, it wasn't that bad, sir." Dak's tone was humorous. "For one thing, I finally got to see what that alien looked like. She was a fine figure of a woman, and I don't blame you for nailing her. You being an officer, I just naturally assumed she was fuck-ugly, but she was okay. Until the acid started eating her, of course."

Small, frustrated laughter bubbled up from inside him, and Mortas laid his hand on Dak's shoulder. He was about to speak when Dassa called out to him.

"Jan, can I have a word?"

He slapped Dak's armor once, and walked back to the blast doors where Dassa stood. The twenty-year-old company commander looked uncomfortable, and Mortas steeled himself for more revelations of barbarity from the chamber of horrors under their feet.

"Yes, sir."

"The Step's been reinstituted, so we'll be getting a resupply of everything the *Dauntless* doesn't have." The news didn't fit Dassa's demeanor, so Mortas stayed silent. "Listen, Jan, I only just got this. It's the explanation for why the Step was suspended for so long."

"Go on, sir."

"It's about your father."

CHAPTER SEVENTEEN

Smoke from McRaney's crashed ship hung in the air like a shroud. The saucer had broken in half when it hit, the rear portion resting against the hill where Ayliss's house had been and the front half burning not far from the tunnel entrance. Ayliss had carried Tin down the back side of the ridge when she'd regained consciousness, delivering the Banshee to a makeshift aid station at one of the rear exits. Elated colonists had told her about gunning down the few survivors among the pirates who'd emerged from McRaney's ship.

Movers kept arriving with more dead and wounded, but she didn't wait for a ride. The climb back up the escarpment had been painful, but Ayliss had kept her Scorpion ready as she walked through the forest of black spikes. Coming to the far side, she'd looked down to see a group of the veterans admiring the wreckage, pointing and laughing. She recognized two of them, and felt the anger welling up inside her again. Good.

Skittering down the slope, Ayliss kept her eyes fastened on the pair of missile gunners who had abandoned the one launcher Lola had left them. The same weapon Blocker had used to fell the steaming brown disc that they found so funny. Happy faces turned in her direction when they heard her boots scrunching on the scorched dirt, and then she was swinging the Scorpion's butt straight into Birthmark's cheek.

The man fell hard, grabbing his face while the others took several steps back. It was only then that Ayliss realized what a fearsome sight she must have presented. Her fatigues were covered with dirt and blood, her hair was matted with camouflage paint and more dirt, and the right side of her blackened face still stung from the pebbles embedded there.

"What was that for?" Birthmark finally managed to say.

"Get on your feet. You and your partner are going to help me find Blocker."

"Who?" the other one blurted, so she knocked him down too. The rest of them decided they weren't with the unlucky pair and quickly backed off toward the tunnel.

"Blocker. The man who picked up the missile you threw away and shot down this stinking cow pie of a ship. It landed on him, and we're going to find his body. Now let's go."

They came to their feet slowly, uncertain and afraid, but an angry motion with the rifle got them moving. They had to skirt the wreckage for several hundred yards, and then she made them climb the slope in front of her. The hospital was completely gone, but she knew Blocker would have run for it.

The incline was steep because so much of the ground had fallen away with the ship's impact, and the ascent was made far more difficult by the field of debris. Huge rocks, many of them black with Go-Three, had been tumbled everywhere. Up the hill, a large segment of the mine's security fence had been yanked down the slope in a twisted tangle of bent poles and shredded wire. It was like that for two hundred yards on either side of the wreck, and Ayliss began to sense that the mission was pointless.

Birthmark and his buddy stopped climbing when they reached a ledge formed by a large slab of Go-Three, and she joined them in order to get a good look around. Her eyes stung with the smoke, tearing up.

"I'm sorry, Minister. Really. But do you think there's any chance we'll find . . . anything in all this?" Birthmark spoke in a halting fashion.

"We're going to keep looking until we find him."

"Maybe he got away. Maybe he's down at the tunnel right now. Did you think of that?"

Ayliss felt the tide surging inside her again, and welcomed the rage. She'd had this same chickenshit in her sights once before, and because of his cowardice Blocker was dead. If the two of them had just done as Lola had commanded, they would have shot down the pirate vessel and then been entombed beneath it. The thought almost put her over the edge, but she needed their help, and so instead of shooting, she yelled at the top of her lungs.

"Because of *you two*, the best man I ever knew is *dead*! It should be *you* buried here, not *him*!" Tears ran down her cheeks, stinging the cuts, and Ayliss knew that she couldn't blame them all on the smoke. "Now I *said* we're going to keep looking until we find him, so *get looking*!"

"Would you please stop shouting? I have one hell of a headache." The voice came from just above them, behind a heap of mangled wire and tangled cable. Eyes wide, heart thundering, Ayliss went right over the obstacle, mindless of the way it tore her trousers and cut her hands. Finally freeing herself, she saw the face she'd never expected to see again, caked in dust, but alive.

Blocker was pinned with his back to the hill, an enormous utility pole resting on his torso armor. His legs were buried under a slide of shale and dirt, but he was smiling when she reached him. The Scorpion bounced on the ground when Ayliss dropped it, and she was reaching to embrace him when she remembered he might be grievously injured. Squatting next to him, her hands fluttering in the air, she asked in a tiny voice, "Are you hurt?"

"A little. One of my legs is folded the wrong way, and I wouldn't be surprised if the other one's broken too. Hard to tell." He glanced up at the crest. "I almost made it. I was just topping the rise when the whole thing went out from under me. Fifteen years in the war and barely a scratch, and look what happens when I take my old job back."

Now her arms were around his neck, and she was crying and whispering directly into his ear. "Don't you ever leave me again, Big Bear."

His hand came up, grasping the back of her shorn head. "I left you once, Little Bear. Never again."

Birthmark and his partner were gingerly picking their way over the wire when Ayliss remembered them. Snatching up the rifle, she came to her feet. "Get over here right now, and dig him out! And if you hurt him—"

"Ayliss," Blocker barked.

Her eyes turned, alight with joy and anger and relief, and she flashed him a smile before turning to the others.

"Just don't hurt him. All right?"

CHAPTER EIGHTEEN

In his palace in the city of Fortuna Aeternam, Horace Corlipso awaited the imminent attainment of a life-long goal. The midafternoon sun streamed into the room from the windows facing a long balcony, and the rays warmed him through a thin robe emblazoned with the Corlipso family crest. The server girl Emma walked out of the bedroom, slipping a strapless blue dress over her head, wincing slightly. Fresh bruises were rising on her back, and displaying pain was a sure way of getting more of them.

"Pay attention to this. History in the making," Horace instructed her while activating a button on a remote control device. The nearest wall, normally a plane of gilt and filigree, opened to reveal a wide screen on which the face of Reena Mortas, nee Corlipso, soon appeared. At his urging, the Emergency Senate had unanimously selected Reena to fill in for her missing husband as the supreme political leader of the settled planets. Horace found it amusing that they felt the promotion was temporary.

"It is with great sadness that I must now tell you that our leader for the last six years, our brave member of the hallowed Unwavering, our Chairman, and my beloved husband, Olech Mortas, is missing." Reena wore a dark suit with a high collar, and her red hair was pulled back in a bun. Seated behind Olech's desk, she was addressing the entire race over the Bounce.

"Hear that?" Horace asked, his voice giddy. "He's gone. The fool didn't realize he became superfluous the moment he married my sister."

Emma almost didn't hear him. She recognized Reena Corlipso, and knew she'd married Chairman Mortas a few days earlier, but none of that seemed to matter. Reena was explaining that her husband had gone missing while visiting the war zone just after their wedding, and that something had gone wrong with the Step. It was hard to focus on the words, or to care very much about them, because Emma knew that the end of her torment on this terrible planet was about to end.

"Good old Olech thought he had the best spy network in the galaxy, but I had the one thing I needed— the man programming his little journey." Horace's excitement was growing, and he stepped closer to the monitor. "Not sure why he disappeared on the very first leg, but Woomer got rid of him and that's all that matters."

"We hold out every hope that my husband will be found safe and sound somewhere, and the search goes on," Reena continued. "I want you all to know that the functions of state and the prosecution of the war are in good hands, and that I have reluctantly accepted the request from our Senate to temporarily stand in for my husband."

"Very good, dear. Use that 'my husband' phrase as much as possible. Just like I told you." Horace looked at Emma, wearing an idiotic expression that she recognized as overpowering pride. She'd seen it many times, and it was often accompanied by the revelation of secrets that made no sense to her. "She's not really my sister, did you know that? Her mother was a lot like you, a household server, but with red hair. I wasn't married yet, and so my parents raised her—after silencing her mother, of course."

"It is my fervent wish that I hold this position for a very short time, but I promise you the same honor and integrity that my husband brought to this office. I would have mentioned his courage as well, but there is no way I could ever measure up to the bravery of that man. He chose to travel to the war zone even though the trip was perilous, and all because he so valued the efforts of the men and women shouldering the burden in humanity's fight for survival."

Reena stopped speaking for a moment, appearing to fight off an attack of tears, and Horace wrapped an arm around Emma's bare shoulders. He pulled her close, aggravating the bruises, and pressed his lips against her ear. "Listen closely. I gave her these lines."

Regaining her composure, Reena fixed the audience with an expression of resolve. "I know you all join me in the sorrow and concern I feel for my missing husband, but I promise that I will not fail him—or you. I am Reena Corlipso of Celestia, and I am Reena Mortas of Earth, but most importantly I am simply Reena, of the race human, and I ask you to go forward with me as we continue the work so nobly begun by my husband. Thank you."

"Draw my bath," Horace released his hold, giving Emma a hard slap on the buttocks. His eyes turned toward the balcony, where he frequently accepted the admiring cries of the people in the square below. There was a price to pay for living as a citizen of Celestia, and loud supplication was a big part of it. A large crowd was gathered out there, watching Reena's address on enormous public screens, overjoyed at having one of their own ascend to such power.

Emma watched him walk toward the balcony as if in a trance, riding the high of having his secret daughter take the place of a man he'd privately hated. She hoped he'd still be in its grip when he settled into the tub, and so she moved quickly into the bathing room. After a quick look over her shoulder, Emma knelt to make sure the knife was still hidden under the mat where she would kneel as she washed Horace's back. The blade was a polished wafer of hard Celestian stone, given to her by the man who had promised to take her family away from this hellish place. He'd been an operative for someone who hated Horace, and came and went so silently that she'd nicknamed him the Misty Man.

Emma had just turned on the water when she heard the transparent balcony doors activating, and a quick glance showed that Horace had decided to go outside. The doors slid shut behind him, and he walked to a console on the vine-covered terrace. His finger punched in a series of commands, and Emma knew that the screens in the teeming square below were changing over to a different feed. Cameras focused on the verandah would give the Celestian citizenry a view of their overlord all across the planet, and even then heads were turning to look up at him.

Outside, the crowd roared, and she guessed that Horace had waved at them or merely smiled.

Horace had his back to her, certain that the doors had locked behind him. Certain that she was too stupid to have learned the code that would open them, that would let her out there in front of the cameras and seal the doors once she'd passed through. She typed in the numbers.

The audience was ecstatic, fully aware that Celestia had finally surpassed Earth to take its rightful place at the head of the alliance. Arms were raised, rows of people swayed, and the cries of approval were like a series of waves crashing against the shore. Horace didn't hear the doors open, but a lull allowed him to detect the sound of the bolts sliding back into place. He turned in surprise, seeing Emma. Seeing the knife in her hand.

She touched the edge of the blade to her forearm. Blood rose up from the thin cut, and red drops fell on the balcony floor.

"How did you get out here?" he demanded, his voice low because microphones all over the balustrade would broadcast his words to the people below.

"I wanted to share this with you," she said sweetly, sounding like a child. Walking toward him, red drops falling, the knife swinging lazily. "This is your big moment, master."

Fear rose with the awareness of his frail clothing and the fact that he was alone. Recovering his wits, Horace summoned the tone that promised errant servers a strict punishment if they failed to obey. "Put that knife down and go back inside."

The girl giggled, and the crowd suddenly became aware of her on the screens. Not seeing her arm or what she carried, only taking in her beauty, they mistook this for part of the show. A gorgeous server girl, appearing with Horace on the balcony at this perfect moment, suggested they were about to witness a physical celebration that would become legend. A roar of approval and exhortation reached up toward them as Emma got within range.

"Haven't I been good to you?" Horace blurted, his eyes dashing around the empty pavilion.

"Oh yes, master. Very good." Emma showed him her teeth. "Let me be good to you now."

She was much younger, and much faster. He dodged the first rush, but she caught his robe with her free hand, and his bare feet went out from under him. His arms flailed blindly when she dropped down with him, the bloody arm wrapping around his neck. Then she'd released him, and he was scrambling to his feet, amazed that she had missed, marveling at the amount of red the cut on her arm had left on him.

Down in the square, the crowd screamed as one. Horace, his robe pulled almost off, staggered back toward the windows while a tide of blood flowed down his front. His eyes opened wide as the realization struck him, and he grabbed at the wound even as his brain began to shut down. He fell back and hit the doors, hard, and then the palace security men were pounding on the barrier while Emma walked away, slowly heading for the spot where he'd been standing.

The howls down below stopped in an instant, an absurd silence descending on the horror-stricken faces. Emma, her dress splashed with crimson, held up the dripping knife at them. Her ghoulish visage was broadcast on the enormous screens and all over the planet.

"I'm not yours! I was never yours!" she shrieked, and then the doors were opening, and she turned just in time to receive the volley that tossed her over the railing, tumbling her through the air toward the crush down below.

"Not good." Hugh Leeger breathed out the words while watching the delayed feed from Fortuna Aeternam. Emma tumbled slowly as she fell, and the crowd rippled while trying to get out of her way. "Not good at all."

The operative—the one Emma had nicknamed the Misty Man—stood next to Leeger in his office in Unity Plaza. "Reports from my network say it's utter chaos there. The crowd in the square went crazy and grabbed every slave in sight. They ripped them to pieces with their bare hands."

"Did she not understand she was supposed to do this privately?"

"These things are hard to manage. As you know."

"Is it spreading?"

"Worse. The broadcast went out all over the planet, and there was an uprising anyplace with a significant concentration of slaves. They've seized control in several of the mining areas, and the slave neighborhoods in the cities have risen up as well. Celestian authorities have shut down all incoming communications, especially the Bounce. I need to get back there right away, to protect my network."

"We took you out of there so you couldn't be connected to Horace's killing. You're not going back, even when order has been restored."

"And what if it isn't?"

"Then the whole war effort is in jeopardy." Leeger stood, straightening his tunic. "I need to go brief Chairwoman Mortas."

Seated behind Olech's desk and still dressed in the same outfit from her earlier address, Reena watched the memorial for her late husband on the Bounce. A somber Hugh Leeger stood with her. On the screen, a teenaged Olech Mortas in a dress HDF uniform smiled at them.

The image shifted to a famous photo, Olech after weeks of combat, wearing muddy fatigues and no helmet. Though only a private, he'd been directing the defense of a hill that had been the target of numerous Sim counterattacks. His face was haggard, and he appeared to be scanning the terrain in front of his position for the enemy.

"What's the latest news from Celestia?" Reena asked, her eyes on the monitor.

"Security forces have regained control of Fortuna Aeternam, but only after shooting anyone who was still in the streets. The uprisings are gaining strength, especially in the mining zones. Every Force unit held in reserve for defense of the settled worlds has received your orders to prepare for movement to Celestia. We're receiving a lot of vague reports from the Celestian authorities, and much of it's contradictory. They're screaming for help while insisting they have things under control."

"Your man's network is still sending information?"

"Yes, but a few of them have stopped transmitting. I'm assuming they had to flee the unrest."

More pictures of Olech moved across the display. The badly wounded boy in a bed in some warship's sick bay. The too-thin veteran, lifting weights as part of his recuperation. A strikingly handsome young man, walking across a university campus, assisted by a pretty girl who would become Lydia Mortas.

"What's the reaction on the other planets?"

"The Bounce is working overtime, but the only thing anyone knows for sure is that Horace was attacked by a slave girl. Luckily he collapsed below the cameras' sightlines, so we're already spreading a story that he was only wounded. The official line is as you directed; Celestia has declared a state of emergency that has grounded all spacecraft and suspended all communications."

"That won't hold up for long. Especially when they order their commanders in the war zone to send their troops home." Reena laughed with bitterness. "Too bad we couldn't keep the Step suspended."

"We're pushing the news of the latest war-zone victories into the feed even now."

Leeger changed the Bounce channel from the memorial to the latest military news. A series of clips appeared, showing billowing smoke and charging human infantrymen. "Command botched a number of good opportunities, so most of the Sim ships raiding our outposts managed to get away. The sudden reinstitution of the Step did catch the enemy off guard, and so their troops were abandoned on two of the planets that were under attack. They weren't large elements, and Force units quickly mopped them up. We're exaggerating the size of the enemy formations a bit."

"Understood."

"Of course we're exploiting the stories involving Jan and Ayliss. The Bounce directors were beside themselves when they heard what had happened on Verdur and Quad Seven, especially the fact that the Mortas siblings had fought off their opponents while the Step was still suspended."

The continuous news loop came back to Quad Seven, and Leeger stopped talking.

"Under the direction of the newly appointed colonial minister, Ayliss Mortas, discharged veterans successfully defended their new home of FC–7777 against a Sim raiding fleet that had taken advantage of the Step's unavailability."

McRaney's ruined ship appeared before them, broken in half and still smoldering. The camera panned away carefully, not showing the abandoned Zone Quest mining operation and instead focusing on the entrance to the tunnel system. Weary men and women, many of them wearing bandages, were removing fallen rocks from the tunnel mouth while newly arrived medical teams were treating the wounded out in the open.

"Showing the same kind of battlefield leadership as her father, Ayliss Mortas personally commanded the defense of the underground colony the veterans had dug out of nearly solid rock. Despite ferocious casualties, the outnumbered colonists soundly defeated the Sim invaders and drove them off before the Step was reinstituted."

A flatbed mover slowly came down the road, passing close to the film crew. An almost unrecognizable Ayliss was kneeling in the back, holding a scarred Scorpion rifle in one hand and the upraised palm of a wounded man in the other. Her blond hair was almost completely cut off, and it looked as if it had been dipped in tar. Her torso armor was covered in brown dust, and the visible side of her face was streaked with what looked like sweat and ash.

The mover stopped and two men riding with her, also covered in dust, hopped off before gently pulling the stretcher down. The man on the litter was large, and he gritted his teeth as they carried him toward the field station. Ayliss strode along next to him, never releasing his hand.

"Minister Mortas, how are you feeling?" called a voice near the camera.

Ayliss turned to face him, as if noticing the crew for the first time. The black camouflage paint had morphed into a gray paste, but for the first time the audience could see the right side of her face. Dried blood covered her cheek, and numerous small wounds were evident. The volume cut out as the group passed, but Ayliss's lips moved in an unmistakable dismissal.

"Was that Blocker on the stretcher?" Reena asked.

"Yes."

"Did Ayliss say what I think she said?"

"I believe she told the reporter to get the fuck away from her."

"Nice to see we were able to teach her a little diplomacy."

The scene changed, flipping to a flat hilltop ringed by lush foliage. Shuttles were landing and taking off, and dirty infantrymen were breaking down supplies and cleaning weapons.

"On Verdur, Lieutenant Jander Mortas and a company from the famous Orphan Brigade were likewise engaged by the Sims. An ecological monitoring facility was under attack by a Sim force estimated to number in the thousands, and Lieutenant Mortas's company force-marched through miles of dense jungle before assaulting straight up the side of the hill where the station is located. The Orphans destroyed the Sim attackers, and are now enjoying a well-deserved break."

The view swung from the landing zone to the pristine white of the Victory Provisions building. Armored Orphans stood guard at the open blast doors, and Emile Dassa could be seen just inside, speaking to Jander. His hand was on Mortas's armor, and they'd both removed their helmets and goggles. Dassa clapped him once on the shoulder, then disappeared into the darkness. Standing there alone for a moment, Mortas fastened his helmet's chin strap before hanging the headgear on one of his canteens. Dangling his goggles in one hand and holding his rifle in the other, he walked out into the sunlight as if unaware anyone else was near.

This film crew had the sense not to engage its subject in conversation, but it slowly zoomed in on Mortas's face as he looked at a segment of defensive wire that had been taken down. The ground beyond it looked like a logging trail, and several of Almighty's vehicles were visible at different points along the shattered slope. Work parties were gathering the broken bodies of the Sims who had rushed up that incline with no thought to their own safety the night before. Mortas stared at the scene for several moments.

Notches cut into his cheeks where the goggles had rested for days, and a spray of dried soil covered much of his face. His dark hair was matted and pressed down onto his scalp, and he gazed out over the devastation as if seeing it for the first time and not understanding any of it at all.

ACKNOWLEDGMENTS

This book is the result of a great many collaborations on a wide range of subjects. I want to extend special thanks to my editor at Harper Voyager, Kelly O'Connor, for her insightful and instructive editing of *Dire Steps*. Additionally, I'd like to acknowledge the marvelous work of the Harper Voyager artists who designed the book's excellent cover.

I also want to thank my West Point classmates Michael McGurk, Meg Roosma, and Ginni Guiton for reading earlier versions of *Dire Steps*. Their invaluable observations helped this novel realize its true potential.

ABOUT THE AUTHOR

HENRY V. O'NEIL is the pen name used by award-winning mystery novelist Vincent H. O'Neil for his science-fiction work. A graduate of West Point, he served in the U.S. Army Infantry with the Tenth Mountain Division at Fort Drum, New York and the First Battalion (Airborne) of the 508th Infantry in Panama. He has also worked as a risk manager, a marketing copywriter, and an apprentice librarian.

In 2005 he won the St. Martin's Press Malice Domestic Award with his debut mystery novel *Murder in Exile*. That was followed by three more books in the Exile series: *Reduced Circumstances*, *Exile Trust*, and *Contest of Wills*. He has also written the theater-themed mystery novel *Death Troupe* and two books in a horror series entitled *Interlands* and *Denizens*.